ELIZABETH'S ENCOUNTERS

By

Edward G. Schultz

Revision 2

Cover painting by William J. "Bill" Schultz

Used by permission of Nadya Schultz

ELIZABETH'S ENCOUNTERS

By Edward G. Schultz

CHAPTER ONE

An Encounter with Hope

Sebastian was weary. He had been on the seat of his wagon since a few hours after sunup. Before leaving home he had already spent several hours loading additional grapes onto his wagon. He had spent most of the day yesterday too, loading his Elbling grapes. Now it was almost midday. After loading them yesterday and early this morning he had wet them down well and covered them with moistened burlap, hoping that they will look still fresh when he reaches the agent at the river port. He reached behind the seat of the wagon to feel the condition of the grapes.

Now looking ahead he saw that there were still five wagons awaiting their inspections. He had been through this process many times before, both as a vineyard worker and, for these past three years, as a worker in his own rented vineyard. The soldiers never hurried. They always seemed to purposely delay the wagons. And as they delayed, their comrades helped themselves to some of the cargo in the wagons. Sebastian wondered why these soldiers, arrogant mercenaries of the Duke, were so hostile.

He thought, 'Aren't we all Germans? When the Duke had his local soldiers conducting the tariff inspections they were not hostile. They inspected the loads efficiently, affixed the duty and allowed the wagons to move on, and without badgering the drivers. But these damned mercenaries seem to feel they are more important than their countrymen. They seem to enjoy tantalizing the workers and poor old men.'

Continuing in line to await his inspection, his mind again went into reverie. He thought about his family and the village where everyone knew each other, and every bit of gossip about each family. Sebastian had moved away from the village more than ten years earlier, first working as a laborer in the vineyards of the wealthy land owner Herr Morganstern, then later as a vineyard share-cropper, with his own piece of rented land and a small cabin that he had built there, in what he considered now to be "his" vineyard.

Sebastian had decided to grow Elbling grapes, because he thought that he could obtain a better price than the much more popular Riesling variety which was being grown by most of the vineyards. He was wrong, for although the Elbling was more rare, the Sekt wine that it was used to produce did not always have the flavor of many more popular wines. Still, Sebastian did not feel badly about his decision because he had less risk when growing this sturdy variety, which had been first grown by the Romans when they occupied this part of Europe.

Sebastian's reverie continued. He recalled the day that he had received an invitation to visit Herr and Frau Bleier. The Bleier's had a young daughter, a pleasant and somewhat attractive young woman. Sebastian smiled to himself as he thought of the day that he saw young Elizabeth, whom he had not seen for several years. My! how she had grown.

On that cold January day, as he sat with Elizabeth's father and mother he

2

was at first astounded, then embarrassed, by what they told him. Elizabeth had been raped a few months before and now they knew that she was pregnant. ('Oh my God' he thought.) The parents explained; she needed a husband. Although Sebastian was much older than she, her father expressed great confidence that Sebastian would be a caring husband. He felt that in spite of Elizabeth's condition Sebastian would accept her as if she were still chaste. Her father explained that he knew how diligent Sebastian was, that even as a youth, he labored harder than most of the other young men in the village, and now that he was a sharecropper he was providing an income for himself better than most of the young men. He said that he was confident that Sebastian would provide well for Elizabeth and her soon to be born child. Herr and Frau Bleier both said that they trusted Sebastian, that they knew that he would be a good husband.

Sebastian listened intently. He knew that he was eligible, for although he was twenty-seven years of age, he had never been married. He had a plain face, neither handsome nor homely. The village girls never fancied him as a beau however, because he was much too serious of nature, not as enjoyable to be with as many of the other young men. Sebastian was very appreciative of Elizabeth's parent's suggestion, for he would certainly enjoy having the companionship of a wife. He assured them that he would accept her child as his own. But Elizabeth was only fifteen years old. How would she feel about having a husband nearly twice her age? When Sebastian raised this question, Elizabeth's parents assured him that Elizabeth was aware of all of the conditions of the marriage, that they were not offering her for a price, but had prayed that Elizabeth would secure a devoted husband, one who would faithfully provide for her. They again assured Sebastian that they felt he was the one man that would sincerely provide for their daughter and their future grandchild. And they assured him as well, that Elizabeth would be a wonderful homemaker, mother and dutiful wife.

Suddenly Sebastian was awakened from his thoughts. The soldier at the head of the wagon line shouted to Sebastian,

"Wake up old man! Move up here now".

Sebastian shook himself back into the present. He drove up to the inspection barrier.

"What's in your load, old man?"

Sebastian did not mind being called an "old man" because he had applied ashes to his beard and hair to make himself look older. In that way he would not be questioned about why he was not in the Duke's army, like many of the other young men.

"Grapes, I have Elbling grapes", Sebastian replied.

Then the soldier asked for Sebastian's identification papers. Most of the men carried their baptismal certificates with them, but if Sebastian showed that it would reveal his true age.

"I used to have my baptism paper, but I lost it a few years ago, and never had a chance to go back to see the priest in my village. It's quite far away, you know".

Sebastian had offered this explanation many times before and the soldiers accepted it with indifference. Sebastian was trying to act a little stupid and hoped that the soldier would show no concern at the lack of his papers. At the back of the wagon another soldier had taken a large cluster of grapes, tasted a few, then threw the bunch to the inquisitor soldier. He tasted a few and said to his comrade,

"These are excellent. Get some more of them."

Sebastian did not mind the distraction of the inquiring soldier. Upon hearing the comment about the grapes, two more soldiers came from their guardhouse and took many more bunches. They removed some of the burlap sheets, throwing them to the ground. Sebastian wanted to get down to retrieve the scarce burlap, but he knew that if he jumped from his seat the soldiers would physically abuse him. Although Sebastian was of good physique, he was several inches shorter than most men. He did not want the soldiers pounding on his head and shoulders. He stayed on the wagon, hoping that the soldier would allow him to pass. The inquisitor continued,

"Oh, so no papers, eh? What is your name, old man?"

Sebastian replied, "Sebastian Mueller".

The soldier replied sarcastically,

"Sebastian Mueller, what!"

Sebastian was inwardly angry but he had to continue to act subservient.

"Oh, Sebastian Mueller, sir." The soldier smiled at his subjugation of this peasant.

He asked, "In what year were you born?"

Sebastian was prepared for the question.

"In 1811, sir", he replied. The soldier appeared to be calculating.

"So, you are forty seven years of age, eh, old man."

"Yes, that is correct, sir" Sebastian lied.

"Alright, old man, that will be four pfennigs.", the soldier demanded. Sebastian searched inside his pocket for the coins. He knew that he must be careful not to extract more than four, or the soldier would demand all of them. He also had to be sure that he had a few more pfennigs secreted in his pocket, a couple to pay the 'river rats', enough to buy a loaf of bread and some ribbon for Elizabeth, and a few to pay the exit tariff when returning home.

Sebastian gave the four coins to the soldier and was told to move on.

'Oh finally', Sebastian thought, 'I am through that encounter'.

He then drove his wagon to the wharf alongside the Mosel. Immediately, two of the 'river rats', men who loitered on the wharves all day, helping to unload wagons so that they could earn enough pfennigs to buy more wine, came to Sebastian.

"Need help to unload sir?" one asked solicitously.

"Yes", Sebastian replied, "help me unload these grapes and do so carefully."

The ship's boatswain had already ordered the lowering of the net to the wharf. Sebastian and the two men started moving the grapes by hand into the cargo net. Sebastian had to caution the two 'river rats' several more times to be careful. After the net was loaded, the boatswain ordered the net raised and swung onto the ships deck. Soon the net was again lowered near Sebastian's wagon. He and his helpers filled the net with a second load. It too was swung up to the ship. Then the ship's agent came ashore. He paid Sebastian twenty Deutschmarks for the grapes. Sebastian was pleased well enough, but he acted not so. He protested,

"Three weeks ago you paid me twenty-two Deutschmarks for the same amount!"

The agent was indifferent, replying that the vintage of this load was a not as good as the previous load. Then with a shrug of his shoulders, he gave Sebastian another Deutschmark. The agent added,

"If you bring these grapes to me in barrels, I can give you a much better payment."

Sebastian replied,

"Yes, I know, but I am unable to afford barrels, nor can I afford to hire a cooper."

With that the agent shrugged his shoulders again and walked away. Though he wanted not to show it, Sebastian was satisfied with his payment. He then reached into his pocket for two pfennigs for the 'river rats'. They took them gleefully and ran to seek another wagon that needed to be unloaded.

It was now mid-afternoon. Sebastian drove his wagon into the village and tied the horse's reins to the rail in front of the general store. He went in and purchased one-half meter each of blue and white ribbon. He knew that Elizabeth would be pleased with these colors because they were the colors of the Virgin Mary, Elizabeth's most revered saint. He also bought a loaf of freshly baked rye bread. It was still warm, and the aroma was mouth watering. How he would have loved to break off a piece, but no, he must bring the loaf home intact. Elizabeth would cut a few pieces for Sebastian and herself, then would remove some of the doughy interior, soak it in goat's milk, and place it in baby Paul's mouth. Paul would suckle it with much pleasure, because Elizabeth, being quite small breasted, was having difficulty providing enough milk for her baby. Paul was reluctantly adjusting to the goat's milk.

Sebastian then went to the local livery stable. He spoke with the liveryman for a few minutes. They both nodded. As the man left to go into one of the stalls, Sebastian noticed the pile of ashes beside the wood stove. He looked about quickly and removed his hat. He took a hand full of the white ash, rubbed some into his hair and beard, then replaced his hat. The next soldier would not question his age, Sebastian was sure.

He boarded his wagon for the ride home. It would take about three hours, but he felt that he must stall a little more so that he would arrive at the exit sentry barrier just before the soldiers would be relieved of their shift. In this way he hoped that the soldiers would be too tired to cause any trouble for him. But when he arrived at the checkpoint, the soldiers were in a nasty mood. They had pulled an old farmer from his wagon and were beating him. The soldiers cursed terribly and continued to pummel the poor man for several minutes. From their calls and curses, Sebastian realized that the poor man had stayed in town too long, had had an extra drink of lager, and was now without money to pay his exit tariff.

Sebastian wanted to get down from his seat and go help the poor old man, but he knew that he would then be beaten also. He was ashamed of himself for his cowardice. But he knew that he had to do something to try to stop the soldiers from continuing to vent their rage on the old man. Sebastian called to one of the soldiers, one that was an onlooker to the melee.

"Say, Herr soldat", Sebastian called. "I have three pfennigs. Can I pay the man's tariff and my own with these?"

He held out the three coins, trying to entice the soldier. The one who seemed to be in charge blurted,

"Oh, I suppose so. We'll demand the other pfennig from this man the next time he comes to town."

Now that they had finished the pummeling, the soldiers were so tired that they hardly questioned Sebastian. They allowed him and the old man to move along after receiving the three pfennigs.

'Lucky that I had saved an extra pfennig', he thought. He was thankful that the sentries did not make him come down from the wagon and search him. He had hidden his newly acquired twenty-one Deutschmarks in his boot.

As Sebastian drove home it was quite dark, but a partial moon had helped to light the trail. And the horse knew the way anyhow. Sebastian succumbed to his reveries again. He recalled the night that he had first embraced Elizabeth. During the first many months after their wedding by the village parish priest in March, Elizabeth had stayed at her parent's home until Paul was born in June, then about two months later moved to the cabin that Sebastian had built. She had been with him now for almost two months. Although Sebastian had become anxious to have his wife in his home, he realized the circumstances and waited patiently for that long seven months for Elizabeth's arrival. After she and the baby moved in, Sebastian had never touched her, except occasionally on her shoulder or had brushed against her arm. He thought of her as still being a child and although he was anxious to embrace her, he felt that he should not offer any amorous movements. Further, he was afraid that any attempt at bodily contact might stir up bad memories of the rape that she had endured. He had to be content to wait until Elizabeth was older and adjusted to her husband and his companionship. She had just turned fifteen in September. He resigned himself to remaining celibate for a while longer. Elizabeth's baby Paul, was born three months after their marriage, on June 19th of 1859, and Sebastian knew that for some time she would only have thoughts of her darling baby, and not of him.

The fall months of 1859 were pleasant. Sebastian nurtured his vines, harvested his grapes, then prepared the vines for the long winter months. He also improved the warmth of the cabin by filling in many of the cracks with thick mud, and adding more pine boughs to the bottom set of logs, to keep the snow from blowing under the logs and into the cabin floor. He covered the floor with several layers of hay. All was now ready for the winter winds and snows. It was a long winter, however, with little to do but wait out the time. Paul was growing and Elizabeth and Sebastian spent many hours being entertained by him, and entertaining him. When their first wedding anniversary had arrived, Sebastian had still not embraced Elizabeth with any passion. He still felt that he dared not.

But in mid-April there had been a very severe storm during the night. There was much thunder and lightning. From his own cot Sebastian knew that Elizabeth, in her own bed cuddling little Paul, was very frightened. He rose, knelt by the side of her bed and embraced her around the shoulders. She instinctively accepted his assurance of protection. They remained in this embrace for many minutes. Finally the storm began to subside. As he loosened his embrace he instinctively kissed Elizabeth on the forehead, then Paul on the top of the head. Elizabeth smiled her approval and thanks. Sebastian reluctantly returned to his cot, continuing to remind himself that he must wait longer for any enjoyment. But after his patient attention that night, Elizabeth seemed much more relaxed around Sebastian, as if no longer fearing that he would demand conjugal satisfaction. Now Sebastian wondered,

'Does she wish it, or fear it?'

Sebastian aroused himself from his reverie. He was approaching his cabin. There he unhitched the old mare and wiped her down, then placed her in her stall. Sebastian then entered his cabin very quietly. Elizabeth was dozing, seated in front of the barely flickering fire. Paul was nestled quite comfortably in her arms. Although Sebastian had been as quiet as he could be, Elizabeth heard him.

"Oh, Sebastian, I'm so glad that you are home. Did your trade go well? Are you happy with your payment?"

Sebastian replied very quietly, but very gleefully,

"Yes, dear Elizabeth, it went very well. As I had told you, I have accumulated many marks over the past three years, even after paying Herr Morganstern his share of my profits. And I have carefully calculated the cost of our travel. Now I am sure. We possess enough Deutschmarks for the fare to Amerika."

CHAPTER TWO

An Encounter with Consideration

A few days later, Sebastian and Elizabeth had loaded their meager possessions into one box. Sebastian lifted it onto the wagon, looked about their cabin one more time, then helped Elizabeth to mount the wagon. He handed little Paul up to Elizabeth. They both wondered how he would behave on their long journey. Sebastian gave a reassuring smile to Elizabeth, climbed onto the wagon himself and snapped the reins to start the horse forward.

Sebastian had made the pine box for their belongings. It was nicely made, and varnished to withstand the moisture of the sea voyage. Elizabeth had placed their heavier clothing at the bottom, lighter clothes, those that would need more readily, on the next layer, and on the top were the clothing and swatches that Paul would need, as well as some cheese and bread. Elizabeth wondered if she had prepared enough swatches for the many changes that Paul would need but even if she wanted to take more, there was no more room. She hoped that she would be able to wash the soiled swatches on the ship. She had also placed a large tin of ground meal that she could mix with water, to feed Paul on the ship. She had tried feeding him some of this as a test and he showed displeasure with the mush, but lacking the availability of goat's milk, or possibly her own, Paul would have to adjust to his new diet. Elizabeth dreaded, but happily anticipated, their four or five week sea voyage.

After riding for nearly an hour, they were approaching the outskirts of their village. Elizabeth looked nervous. She asked Sebastian,

"Do you want to go to say goodbye to your father?"

Sebastian looked sad, shook his head and said,

"No, Elizabeth. There is no need. He is probably drunk as usual and would not even remember that I was there."

Elizabeth squeezed Sebastian's arm in sympathy. Sebastian had already related to Elizabeth the sad story of his young life. His mother had died of the terrible coughing disease. It seemed to Sebastian that he never remembered when his mother did not cough. Then one day, much blood erupted with each cough. Within a few days she died, leaving Sebastian and his older brother Rudolf to be reared by their heavy-drinking father. Two other children, a boy and a girl, had died as small infants. Sebastian was twelve and Rudolf was fourteen when their mother passed away. After their mother's death their father was inconsolable. He started drinking even more heavily. The parish priest and many friends tried to help him adjust to his new circumstances, but he continued to imbibe, more and more each week. When he would be in his greatest drunken state he would beat Rudolf and Sebastian, as if they were the cause of their mother's death. Finally, after two years of such treatment, Rudolf left home, never to be heard from again. Soon after that, Sebastian also left home, going to work in Herr Morganstern's vineyards.

They were nearing Elizabeth's house. To improve the mood, using a lighter tone, Sebastian stated,

"Your papa and Mama will be happy to see Paul again"

"Yes", Elizabeth replied sadly, "but it will be for the last time."

She looked pensive. Now Sebastian squeezed her arm. Soon they arrived at Elizabeth's house, or rather, her former house. Her parents came out showing great excitement. They had seen the wagon coming and were anxious to greet the young family. Elizabeth's younger sisters and brothers, there were five of them, also came out showing excitement.

After a few minutes of joy, with Paul being the center of attention, Elizabeth began saying her goodbyes. Now the mood became somber, then after a few hugs and kisses, everyone was tearful. Finally, Sebastian spoke,

"Well, Herr and Frau Bleier, we must leave. We have to reach Brauneberg by noon."

He helped Elizabeth onto the wagon. Elizabeth's mother was holding Paul. After she and Herr Bleier gave the baby their last kisses, she handed Paul to his mother. Sebastian again gave a snap to the reins and as the horse began to walk ahead, Sebastian and Elizabeth looked back at the waving family that they were leaving forever. Elizabeth dabbed her eyes, but smiled confidently to Sebastian.

When they reached Brauneberg, Sebastian drove straight to the livery stable. The two travelers and their baby dismounted. Then Sebastian removed the box, which held their only worldly possessions. He conferred with the liveryman, gave his old horse a pat on the rump and collected the money that the liveryman had agreed to pay for the horse and wagon.

"Well, Elizabeth", Sebastian commented, "now we have enough to pay for the barge fare to Rotterdam."

Elizabeth nodded to show her approval of Sebastian's prudent planning. They walked to the wharf, with the box on Sebastian's shoulder. After paying the required fare, the family boarded the barge for their six day trip northward.

The afternoon sun was bright. The couple were enjoying their first trip on the Mosel, for neither had ever been very far from their village, and had always traveled on land. As the Mosel River joined the Rhine, they passed the city of Koblenz, gawked at the many castles that bordered the river, admired the vineyards on the upper banks and marveled at the beauty of their native land. They looked into each other's eyes, and in silence each said to the other,

'Are we doing the right thing?'

The barge continued its sail northward. The sun, the view, the exhilaration of the wind sweeping by them made them giddy. It was if they were on a day's outing, with not a care in the world. As evening approached, the lights of the villages and towns along the river began to flicker, becoming brighter it seemed as the sky became darker. Sebastian opened their box, extracted some cheese and a piece of the loaf of bread. They acted like lovers on an evening cruise, even though the two had never embraced with passion, nor even kissed on the mouth. Elizabeth broke the mood, for she had to tend to Paul's needs for food and a clean swatch. She fed Paul the last of the goat's milk. He took it agreeably but she knew that the next feeding would not be so pleasant.

Although the evening was cool, they slept on the deck, for barges had no cabins for passengers. A kindly crewman had come along and provided them a heavy blanket. They thanked him with shivering voices, then crowded close together and tightly covered themselves and their baby. The next two days were again sunny and as the mornings wore on, the days became even warmer. As the barge slipped along the river's smooth surface, every few minutes it seemed that Sebastian and Elizabeth were treated to another magnificent sight. Town after town, Neuwied, Bad Honingen, Linz, Remagen, Bad Honnef and cities like Bonn, passed before their eyes. They were amazed at how many towns, villages and cities that their homeland possessed. Though they knew it not, many had been established hundreds of years, some even a thousand years earlier. When they reached Cologne they were awe struck at the beauty of the ancient cathedral and the medieval buildings surrounding it. At about eleven o'clock of the fourth day, the barge pulled up to a wharf. The barge captain explained that they were about to enter The Netherlands, and all must now submit to the border interrogations. The Captain also had to declare his cargo since he was leaving the country.

Sebastian, Elizabeth and Paul were soon at the office of the border officials. They presented their baptismal papers as proof of identity, nationality and age. This time Sebastian provided his paper to the official without reluctance for he wanted no confusion now. In answer to the questioning official, they declared that they intended to move to Amerika, never intending to return. The agent filled out the necessary exit papers then asked for payment of two and one half Deutschmarks.

"Oh but sir", Sebastian complained, "I believe that the tariff is only two marks, one per person."

The official replied in a matter of fact tone,

"Ja, that is correct. But the baby's fee is one-half mark."

Clearly Sebastian had not anticipated this cost.

"You would charge for this tiny baby?" he asked.

Again the official spoke with finality,

"Yes. Now do you want the baby to go with you or not?"
He and the parents all knew the answer to that question. Sebastian extracted the extra half mark from his pocket and placed it on the table. The official signed the documents and handed them to Sebastian. The two parents and the baby returned to the barge. As they re-boarded the captain asked,

"Are you all set now, young man. We are ready to depart."
Sebastian nodded 'yes' but was still in a slight state of shock. He was upset with himself for not anticipating the baby's tariff.

The afternoon wore on. It was a repeat of the previous afternoons and evenings, but somehow Sebastian was not as joyous. He was now worried about the departure fees at Rotterdam. Elizabeth tried to take his mind off of his trouble by pointing out the lights and the sights of the shoreline. It was indeed a beautiful evening. Paul had to be fed the cornmeal mush, which at first he refused, but later accepted a little and then fell to sleep. The next day was again a repeat of the previous days but as Sebastian and Elizabeth peered at the terrain, it was now flatter, not as picturesque as the hills and vineyards of their Germany.

Shortly after dawn the barge again tied up at a wharf.

"We are at Rotterdam. Time to go ashore for good", the captain shouted.
With much apprehension, Sebastian picked up their box, Elizabeth grasped her baby and they went ashore. Sebastian made several inquiries and finally decided where they must go and how to get there. They must walk to the section of the city called Delfshaven, from where the seagoing vessels depart.

As they walked, each carrying their responsible load, they were gawking at the sights of the city. Neither had ever seen such large buildings, nor as many people hurrying about. After three-quarters of an hour of walking, resting, and walking, they arrived at the seaport area. Again Sebastian inquired and was told where the office of the emigration service was located. With another few minutes they arrived at a building marked "Auswanderung". They entered, only to find that they were at the end of a long queue. Sebastian placed his box on the floor and Elizabeth quickly sat on it, still holding Paul. She knew that it was time for him to complain about not being fed. She unbuttoned her blouse in anticipation. Paul immediately demanded his milk. Elizabeth placed him on her breast with as much modesty as was possible and offered him nourishment. Fortunately, this time, Paul found contentment there.

When Sebastian and his family reached the front of the line, and after submitting to the questioning and offering their German identification, the Dutch emigration officer commented, "Germans, eh, lots of you folks leaving. What's wrong over there?"

Sebastian made no reply. The official then requested three guilders. Sebastian reached for all the coins remaining in his pocket. He said,

"I have two Deutschmarks. Will that be enough?"

The official calculated the conversion in his head then said,

"No, you are short one guilder."

Sebastian complained as he had previously to the German official,

"Why should such a tiny baby have to pay?"

With exasperation beginning to show, the official stated,

"I don't make the rules, but I do have to enforce them. Now, please, either pay or leave the line. Many are waiting."

Just then the man behind Sebastian reached around him. Thinking that the man was being impolite and trying to move him aside, Sebastian began to complain. But then the official said to Sebastian,

"Alright sir. Now you are properly paid."

He signed the papers and handed them to Sebastian. Suddenly Sebastian realized that the man behind him had paid the necessary additional guilder. He turned to the man, shook his hand vigorously and said,

"Oh! Danke schon! Danke sehr! Thank you sir! You are indeed an angel come to earth." Sebastian looked at Elizabeth who was now tearful.

"Elizabeth, this kindly man has helped us greatly, even though we are strangers."

Then Sebastian thought,

'Maybe God provided this man to repay me for when I saved the poor farmer from being beaten.'

They now walked to the pier where the ship *George Washington* was tied up. Sebastian found the ticket agent's office, paid the fare using a good sum of the money secreted in his boot, and received the boarding tickets. Turning to Elizabeth, with an air of self-satisfaction, he said,

"Well, my dear, before the end of 1860 we will be in Amerika."

Elizabeth smiled broadly and raised herself up on her toes to kiss him on the cheek. Sebastian reddened somewhat, looking about to see if anyone had seen their intimacy.

Although the ship would not sail until morning, they were allowed to board, and were directed below decks. Sebastian descended the ladder, balancing their box on his shoulder. Placing the box on the lower deck, he then reached up for Paul. Elizabeth handed him down then descended herself. At the bottom of the ladder she let out an involuntary gasp. Although the cabin had been cleaned since arriving in port, the stench of the seasickness of previous passengers was still nearly nauseating. She immediately wondered if she or the baby would them selves become ill with seasickness. The lower cabin had only one lantern burning. It was dark and very dingy. Several other families had already come aboard and had selected their locale for the voyage. Sebastian looked about, sighted what looked like a corner that might be endurable, then led Elizabeth there. Through it all, Paul was peaceful, for which his parents were very grateful.

The pair were tired, but anxious for morning to arrive so that they could see what the conditions of their passage would be like. But right now, they needed rest. Sebastian opened the box, removed their only blanket and several swatches for Paul, a small portion of cheese for Elizabeth and himself, and settled down for the night. He was just about dozing off when Elizabeth whispered,

"Sebastian. We should say a prayer of thanksgiving to the Lord for all that he has given us."

The two joined hands and recited the Hail Mary, a favorite prayer of Catholics everywhere. Again Sebastian was about to drift off to sleep when a commotion began on the ladder. A family, no, several families were descending. There were several sets of parents and many, many children. They spoke in a language that Sebastian and Elizabeth had rarely heard in their village. Occasionally a German word was uttered but mostly the arriving passengers spoke their own language. Although Sebastian had never seen one, he sensed who these families were. He whispered to Elizabeth,

"They are Jews, Elizabeth. They speak Hebrew."

Elizabeth accepted his explanation.

"Oh, I see.", she said.

Everyone was tired so that all settled down and within minutes were apparently asleep, Sebastian, Elizabeth and Paul included.

Starting in the early morning more and more people descended the ladder to this lower deck. Everyone grumbled, wondering how all the people would be accommodated. Sebastian wanted to go up on deck to determine what was happening. Were more people coming aboard? How would they obtain the food that was to be included in their passage cost? What was the sailing time? But although he was very anxious about all these matters, he dared not leave Elizabeth and the baby, at least not right now. There was too much confusion, too many new arrivals grappling for space, too many distrustful looking people.

Finally things began to settle. It seemed that all who were assigned to steerage were now aboard. People were settling down, apparently satisfied that they had obtained all the space that they would be able to inveigle. Crewmen now came to the top of the ladder.

"Hear ye down there! Bring yer cup or dish fer yer food. Don't rush! There's enough for alla ya!"

But most people did rush. Sebastian was the twentieth or so person in line. Each person had to scramble up a few rungs of the ladder, reach up so that the crewman could ladle some stew into their utensil, then scramble off the ladder. The process took quite some time. As he waited his turn, Sebastian looked often towards Elizabeth to be sure that she and the baby were alright. Elizabeth always smiled back bravely, though in her heart she was worried about how they would survive the next four difficult weeks.

In the corner of the deck where the Jewish families had gathered together, they began to pray aloud, in Hebrew. Most of the other passengers did not understand their words but they tried not to intrude into the Jewish rite. But considering the crowded conditions and the scramble for food, it was very difficult not to disturb the praying families in some way. Sebastian struggled to bring the tin plate of stew to Elizabeth without spilling it upon others, nor to lose any of the precious contents. He, nor any of the other passengers, knew when next they might be fed.

When they finished their meager meal Elizabeth wiped clean the tin plate then poured a small amount of cornmeal and water into it. Sebastian had obtained fresh water from a barrel on the main deck. While he was there he learned from a crewman that the ship would sail with the outgoing tide just after mid-day. Elizabeth stirred the cornmeal and water then fed it to Paul in small and carefully timed increments. At first refusing the mixture, then wiping it from his lips with his tongue, then finally accepting some from the spoon, Paul learned to accept the meal. He would have many more like it, though he knew this not.

Through the few portholes it could be seen that the sun had crossed over the center of the ship. Everyone anticipated the ships departure, and then finally they realized that the ship was moving. When they heard the crew singing above, as they hoisted the sails, the entire cabin was filled with cheering voices. All hundreds of them were on their way to America. After the shouts died out, many knelt in prayer. Paul kicked in his mother's arms as if he too, knew the importance of their departure to Amerika.

CHAPTER THREE

An Encounter with Tolerance

By the next morning the ship was well out in deep water. Below in the steerage deck the motion of the rise and fall of the hull in the water was beginning to affect many of the passengers. If they were able, they scrambled up the ladder to the top deck and gulped in as much fresh air as they could. For some it did not provide enough invigoration and they vomited over the side of the ship. The wind blew it aft, onto some of the other surprised and then disgusted passengers.

Sebastian was feeling well enough so he climbed to the upper deck. He had a glorious feeling as he rode the deck and felt the ships pulsating rhythm as the hull struck the waves. After a few minutes he went below again. He coaxed Elizabeth to leave their space. Reluctantly she did so. Sebastian climbed up and reached down as far as he could. Elizabeth held Paul as high as she could and Sebastian pulled him up to his chest. Elizabeth then followed. Holding Paul with just one arm, Sebastian caught her hand at the top and pulled her upward. Now she smiled broadly, feeling the wind in her face and the sense of the speed of the ship. They looked upward at the billowing sails that seemed to fill the beautiful blue sky like cumulus clouds on a summer day. They were both laughing because they felt so exhilarated at the thought of starting a new life. Neither had any doubt now that they had made the right decision. Sebastian was holding Paul on the leeward side so that he would not lose his breath to the wind. Paul's face showed that he was plainly astonished at the new feelings that he was experiencing.

After a few more minutes the three went below again. Upon smelling the odors below, Elizabeth wished that she could spend the entire voyage on the top deck, but she knew that was not possible, for soon they would likely be experiencing much more hostile weather.

Each day passed as the one before. The scramble for a little food, then obtaining water from the barrel while straddling bodies laying everywhere, then an occasional very short visit to the top deck. Upon return Sebastian would have to insist on repossessing their space which was quickly filled by the horde of overcrowded passengers. Elizabeth found it very difficult to feed and change Paul's clothing, but all around them everyone ignored the child's pleadings for food and dry clothing. And worst of all was moving through the crowd to get to the ship's toilet and when arriving there, enduring the offensive stench and unimaginable filthy conditions.

When Elizabeth returned to her space next to Sebastian, Paul was crying loudly. Elizabeth had tried to feed him the cornmeal mush earlier, but Paul had refused it. Elizabeth tried to suckle him with her milk but she had great difficulty, not just in supplying the amount of milk that Paul seemed to want, but now her breasts were hurting very much. Elizabeth again tried the cornmeal food. Although Paul now accepted a small amount of the cornmeal mush, it was obvious that he was not feeling satisfied with that nourishment. It was evident that he wanted his mother's milk. Elizabeth had tried to wean Paul, knowing that it would be difficult to breastfeed him on the ship, but Paul had difficulty in accepting the substitute method of feeding, and Elizabeth was too loving to force the matter.

Elizabeth looked at Sebastian with pleading. Her eyes seemed to say,

'What am I to do now, Sebastian?'

In reply, Sebastian only shrugged that he knew not what to do either. Sebastian took the boy from Elizabeth and cuddled the baby close, trying to convince Paul that the warmth of his body would ease his yearnings.

One of the nearby Jewish ladies, a stout one who had an infant herself, had interpreted Elizabeth's helpless look, and Sebastian's equally helpless none reply. She reached out for Paul. Sebastian looked surprised, then pleased that someone else would be willing to coddle poor Paul. The lady took Paul, opened her dress top wider than it already was, and placed Paul on her breast. Her own baby was suckling on the other breast. Paul now began to suckle the stout lady's very abundant breast. From his sounds he appeared to find satisfaction in his effort.

"He may not get much milk, but he's happy to have the warmth and the softness of my flesh to comfort him", she told Elizabeth. Soon, both infants fell asleep. Elizabeth started to reach for Paul but the Jewish lady motioned for her to let Paul sleep at her breast.

"The little darlings need their sleep, and I'm a fine cushion for them to rest on."

Elizabeth smiled her gratefulness and Sebastian relaxed his whole body from the tension that he had developed while hoping that Paul would settle down. He placed his arms around Elizabeth who was now finally able to sleep without worry about her inability to satisfy Paul.

During the next few days Elizabeth and Sebastian became good friends with the Jewish lady, whose name she said, was Sarah. She had introduced her husband, a frail man with the name of Efrom, but he maintained silence throughout most of the voyage. Elizabeth and Sarah enjoyed many hours of laughter as they breast fed their infants and Sebastian was very pleased that both Elizabeth and Paul were much less burdensome to him.

Although Efrom and Sarah's family and all of the other Jewish families were enduring the same hardships as the rest of the passengers, they acted as if all was well. Each morning and each night they prayed, aloud as a group. Sebastian and Elizabeth understood not a word, but they knew that they were praying to their God, in thanks for the opportunity granted them, and in supplication for a better future life than that which they were leaving.

Sebastian and Elizabeth prayed too, quietly and in unison, with hands held to each other. When they finished their evening prayer, Elizabeth always smiled at Sebastian, demonstrating to him that she was happy to endure these temporary hardships, for the sake of a new life. Then, before falling asleep each night, Sebastian made a knife mark on one of the planks, indicating the number of days since they had left port. Now he scratched the sixteenth mark, and then smiled at Elizabeth, his face indicating to her that it would not be long now to their arrival in the new world.

In the afternoon of the seventeenth day the weather changed for the worse. The sea was now very choppy. The ship was bounding up and down with great ferocity. The ocean treated the ship as a toy being swept along a swiftly moving stream. From below deck everyone could hear the howling of the wind and the shouts of the sailors. Soon one of the passengers called out,

"Hurricane! She be a damned hurricane!"

Hearing this, the children all began to cry. The adults looked anxiously at each other, then pulled their smaller children tight to them. Sebastian and Elizabeth huddled and squeezed the baby between them.

"Oh my God, Sebastian. What will become of us?"

Sebastian, tried to give a reassuring reply.

"Don't worry my dear. This ship and its crew have no doubt experienced this kind of weather before. They know what to do. The ship will endure the wind and rough water, and all will be fine in the morning."

There was nothing else for anyone to do except pray. Sebastian and Elizabeth held hands as was their custom, and in low voices recited their Hail Mary prayer. The Jewish families again began to chant their prayers aloud. Several others, mostly men, began to shout prayers to the Almighty, overly emoting as they beseeched Him to protect them from the turbulent storm. Sebastian leaned close to Elizabeth, whispering in her ear,

"No doubt these people haven't prayed in years. Now they want us to think that they know God personally. Do you remember the story of the Pharisees?"

Elizabeth giggled a little, easing the tenseness of the moment.

The wind and turbulence worsened. The ship creaked as the hull was being contorted by the twin forces of nature. Everyone mumbled that they did not believe that the storm could go on much longer, but it did. The steerage deck, and no doubt the upper decks as well, began to become places of unimaginable din. Everyone was either screaming, praying aloud, or cursing, depending upon their beliefs about life. Children became even more frightened by this incessant and raucous noise. The night seemed to drag on forever. While everyone was eager to see the dawn, they simultaneously wondered if the dawn would really bring gentler waters. Finally, although the storm did not subside, the din did. By the hours just before dawn, everyone was so exhausted that some fell off to sleep, while the others at least became less boisterous, seeming to accept whatever fate was in store for them.

Sebastian and Elizabeth, and even Paul, had fallen asleep. They were suddenly awakened by someone shouting

"The storm is past! We are still afloat! The Lord has answered our prayers."

The Jewish families began again to chant their prayers, this time in thanksgiving, rather than in supplication for security as they had before the storm. Many other passengers made the Sign Of The Cross or knelt as best they could, their lips also giving praise and thanks to the Almighty. Throughout the ordeal, although Sebastian had shown Elizabeth many signs of confidence that they would survive, during the middle of the night he actually felt quite the opposite. Now, like everyone else, he was elated. He signaled to Elizabeth that he was going to then upper deck. He had to step carefully to avoid the many who were lying on the deck, and stepped even more carefully to avoid the many splotches of vomit left by the ailing passengers.

On the main deck the air was again very exhilarating. The sun was shining brightly and the sails were filled with the air of the Atlantic's new-world side. The top deck was filled with passengers, all enjoying the same sensations as Sebastian. He glanced about over the heads of the many, seeking the location of a crewman. Toward the bow he saw one, snaked his way to him, and inquired of the time remaining until landfall. The seaman, who looked very experienced to Sebastian, replied, "I would dare say that by the day after tomorrow, we should see the coast of Newfoundland." Sebastian literally danced his way back through the crowd, scrambled down the ladder to his deck below and shouted the news,

"By the day after tomorrow we shall see land!"

Hundreds of voices in unison shouted out their jubilation. When the initial cheering ended, many asked Sebastian how he knew of this wonderful news. He explained that a very skilled seaman had told him, and he doubted not this man's knowledge of the seas.

The following two days, being of pleasant weather, found nearly every passenger on deck, eagerly looking ahead for signs of land. Joviality reigned supreme. Most began conversations with other travelers, be they of the same deck accommodations or not. It soon became apparent that the common subject of the moment was the question,

"After we land in New York, where are you going.?"

The answers were as varied as there were passengers. Some were planning to remain in the huge city of New York because they already had relatives that had migrated and settled there, some recently and some many years before. But most stated that they planned to move inland, to places called upper New York,

New Jersey, Pennsylvania, and some even further west, to a new area called Wisconsin, where it was said that thousands of acres of beautiful farmland was available to new settlers. Many now excitedly displayed the letters that they had received from relatives or friends, describing how they should take a steam train or a boat to places like Philadelphia, Pittsburgh, even Chicago. Everyone seemed confident that they would have no trouble reaching their destination, for wasn't Amerika overflowing with an abundance of steam trains, river boats, canal boats, or of course, stage coaches.

Sebastian too, was confident that Elizabeth's cousin Johan would meet them at the pier. Johan had written to Elizabeth's father a year earlier, offering to help his family to come to Amerika, where there were good jobs for everyone, in the city or on the farms. Elizabeth's parents did not feel that they could migrate for they felt that they could not obtain the required tariff for themselves and all their children. And they certainly would not leave without their children. In his letter Johan had indicated that the girls in the family could find employment as housemaids among one of the many wealthy families of the village where he lived in upstate New York. Elizabeth's father had replied that although his family would not be emigrating, Elizabeth looked forward to this opportunity. His letter was sent before the rape incident and the changes to her life as a result of that heinous offense. Later, Elizabeth's father had sent another letter to Johan to tell of the details of Elizabeth's arrival, though he did not mention the baby or Elizabeth's marriage. By the time of posting that letter, Sebastian had made arrangements for their passage on the brig *George Washington*, sailing from Rotterdam in very early November. Sebastian hoped firstly that Johan had received the letter, and secondly that Johan had a way of learning the date of the ship's arrival. He and Elizabeth realized that there might be difficulty in finding Johan on the pier among the hundreds that were expected to be greeting passengers. Further, Johan had not seen Elizabeth for five years now. Would he recognize the girl of ten that he knew, when she is now much older. And had Elizabeth's father told Johan that she would arrive with a husband and a child? Would he now wish that he had not made his generous offer to help Elizabeth? Sebastian and Elizabeth discussed the many possibilities but remained confident that they would find happiness in the New World. Of course they did not anticipate the confusion and time-consuming interrogations that would soon delay them at the pier in New York City.

As the many passengers returned to their respective accommodations and decks for the evening, a somber mood had now set in. Although earlier in the day all had spoken with confidence about their new life, now they began to show some worry about reaching their final destination and whether the rendezvous arranged with their relative or friend on the pier would be effective. Sebastian was just as worried. Would Elizabeth recognize Johan? Did she still remember him? She might, because he was already a young man when he left, the last time that she saw him. Although Elizabeth felt confident that she would recognize Johan, Sebastian spent a restless night, worried about the possibility of being stranded in the great city of New York, for even in the remote villages of Europe, all had learned of the huge city, the city that graciously welcomed travelers from everywhere in the world.

It was the evening of the nineteenth day at sea. The exhilaration of the morning news had subsided. The rigors of the voyage were exhausting. Many people began to show their tension, and even anger, by snarling at one another. Families were squabbling among themselves. Small children complained that they had not enough to eat. Fathers retorted angrily that they had had as much as was available, that no one had enough food. Older siblings complained that during the night one had usurped more of the blanket that they shared. Mothers were showing their exasperation at trying to keep their family peaceful, and remain as one.

At sunset the Jewish families began their usual prayers. It did not seem to Sebastian that they were any louder than before, but one man, no doubt also exasperated and tense due to the long voyage, shouted,

"Will you damned Jews shut up!"

Everyone quickly looked up with shocked expressions, but no one said anything. After a few seconds of silence, Sebastian felt that something should be said to relieve the tension and to make the Jewish families feel less insulted.

"Hey there! Stop that. That's not the way to speak to others. These families are just praying in their traditional manner. Do you not also pray in your own tradition?"

"Well", the man retorted, "I don't shout my prayers, annoying others. I say them quietly, to God."

Sebastian wanted to show calmness. No loud retort; just a conversational tone was best, he thought.

"Look, we are all here because we chose to find a new life in a new country. One where people are said to be more tolerant of each other. We're all tense and greatly exhausted by these many days at sea in these tight quarters. I don't think that you really meant to criticize these families for the way that they pray, did you?"

The man looked sheepish,

"No, I guess I didn't mean to criticize. And I really didn't mean to insult anybody. I'm just tired. I'm very tired. I'm sorry that I shouted at you folks over there."

The Jewish men, especially the oldest that seemed to be their leader, nodded several times but said nothing. Everyone interpreted the nods of the Jewish man as an acceptance of the non-Jewish man's apology. No more words were spoken. Elizabeth squeezed Sebastian's hand. She was very pleased that he had interceded. Her Jewish lady friend also nodded and smiled at Sebastian. Everyone now settled down in their restricted spaces, trying to find the sleep that they had lost by the brief incident.

Elizabeth and Paul were now settled and appeared to be asleep. Finally Sebastian too, fell asleep, but he was listless. Dreams filled his subconscious, dreams of being engulfed by a throng of people, of losing Elizabeth and Paul, of wondering what would become of them and of himself, and of wandering in what must be the cavernous streets of the city that was the largest in the whole world. When the many passengers began to stir at dawn, Sebastian was glad that he was now awake, hoping that his terrible dreams were just that, dreams, non-existent realities. As soon as Elizabeth stirred a little, Paul began demanding attention. His bellowing brought Sebastian back to the present, the day that they might sight land, the day, he mistakenly thought, that they would

Encounters Elizabeth's
arrive in New York's magnificent harbor.

CHAPTER FOUR

An Encounter with Anxiety

As was his practice, as soon as Sebastian awakened and attended to any needs of Elizabeth and Paul, he went to the top deck. As soon as he looked over the starboard railing he let a whoop. A few other passengers were also on deck. They had already seen the land. When they saw Sebastian's reaction they laughed. A well dressed stranger said,

"A beautiful sight eh, young man!"

Sebastian's broad smile was his answer. He instinctively ran back to the hatch, scrambled down the ladder and shouted,

"Take a look out the starboard portholes everyone! We're in sight of land!"

Everyone scrambled to the right side of the ship, jostling each other to get a view out of the small portholes. All began cheering, shouting to each other, some even dancing.

Sebastian took Paul in his arms then led Elizabeth to a porthole. She stretched on her toes to peer out.

"Oh Sebastian! How wonderful! Will we land today or tomorrow?"

Suddenly Sebastian realized that the sight of land had surprised him so much that he forgot to inquire about the time of reaching port. He pretended to know,

"Oh, it won't be long now Elizabeth."

The mood of the passengers became jubilant. Some prayed, most sang or

36

called out joyfully in acclamations.

"It won't be long now! By tomorrow we'll be Amerikans!"

"Let's start packing our goods."

Every husband hugged his wife, every mother held the hands or hugged their children. Everyone laughed, some trying to dance in the tiny space that they occupied.

After the celebration calmed down somewhat, Sebastian quietly bade Elizabeth goodbye again and scrambled up the ladder once more. The deck was crowded with many more of the passengers, all in the same joyous mood as those below. Sebastian looked anxiously about for the seaman that he had spoken with a day earlier. He spied him again near the ship's prow. Making his way through the crowd, he approached the sailor.

"My good man, when do you expect that we will arrive in New York?" The sailor looked up from the coil of rope that he was arranging, looked somewhat pensive, then spoke aloud his mental calculations.

"Well, now, we be off the coast of Maine, have to sail 'round Cape Cod, then Long Island. Oh, I'd reckon that we've another day and a half, mebbe two, to get to the Hudson river's mouth. That is, if we can keep hold of this spankin' breeze we've got".

Sebastian had never heard the names of any of the places that the sailor recited, but he assumed that the seaman was describing the end of the journey.

"So, New York in about two days?" Sebastian asked.

"Yep, I reckon", was the sailor's terse reply.

With that Sebastian began to run towards the hatch to go below again. Halfway there he stopped himself.

'Calm yourself now Sebastian. Don't go down there and get all the folks riled up again. The sailor said *maybe* two days, if the wind keeps up. I better not start getting the folks anymore anxious than they are already.'

Sebastian clambered down the ladder slowly. As he approached Elizabeth, she asked anxiously,

"Did you find out when we'll land, Sebastian?"

With a small shake of his head up and down, and with an unnoticeable finger to his lips, he signaled Elizabeth that he could not speak of it now. She nodded that she understood. Later, when all was quiet, Sebastian gave Elizabeth a nod and secretly held up two fingers. She returned the nod, indicating that she understood. They continued the day in a casual manner, tending to Paul and themselves as needed. Sarah, the Jewish lady, looked at the two of them with a smile, indicating that she too, knew their secret.

The next morning produced even more anxiety. Everyone that could possibly do so went to the main deck. The Captain shouted into his bull-horn,

"Here, you folks from steerage. You've got to go below. You're crowding the deck so much that my seamen can't tend their duties. Get below, all a' ya!"

With this order, some went slowly below, many did not. The Captain gave the order a second time. Now most of the steerage passengers, including Sebastian, Elizabeth and Paul, went below again. The rest of the day dragged on it seemed, because everyone was awaiting the grand day that they would see New York.

Shortly after noon of that next day, a sailor up in the crow's nest, shouted.

"There be New York. Look ahead to the starboard side."

Those on deck raced to the right side of the ship, craned their necks and stretched on tip toe, but they were not able to see the city. The sailor above had the advantage of being able to see a few miles ahead more than those on deck. But the word spread throughout the ship very quickly. Every person in steerage as well as all the other passengers came to the starboard side of the ship. Now the Captain showed great concern,

"Ye damned fools! What are ye tryin' to do? Capsize my ship? Blast it, some a' ya get to the leeward side or we'll take on water through the gunnals. Then none of us will see New York!"

Fortunately, some of the passengers heeded his warning and moved back to the opposite side of the deck. As everyone anxiously peered over the water, someone shouted,

"I see 'er. I see New York. See the water towers!"

Then everyone shouted as they began to make out the top of the buildings.

'What a sight!', most were thinking, for none had seen so many buildings, spread over such a large area. After another hour, the ship turned northward, into the harbor. Hundreds of boats of all kinds and sizes now came into view.

"My God, Elizabeth, did you ever see such a sight?" Sebastian exclaimed more than he asked.

"Oh my, Oh my!"

was all that Elizabeth could express. She repeated it over several times. Now the Captain shouted instructions to all through his megaphone. No one was to interfere with the crewmen. Everyone was to remain calm. Everyone was to prepare their personal belongings for departure from the ship. All passengers must be interrogated and examined by the officials as soon as they stepped off the gangplank.

"Hurry now, get your gear together. Return to the main deck for disembarkation. Don't crowd the gangplank. Listen here! Due to the many passengers and due to the other ships that have also just landed, some a' ya may not get off this ship until very late, or even tomorrow. The officials can't move everyone that fast. Just wait your turn, and be calm." Calm? How could any human be calm at this moment of their life? Everyone had that same thought. Sebastian, in addition to a lack of calmness, was very much worried about the possibility of not finding Elizabeth's cousin Johan, who was to meet them.

The steerage passengers were, of course, the last to be allowed to disembark from the ship. Although the ship had docked in mid afternoon, it was now nearly ten o'clock at night. When it came time for Sebastian, Elizabeth and Paul to be allowed on the main deck, they peered as best they could into the crowd of people on the wharf who were waiting for their loved ones to depart the ship. The few lanterns burning on the wharves made it almost impossible to discern faces. Still, everyone stared into the semi-darkness, straining to see, and hoping that they would find the one face they sought, among the many hundreds of faces in the crowds on the wharf.

Sebastian, holding their treasured box of goods on his shoulder, and Elizabeth, holding onto Paul tightly, scrambled forward, all the while being pressed hard by the many other passengers. They tried nevertheless to look over the heads of fellow passengers to see if any one might be identified as

Johan. Sebastian asked Elizabeth several times,

"Do you think that you will recognize him?"

For her part, although she nodded 'yes' each time the question was asked, she herself wondered how she would locate Johan in the throng of people. She then realized that many hundreds of other passengers had been processed already during the afternoon. Did many of the waiting relatives and friend already leave the wharf? If so, the earlier crowd must have been even more gigantic.

Sebastian, Elizabeth and Paul finally reached the top of the gangplank. Their view was better now, but in the dim glow of the many gaslights, they doubted that they would find Johan. Suddenly Elizabeth screamed,

"There he is Sebastian! There he is!"

She pointed into the middle of the crowd.

"How in the world do you know?" Sebastian asked incredulously.

"See the man with the Tyrolean hat, the one with the long white feather sticking up into the air", was Elizabeth's confident reply.

Sebastian looked doubtful and puzzled. Elizabeth explained,

"My father gave that hat to Johan when he was leaving Germany. And Mother added the very long feather as a good-luck token. It's an ostrich plum that she had for many years." Sebastian now smiled broadly. The two began waving frantically to the man with the feathered hat. The man waved back, but no doubt wondered why the man near Elizabeth was also waving.

They reached the bottom of the gangplank. An official directed them to follow the line of other immigrants who were walking towards a building that looked like a fortress. When they reached the inner part of the building, they realized that indeed, it was an old fortress, but the inner court had been roofed over. Many tables were lined there, with two officials at each table.

When they reached the front of the line they were directed to a table that a family had just vacated. The lady of the family looked back. It was Sarah. She waved madly at Elizabeth, threw her a kiss in the air, waved goodbye and was gone. Sebastian had been distracted by the goodbye to the Jewish family. One of the officials abruptly demanded their attention.

"What is your name mien Herr?"

The official asked, speaking in broken German. Sebastian replied for the entire family.

"Mueller, sir. Sebastian Mueller. And this is my wife Elizabeth and our son Paul."

He had emphasized the *our*, to which Elizabeth smiled proudly.

"Alright Mister Miller. Show me your papers."

Sebastian reached into his pocket to extract his own and Elizabeth's and Paul's baptismal certificates. As he handed them to the official he corrected the pronunciation of his surname.

"My name is Mueller, sir."

The official reached for the three certificates and replied a little sarcastically,

"Well, you had better get used to being called Miller, because that what most Americans will call you from now on."

As the official verified the three identification papers, Sebastian looked at Elizabeth with a puzzled look. His expression asked,

'Why cannot I be called by my own name?'

Elizabeth shrugged, for she had no answer to give Sebastian.

Now the official addressed Elizabeth.

"This paper says that your name is Elizabeth Bleier. Is it Miller or Bleier?"

"Oh", Sebastian started to explain. The official placed his hand up in front of Sebastian.

"I'm asking this lady, not you sir."

Elizabeth quickly explained,

"Why sir, that is my madchenname, how you say, unmarried name. Of course I was not married at baptism" Elizabeth giggled slightly.

"But you are married?" the official prompted.

Now Sebastian came to the realization that he had better show their marriage certificate. He quickly reached into another pocket, extracted the paper and presented it to the official. The official studied the paper for quite some time, looked strongly at both Sebastian, then Elizabeth. Looking again back at Sebastian, but addressing Elizabeth he stated,

"Well, young lady, you are quite young to be a mother. But you are married, eh?" Sebastian reddened a little, somewhat in embarrassment, but more in indignation. He replied with a reassuring tone.

"Oh, yes sir, we are married. Vater Kirchner, our parish priest married us. We had a wonderful wedding, and Elizabeth's parents and family were all there."

He was trying hard to allay any question of why two people of such diverse ages had gotten married. The official looked once more at the marriage certificate, handed it back to Sebastian then asked,

"Who is sponsoring you? Is someone to meet you?"

Sebastian quickly answered,

"Ja, oh ja. My wife's cousin is waiting on the pier at this time. His name is Johan Bleier."

"Good!" the official replied.

"Now a few more questions. Do either of you two, or the baby have a strong cough?" Before Sebastian could answer, the official asked,

"Do either of you or the baby have any running sores?"

Sebastian quickly answered both questions,

"No sir, absolutely not."

The official seemed satisfied but nevertheless asked one more question,

"How much money do you have, mien Herr?"

Sebastian, in an effort to satisfy the man's question, extracted several German paper notes from his deepest pocket.

"I, er, we have eighteen Deutschmarks, Sir."

Sebastian proudly showed the money that he had managed to sequester during the entire voyage. The official made a quick mental calculation.

"Good, that's enough", the man replied. "Now put it back in your pocket, and be very careful not to show it around too much."

Sebastian seemed puzzled at the man's warning. Then the official smiled and said,

"Alright, you may enter. Welcome to America."

As Sebastian and Elizabeth hugged each other strongly, with Paul between them, the official laughed. Then looking at the large clock on the wall, the immigration officer said,

"Well, it's not midnight yet. It's still the twenty-eighth of November, 1860".

He stamped a card for each of them, handed them to Sebastian and said,

"Go ahead you two, oh I mean three. And may the good Lord be with you!"

For Paul's part, he did not even realize that while he slept, he came into a new world.

In their hurry to find Johan, Sebastian almost forgot their box. He had started to depart the area of the tables and the queues, then quickly ran back a few steps to retrieve the box. Many others in the line laughed at Sebastian's excited condition. As soon as they left the large fortress building, they walked onto the wharf where they hoped to find Johan again. Johan had been watching for Elizabeth. He really did not recognize her at first but Elizabeth spotted his unique hat and feather. She called loudly,

"Johan! It is me, Elizabeth, over here!"

The feather traveled through the crowd until it, and the man under it, broke from the crowd and ran to Elizabeth. He hugged her madly, turning several circles. Luckily, Sebastian had placed their box on the ground and was sitting on it while holding Paul, otherwise Paul would have been smothered by Johan's robust hug. Elizabeth finally broke free of Johan. She pulled Johan towards Sebastian.

"Johan, this is my husband Sebastian Mueller, and my son Paul."

Sebastian rose, extended his hand, and waited for Johan's amiable greeting. But Johan was obviously flabbergasted. Instead of extending his hand, he clearly showed his lack of comprehension.

"Husband? Baby? Elizabeth, I do not understand. You are too young to have a baby, or a husband!"

Elizabeth replied sounding apologetic.

"I know that this is a shock to you Johan. But we had no time to write you of the events of the last many months. I am indeed the mother of this little boy. He is Paul, and he is now seventeen months old. And this is my wunderbar hazband Sebastian."

Then looking Sebastian squarely in the face, she added,

"who I love most dearly."

With that, Sebastian hugged Elizabeth and Paul at the same time and rejoiced,

"And I love you, dear Elizabeth."

They both realized that that was the first time that they had spoken openly of their love.

Now Johan showed impatience.

"Come, it is now late. We must find shelter for the night. I have been here since early morning. I am very tired."

Because of the tone of his voice, Elizabeth wondered if he now wished that he had not come to meet them. Sebastian too, heard the annoyance in Johan's words. Sebastian tried to sound conciliatory,

"We are most grateful to you Johan. It is certainly kind of you to help us this way."

Johan continued to walk ahead of them. Soon he stopped in front a building that had sign hanging over the door, having one word, "INN". Johan explained with only one word,

"Gasthaus." He led them in.

The sleepy innkeeper stated that he did indeed have a room with two beds. The charge was thirty-five cents.

"Do you have money, Sebastian?" Johan asked.

Sebastian offered one of his Deutschmarks, which Johan handed over to the innkeeper. Sebastian had no idea if it was the proper amount, but the innkeeper offered no money in return.

'My', Sebastian thought, 'my money will soon be gone if everything in Amerika costs so much.'

They all went to the one available room. Elizabeth and Paul shared one of the beds, Sebastian and Johan the other.

Early the next morning Elizabeth remained in bed with the blanket secluding her as she fed Paul. The two men had arisen earlier. Sebastian was looking out of the window, but all that he could see it seemed, was red-brick walls. As the men waited for Paul to finish his breakfast, Sebastian asked Johan,

"Are all of the buildings made of stone? The building through which we passed on arrival, it looked like a fortress. Is it so?"

Johan's answer was somewhat matter of fact, for he had by now seen enough American buildings that he acted as if he were an expert.

"Yes, many are made of this red clay that you see, baked to harden them, and many are made of large blocks of stone from the many quarries here in America. The building that you were processed through was indeed an old fortress, but has been used for many purposes since. It became a theatre, then a botanical garden, now the immigration center. It was called Fort Clinton, but is now called Castle Garden. When I came through five years ago they were just beginning to use this old fort. You see, because so many of us were coming from our old countries, they needed a larger place. A man told me about the place then. And the red bricks that you see, they are made in many places called brickyards. It seems that the men cannot make them fast enough for the many buildings being erected here."

Sebastian thought about Johan's answer, then mentally compared these buildings to those in his village and nearby towns. There, the buildings were made of stones from the field, or of hewn trees.

Elizabeth had now completed her motherly duties, realigned her clothing, in which she had slept, and stated,

"Sebastian, Johan, I am ready. To where do we now travel?"

As she spoke, Sebastian was rearranging the contents of their box and replacing the lid. Johan replied to Elizabeth,

"First, we will take breakfast at some nearby gasthaus. This one has no rastarant. Then we must take a horse-trolley to the coach stable. Then we will board the stagecoach traveling north, to Altady."

Some snow had fallen during the night so all stepped carefully. Finding a small delicatessen they quickly ate a biscuit and gulped coffee, for which

Sebastian again made payment. Then Johan hurried them outside. He led them, walking quite fast. Elizabeth was breathless but kept up with the men. As they walked, then rode the horse-drawn trolley, Sebastian and Elizabeth looked at each other with wonderment in their eyes. Never had they seen so many people, horses and wagons, children playing and shouting in the streets now covered with a light snow, and merchants and street peddlers everywhere. The resultant confusion, noise and stench were everywhere.

They reached the stage depot at about noon. Sebastian paid for three tickets. Johan stood by, appearing not to feel any responsibility for his fare. After cleaning their boots of mud from walking, they were allowed to board the stage, Elizabeth clutching Paul, and Sebastian tending their large box. They soon departed New York City and as they traveled past the many tall buildings on their departure route, Sebastian wondered if he would be capable of enjoying life in such a crowded place. He thought of his many shipmate passengers who were beginning their new lives here. Now more than before, he longed to reach the farm area that Johan had described. Even more, he yearned for the vineyards that he had heard were not far from the area where Johan was taking them.

CHAPTER FIVE

An Encounter With Disappointment

On the second day of their long and arduous journey, they reached Altady. It too was a bustling city, but not nearly as overwhelming as New York. Here the buildings were not as high and the streets seemed a bit wider. The wagons moved with less congestion and the pedestrians crossed the streets less hurriedly. Nevertheless, they were busy streets, with all of the same activities it seemed, as the huge city to the south.

Sebastian had enjoyed the first day's journey, viewing the beautiful county side after they had left the crowded area of the big city. They had passed though a great number of towns and small villages. Each seemed beautiful to Sebastian, even if the shape of the houses were quite different than those that he was accustomed to in Germany. On some occasions they were able to see a vast river with many boats and barges traveling in either direction. Some boats had passengers on deck waving merrily to the stage riders. Sebastian wished that they were using that mode of transportation. Johan commented tersely that this was the same river that their ship had entered into in the harbor of New York.

Elizabeth, too had enjoyed the first afternoon, but as evening approached and then nightfall, she grew extremely weary. Paul too, who at first seemed content in his mother's arms, and with her feedings, had become very discontented. He cried often, until finally, lulled by the swaying of the coach, he fell off to sleep. When Paul was sleeping soundly, Elizabeth would place him on the seat beside her so that she could rest her tired arms.

Throughout the journey Johan said little. He sat in the seat opposite the couple, glancing out of the window, changing positions often, but offering no social commentary. Sebastian had tried several times to be pleasant to Johan, asking questions about the scenery, or other sights as they passed, but Johan gave terse, if any, responses. Finally, Sebastian gave up on his efforts to appease Johan. Elizabeth was plainly concerned about Johan's attitude. She worried about whether he would assist Sebastian to find employment, and a place for the newly arrived family to reside.

When they reached Altady they alighted from the stagecoach. It felt good to stretch. Johan then spoke to the ticket agent, asking for three tickets to Cheltham, indicating to Sebastian and Elizabeth that that would be their ultimate destination. Again, Sebastian paid for the three fares. The couple showed their appreciation for Johan's guidance with courteous smiles but wondered about his frugal attitude. Sebastian purchased three sandwiches from a vendor in the station house and soon they were ready to board a different stagecoach. They were hopeful that this leg of the journey would not be as long as the one just completed.

It was well into the night when they reached Cheltham. After alighting from the stage wagon, Johan led them down a dim gas-lighted street for a short distance. He approached the door of a house and knocked. Very soon a pleasant older woman appeared at the door. Johan spoke to her.

"Frau Huber, this is my cousin Elizabeth that I had spoken to you about."

The woman looked extremely surprised. She looked at Johan with a questioning expression on her face. Johan recognized her confusion. He introduced Sebastian,

"And this is her husband, Sebastian….and their baby Paul."

Now the woman's facial expression changed from that of con-fusion to that of a smiling welcome.

"Come in my dear child! Come in Sebastian. Oh, let me take that dear baby from you. Your arms must be aching from holding him all the way from New York. Oh, you look so tired. Come! Let me fetch you a cup of tea. Here! Sit, rest yourselves."

Now she looked at Johan and addressing him with like kindness she said,

"Johan, you look tired too. Would you like some tea also?"

His reply showed his weariness,

"No Frau Huber. Thank you. But I will walk to Herr Aldrich's barn to retire. I am sorry that I did not tell you of Elizabeth's hazband and baby, but I did not know of this myself until they found me at the pier at Castle Garden. I hope that you will still be able to employ Elizabeth!"

For the first time, Johan showed concern for Elizabeth's welfare.

"Ja, ja, I can still use a nice girl like Elizabeth. Don't worry about her. Go! Get some rest. Come back tomorrow."

As he left, Johan replied,

"I'll come by after work, Frau. I can take no more time off from my job or Herr Aldrich will be upset with me."

Johan waved a slight goodbye to Elizabeth and Sebastian as he turned to the door, saying not another word. With this comment, Sebastian realized for the first time that Johan had greatly inconvenienced himself to take time from work and to travel to New York. And no doubt he had not enough money to purchase a fare on the stagecoach, so Sebastian wondered if he had walked the whole distance, or was he able to obtain a ride on the wagons of farmers traveling south with their market goods.

'My God' Sebastian thought, 'if he walked he must have worn through the soles of his boots. I'll have to pay him to obtain a new pair.'

Suddenly Sebastian wondered how many Deutchmarks he had remaining. Later, when out of sight of Elizabeth and Frau Huber he had better check.

Paul was stirring from his sleep. Elizabeth put him to her breast but he was now crying.

"I am unable to provide for him",

Elizabeth told Frau Huber.

"Oh, wait darling, I have some milk in my kitchen ice chest. And I have a nipple too. I have used it before to feed the calves, but it is clean."

She looked at Elizabeth, hoping to find an expression of relief. Elizabeth nodded with a smile. The old lady hurried to the kitchen, soon returning with a bottle of milk, one the size of which Elizabeth and Sebastian recognized to be a calf feeding size, with a somewhat large nipple attached. At first Paul had trouble with the nipple but soon took to it and drank the milk with great gusto.

After finishing the baby's feeding, and having already finished their cups of tea, Sebastian looked toward Frau Huber, wondering if this house was to be their resting place for the night. Frau Huber must have recognized Sebastian's quizzical look. Rising quickly, she said,

"I'm afraid that I did not expect a couple to arrive, and with a baby too! I have a nice small room for Elizabeth, and the baby too will fit in the bed with her, but I'm sorry Sebastian, you will have to sleep in the barn with my cow Gretel."

Frau Huber saw the disappointed look on Elizabeth's face. Elizabeth seemed much more concerned about Sebastian's lack of a bed than he did.

"That will be fine, Frau. You are a very kind lady. I'm sure that I will sleep well with your cow."

Then, laughing, he said,

"It won't be the first time. I did that often at my father's house."

Elizabeth still looked disappointed as Frau Huber led her to her small room at the back of the house, behind the kitchen.

"Now darling, if you need help with the baby, or for yourself, you be sure to call me. I'm a light sleeper."

As she entered the doorway back to the kitchen she added,

"The outhouse is just down the path. I think there is enough moonlight tonight that you won't need a lantern."

Sebastian had followed, carrying their box of worldly goods. He placed it in the corner of the small room then returned to the parlor. After being sure that Elizabeth and the baby were settled Frau Huber returned to the parlor herself. She addressed Sebastian,

"Now young man, let me show you to the barn."

Sebastian half laughed and replied,

"Oh, that won't be necessary Frau, I'll find my way easily. Thank you greatly for helping us. And especially for your warm kindness to my wife and our baby."

The lady appeared flushed, giggled a little and said,

"Now off with you. You must be dead tired. Don't you worry about Elizabeth and the baby, they will be fine."

Then in a softer voice she added,

"I'll let Elizabeth sleep as long as she likes in the morning. The poor child must be exhausted. You too! Sleep late! Now get!"

When Sebastian awakened the sun was quite high in the sky. He sat up with a bolt then jumped to his feet. As he hurried to the outhouse he brushed the hay off his clothing. Then he went to the back door of the house, knocked lightly and entered the kitchen. Elizabeth greeted him with an enormous smile, hurried to him and placed a long kiss on his cheek. With tears welling in his eyes he told her,

"Oh! Elizabeth, you are my dear darling. I do love you greatly."

He returned the kiss to Elizabeth, but now placed his lips on hers. Elizabeth did not resist. After some long time, they separated their mouths. He waited for Elizabeth's reaction. She replied tenderly,

"Oh my wonderful man. You have been so kind to me and to my baby. I am so blessed that you came into my life."

They hugged for a long time. Frau Huber had returned to the kitchen as they were kissing. At first she showed embarrassment, then surprise, then quizzical look came upon her face.

"My word, young lady, you have only been without your husband for one night. You act as if you had never kissed him before."

Elizabeth and Sebastian smiled at each other, both thinking,

'If she only knew.'

During that day, the first in the new town to which they would have to adapt, Frau Huber took them out the front door, pointed out some of the houses, naming some of her nearby neighbors. Many had German names, but many had names with sounds that Sebastian had never heard. Then she took them out the back door, repeated the process, but also denoting the extent of her land. Sebastian thought,

'Her property is not large, just enough for her house and barn, and a small field for her cow to graze. And she seems healthy enough. I wonder why she needs a housemaid?'

He decided that this kindly lady must have consented to accept a maid just to allow Johan to bring his cousin to Amerika. Perhaps his thoughts transferred to Frau Huber, for just then she spoke,

"Maybe you wondered why I need a maid. Well, I may look healthy, but I'm getting along in years, and I just can't do all that needs doing around here. The cow has to be fed and milked, and the barn must be cleaned out, and well….oh, lot's of things need doing. And I'm not so able anymore to fetch the water from the well and do the cooking and the canning. Yes, there's plenty for a maid to do around here. And on rainy days my rheumatism acts up something terrible".

The way that she recited it, Sebastian realized that she must have mentally concocted this list many times to convince herself to accept Johan's cousin into her house. Then he wondered, 'Would she have agreed if she knew of Elizabeth's baby and husband?'

The Frau and Elizabeth and the baby were all getting along famously. Sebastian decided to take a short walk around the area. The ladies shooed him out to encourage him to get some exercise. As he ambled along the streets everyone looked at him quizzically. Of course he knew that they all wondered who this stranger was, and why had he come to their town. When he occasionally overheard conversations by the townsfolk, he understood none of their words. He knew that they would be speaking English, and that he would quickly have to learn to speak this language also. But it sounded to him to be a difficult language.

Having satisfied himself that it was a pleasant town, that folks were not belligerent,

'Not like the Duke's soldiers', he thought, and having stretched his legs enough, he returned to Mrs. Huber's house. All was fine there. Mrs. Huber was gooing-gooing at the baby and occasionally explaining to Elizabeth what her duties were to be.

In the early evening Johan arrived. Everyone greeted him warmly and he seemed to be in a better mood than when he left the night before.

"Would you like some supper, Johan?" Mrs. Huber asked. She added,

"There is plenty left over from our supper. You are welcome to it."

Johan declined. He then explained that he had spoken to Mr. Aldrich, the man that he worked for, and the man who owned the largest acreage of farmland in this area, and he was willing to take on another farm hand. Johan explained that he told Mr. Aldrich's foreman that his cousin's husband was an experienced farmer and although short of stature, he was a very robust man. Sebastian could start work tomorrow, be at Mr. Aldrich's foreman's office no later than one-half hour after sun up. Elizabeth smiled, hurried to Johan and kissed his cheek. Johan blushed, then turning to Sebastian asked,

"Is that alright Sebastian. You can work on the farm can't you."

Sebastian suddenly realized that he had not told Johan of his rented vineyard in Germany. Sebastian surprised everyone when he replied,

"Oh yes, Johan, I can do any chore on the farm. I've done them all. But I wonder, does Herr Aldrich have an arbor? Does he grow grapes to make wine to be sold?"

Johan's smile changed to an annoyed look. He seemed indignant when he replied,

"Why no Sebastian, he does not. He may have a few grapevines nearby his house. All wealthy folks do. But he is not a vintner. He's a very successful farmer. Don't you want this job as a farm helper like I am?"

Elizabeth looked plainly worried until Sebastian replied,

"Oh ja, Johan, I want the job."

As Sebastian shook Johan's hand vigorously he added,

"And thank you very much, Johan, for this job and for all that you have done for us."

Elizabeth smiled, Mrs. Huber seemed relieved, and Johan and Sebastian seemed more brotherly. Still, Sebastian wondered about the arbors, for he had heard that there were many in this place called New York Stadt. He had hoped that he could work among the grapes again. Inwardly, he was somewhat disappointed.

Johan bade everyone goodnight. Frau Huber announced that she was now going to retire to her room on the second floor. She ascended the narrow squeaking stairs. Elizabeth and Sebastian wished her pleasant dreams then walked to the kitchen. Elizabeth took sleeping Paul to her room, placing him on the bed, then returned to Sebastian's side. He placed his arms about her tightly. She did not resist. He placed his lips on hers. She did not resist. He again stated his love for her, adding that he enjoyed feeling her body against his. Elizabeth replied,

"Oh, Sebastian, I wish that we could be together tonight. I missed you very much last night." Sebastian spoke softly,

"Oh, dear Elizabeth. Ever since we were married, I have wanted to be a true husband to you. Do you understand?"
Again kissing Sebastian's lips, she replied,

"I do understand Sebastian. I'm so sorry that when I first moved into your home I was still frightened of manly embraces. But you have shown me that all men are not animals, you have been so very patient."
Sebastian squeezed her tighter and said,

"Well, my darling, we will have to be patient a little longer."
She could feel his excited state and she felt her reaction to it. Reluctantly she said,

"My darling, tomorrow we must ask Frau Huber to let us share the bed.

She will understand."

Sebastian left for his sleeping place. As he walked the path to the barn he looked up at the sky, thinking,

'It is chilly tonight. The sky looks like it will offer some snow.'

He first used the outhouse, then entered the barn. He rustled up the hay for more resilience then lay down. He felt the chill and decided that he had better get a blanket. He went back to the house. He tapped gently on Elizabeth's door, saying,

"Darling, I need to get a blanket from our chest."

Elizabeth's reply had urgency,

"Come in, Sebastian. Yes, you will need a blanket tonight."

The candle was still lighted when he entered. He saw Elizabeth kneeling by her bed, just finishing her nightly prayers. Paul was fast asleep on his side of the bed. Elizabeth had removed her dress and was in her underclothing. Her arms and part of her shoulders were bare. Sebastian had never seen her in this state of undress before. He hurried to her. As she rose he placed his arms about her again.

"Oh, Elizabeth. I am very greatly aroused. I don't want to leave you. I want to lay with you! I have waited so long for this moment. All those long months since our marriage!" Elizabeth began to cry. She held to his body.

"Oh Sebastian. What are we to do. We must not affront Frau Huber. She has been so kind to us. But we must speak with her tomorrow."

She pulled away a little, indicating to Sebastian that she felt that he should depart to the barn. As he again walked to the path to the barn he thought,

'Yes, tomorrow we must speak with Frau Huber. We must make a different arrangement.' But how was he to be able to sleep tonight? Gretel heard him enter the barn and emitted a "Moooo", seeming to understand Sebastian's torment.

CHAPTER SIX

Encounters with Frustration....and Anger

Sebastian was surprised at how fast the winter had passed. He found it hard to realize that it was now March of 1861. It had already been two years since his marriage to Elizabeth. With a smile to himself he thought,

'Now I am really a husband to my wonderful Elizabeth'.

He was happy too, that spring was here, for he had been too idle during the depth of winter. Yes, he had much snow to shovel for Frau Huber, and Mr. Aldrich did find chores for him, but they did not occupy the whole day. He worked in Mr. Aldrich's barns, cleaning stalls, feeding the horses, milking the cows and worked in Mrs. Huber's barn also.

But for many of the hours he just sat by the window, looking out at the snowy streets, watching the farmer's sleighs pass by with their large urns of milk, straw, or other farm produce that had been stored in the barns of the farmers.

He thought back to the first days at Frau Huber's house. After that night when he and Elizabeth had such unfulfilled passion, they had spoken to Mrs. Huber. They were honest with her and explained their marriage arrangement. Mrs. Huber's first reaction was one of astonishment. Then she exclaimed,

"You mean that you two have not yet......Oh! Poor darlings. We must make suitable arrangements for your married state."

She excused herself, left the house, but returned in a few minutes carrying a

Encounters Elizabeth's
cradle.

"I hope that Paul will fit into this. I borrowed it from Frau Krause."
With a laughed she added,

"After seven children, she hopes not to have to use it again."
They took it to Elizabeth's bedroom, removed a small stand from the inside
corner of the room, then placed the cradle there.

"A good place for it, darlings. Paul will be nice and warm here."
Then with a smile and a wink she said,

"I believe that that bed is wide enough for two."
Sebastian and Elizabeth let out embarrassed laughs, but let Mrs. Huber know
that they agreed that the bed would certainly accommodate two. That night they
placed Paul into the cradle. He barely fit, but did not seem to mind the change
of bedding. Then finally, the longing couple fulfilled their ardent love. For
many more days their exhilaration was evident. And all had continued well
since.

Their first Christmas in Amerika had passed, but it was much less
eventful than in the southwestern region of Germany from whence they came.
That region was largely of the Catholic faith. Here in their new country, there
was a Christmas day Mass at St. Mary's church in the nearby village of
Lassau. This American village had been given the same name as a village in
Germany many years earlier, by immigrants that settled here after the
Revolutionary War. Many had been mercenary soldiers in that war. St. Mary's
church had been founded in about 1850, because of the ever growing
population of German immigrants. It was closer to Frau Huber's house than the

other Catholic church, St. James, on the other side of Cheltham, where all the Irish immigrants had settled.

Sebastian and Elizabeth enjoyed hearing Christmas hymns in their native German again and they even enjoyed the long sermon preached in their native tongue by Vater Offengeld. But there was no decorated tannenbaum in the town square, nor carolers strolling the ways. They now realized that Christmas in Amerika was not as widely celebrated as in their native country. Mr. Aldrich, however was very understanding, and allowed all of his Catholic farm hands to take the day away from work, after the very early morning chores were completed, that is.

As the days warmed, Sebastian thought more and more about his arbors in Germany. He began to realize that he missed his vineyards more than he thought he would. He held hope that he would someday find employment in a vineyard rather than at the farm. But when he had asked Johan about the vineyards, Johan scoffed,

"My God, Sebastian, these vineyards are several hundred kilometers to the west. You can't drag Elizabeth and Paul there. You don't even know if you will find employment there. Here you have a fine job and a fine employer. Why do you day-dream about those vineyards."

Upon hearing this discussion Elizabeth had worried greatly, but never spoke her concerns to Sebastian.

So Sebastian worked another year on Mr. Aldrich's farm and continued to live at Frau Huber's cottage. Elizabeth did much work for the elderly lady, as did Sebastian when he arrived home from a full day of effort at Mr. Aldrich's farm. The couple did realize that they were fortunate to have the food, lodging, and friends that they enjoyed. Sebastian received two dollars per week in wages, and though he did not have to spend much of this, he wasn't saving much either. Each week he purchased some of the groceries for the Huber household, for after all he and Paul were not intended to be part of the arrangement for Elizabeth's maid service. Her wages were to be only her room and board, and Sebastian knew that Frau Huber could not afford to buy the food for his entire family. But on occasion, Sebastian still dreamed of his vineyard and continued to have hope that someday that would be his future.

In the spring of 1862, now that Sebastian understood more of the American's language, he came to realize that the war between the northern and southern states was becoming a great concern to everyone. He had heard people say that it would be a short war, that the southern states would concede to the conditions of the President, Mr. Lincoln, but now more and more people were talking about a prolongation of the war. No one seemed happy about the prospects. Many young men of Cheltam and all the surrounding villages had volunteered to serve in the Union army. They had been sent off with much patriotic cheering. It was expected that they would return within half a year. Most did not, some never.

Among those who had volunteered was Johan, Elizabeth's cousin. He had joined an artillery battalion that was being formed among men of Columbus county. He said that he did not wish to be an infantry soldier because of all the walking they must do. Artillery units had horses to pull the cannons and the ammunition wagons, and the men. He was paid a bounty by the village of Cheltam and departed in March of 1862.

A few of the earlier volunteers did return because of wounds received, but sadly, a few returned in coffin boxes. A battle with the strange name of 'Bull Run' had taken place. The realism of the situation was now setting in. Most people, even Mr. Lincoln's supporters, did not like the way the war was being prolonged. Soon news came that President Lincoln had appointed a new General who planned to capture Richmond, the Confederate capitol. Many thought, mistakenly, that that would surely end the war. Before this expected capture of the Confederate capitol, however, more astounding news arrived. Two ships, one of the north and one of the south, had fought a battle. But the amazing fact was that these ships were made of iron. Imagine, ships of iron!

The summer dragged on. Sebastian continued to work on Mr. Aldrich's farm. Elizabeth was happily providing help to Mrs. Huber, whose advancement of age was becoming more obvious. She now more greatly needed Elizabeth's help. One part of Elizabeth's job was the most enjoyable to her. Mrs. Huber had taught Elizabeth how to bake. In fact, they were now baking extra loaves of bread, and sometimes pies, and would sell them to nearby neighbors, for some wives and mothers were now working outside of their homes, replacing the income of their husbands that had gone off to the war.

Paul was now almost three years old. Sebastian had made him a new, larger bed, which was in his parent's room. As Paul was growing, it became more difficult for Sebastian and Elizabeth to enjoy each other's comfort. So Paul's bed was moved to the parlor. Mrs. Huber agreed to this arrangement, but not with great enthusiasm. Or was her increasing bout of rheumatism affecting her usual jovial spirits? During the winter months Sebastian had carved wooden soldiers and animals for Paul to play with and to while away the time. Sebastian even created a special toy for Paul, a wooden horse large enough for Paul to sit upon. Making these things helped Sebastian to keep his mind off the thoughts of the arbors that he still dreamed of someday owning.

On March 14th Elizabeth prepared a special meal for Sebastian, to celebrate their third wedding anniversary. The Mueller family was now "American". And the arrangement with Mrs. Huber was continuing well in Elizabeth's mind. But she could not help but recognize the occasional far off look of Sebastian. Is he still hoping for a vineyard, many, many miles away?

In early May Sebastian came from work a little earlier than usual. Elizabeth anxiously asked,

"What is it, Sebastian? Why are you home? Is there something wrong?"

Sebastian's tried to sound casual,

"No, nothing is wrong with me Elizabeth, but the war news is not good. Word has been received that a new Regiment is to be formed, from men of the area all around. Many of the younger men are preparing to volunteer into this special Regiment, and many of the local leaders expect to be made officers."

Elizabeth and Mrs. Huber both appeared very concerned.

"But you will not need to volunteer, will you Sebastian?"

"You are not a citizen yet. You will not need to go will you?"

Sebastian's reply was again very cautious,

"Well, Elizabeth dear, the towns are authorized to pay a bounty to all who do volunteer, whether citizens or not."

Elizabeth gasped,

"Oh Sebastian! You are not thinking of becoming a soldier because of the pay, are you? We are doing very fine here, with what you earn at Mr. Aldrich's farm."

Mrs. Huber agreed,

"Yes, Sebastian, we are all doing quite well. We'll get along just fine, just as we are now."

Sebastian's next statement absolutely astounded the two women.

"Well, you see Elizabeth, Mr. Lincoln is soon to order a conscription of all men. All must serve."

Again Elizabeth protested,

"But Sebastian, surely he will not order foreigners to be forced to serve. This is not their country!"

With this, Sebastian looked at Elizabeth with surprise, and with some criticism in his voice said,

"Elizabeth! We have been here in America more than two years already! We are no longer foreigners. We are Americans! This is now our country!"

Fearing Sebastian's next statement, Elizabeth began to cry. Upon seeing this, Paul also began to cry, for he sensed sadness in his mother. Mrs. Huber came to Elizabeth and placed her arms around her shoulders,

"Oh, this terrible war. It has ruined so many lives already. Will the misery never end?"

In spite of Elizabeth and Paul's cries, Sebastian uttered more justification for his intended volunteering.

"I'm sorry, Elizabeth, but this is an opportunity that I will never have again."

Elizabeth almost shouted,

"Opportunity! Is war an opportunity! Are you insane Sebastian?"

Calmly Sebastian retorted,

"Well you see, darling, Mr. Aldrich's son is to be conscripted with the others, but he fears going. Mr. Aldrich will pay me four hundred dollars to replace his son. The town will also pay me a bounty of one hundred dollars. Don't you see? We will have five hundred dollars. With a fortune like that when I return we can move to the lake region and buy the arbor that we want."

Elizabeth groaned as she slumped into a chair,

"Oh that damned vineyard, that damned dream of yours. Why are you not content here? Everything is just fine. Our lives are very pleasurable. What is so wonderful about starting another journey?"

Sebastian's tone now became determined,

"I'm sorry, Elizabeth, I believed that you shared this dream with me. I want to own a vineyard again, and I believe that this is the only way that I will ever obtain it. While I'm gone, it will be just a few months, you will change your mind. I know that you will see that it is the best for all of us."

CHAPTER SEVEN

An Encounter with Great Anguish

In September of 1862 Sebastian and many hundreds of other men from the towns and villages in the area of Hutson City, were assembled in the County Fairgrounds, ready to officially become soldiers in the Army of the United States.

Sebastian, and most other men from his village had been assigned to Company E of the newly formed 182nd New York Volunteer Infantry Regiment. The nearly one thousand men that were to form the new Regiment came from two Counties of the area. They were to be sworn to duty and commanded by newly appointed Colonel Nathaniel Shores, a prominent businessman of the County seat of Hutson.

Many thousands of spectators were on hand to cheer the men as they raised their right hand to accept the duties as described in the oath read by Colonel Shores. Elizabeth and Paul, along with hundreds of other wives and children watched as their loved ones, husbands, fathers, sons and even a few grand-fathers, repeated the words of the oath. Sebastian was now officially a soldier. Following the swearing-in ceremony, the Colonel ordered the men to march out of the fairgrounds and to the train station. As they did so the loving spectators tried as best they could to march abreast of their soon-to-be departed soldiers. Elizabeth lifted Paul to her waist as she first walked and then ran towards the train depot. All the while she and Sebastian tried to keep in view of each other, but the best that they could do was to catch occasional glimpses. When she thought that he was able to see her, she shouted

"Auf weidersehen Sebastian! Auf weidersehen!"

When it seemed that she would not see him again, she kept saying,

"Auf weidersehen Sebastian.", over and over to herself, even though she knew that he could no longer hear her. Finally, through soft sobs and tears, she mumbled one more time, to herself and almost inaudibly,

"Auf weidersehen Sebastian."

It required over an hour for the embarkation onto many rail cars before the Regiment was finally ready to depart. It was late afternoon when the locomotive let out its first blast of white steam and then belched heavy black smoke. With this, it started its wheels rolling, very slowly as first, then faster and faster. All of the soldiers that were able were leaning out of the windows, waving to those in tears along the train tracks. Elizabeth was not able to find Sebastian. Perhaps he was on the opposite side of the rail car. As she sobbed, she wondered,

'Will I ever see my Sebastian again? Oh, God, what is to become of Paul and me? And what of my dear, dear Sebastian? Will he return safely?'

During all this time Paul showed much confusion and wonderment, but no fear. At three years of age, he only understood that lots of people were all around him. Why, he did not know. He did wonder however, why his Mommy was crying so much.

On the train, which was heading to Washington, D.C., Sebastian began to realize more fully what he had done, perhaps more rashly than he had intended.

'Am I ever to see my beloved Elizabeth and darling Paul again?' he wondered. Now anguish and misgiving began to fill his thoughts. 'Oh, what have I done. Is all this worth the price of the hoped-for grape arbors?'

Sebastian had two days in which to think about his self-created predicament before the train arrived in Washington, D.C., to help with its defense, while simultaneously being trained. Although Sebastian did not then know it, he would have two more years and many thousands of miles of travel, in which he could turn over the same agonizing thoughts many, many, times.

It was November before Elizabeth received the first letter from Sebastian. For the whole two months since he had left, she wondered and prayed, hoping that Sebastian was well, in both health and spirit. Her own spirit was not at all cheerful. She had cried many nights since Sebastian left, sometimes sobbing so loudly that Mrs. Huber would come to her side like a mother, place an arm around her shoulders and try to console her. Paul had asked for his Papa many times and each time that he did, Elizabeth felt tears welling as she tried to explain to the small boy that Papa had to leave them for awhile.

"When he returns will he bring me a new toy?" Paul asked several times. Elizabeth nodded 'yes' each time, but wondered again if Papa would ever actually return home.

Sebastian's letter was in German. Although he had learned some English during the last two years, he could write more readily in German, and he felt that Elizabeth would prefer to read in their native language. There were several other recruits in Company E that were also German immigrants. Many had been in America for several years longer than Sebastian and spoke English quite well. Whenever Sebastian would prepare to write another letter, one of those soldiers would offer to write it in English for him, but Sebastian always declined. He did not wish others to know of his intimate words to his wife.

Although Sebastian had written his first letter to Elizabeth only one week after departing Hutson, he had no immediate opportunity to post it. After carrying the letter in his cap for another week, his Sergeant, a very kindly man, took it from Sebastian and assured him that it would get properly posted very soon. It was posted near the end of September but had taken about five weeks to reach Elizabeth, due to the abundance of letters being sent by the new soldiers of the many, many new Regiments. The postal authorities had great difficulty in processing the many, many thousands of pieces of mail.

Sergeant Henry Van Allstyne was from the town next to where Sebastian had lived. He had entered the local militia about one year before the outbreak of the War Of Rebellion, as the conflict was officially called. Although American born, he under-stood and spoke some German, having learned it from the many German immigrants in the area. He also had heard his parents speak Dutch at home, which had some similarities to the German language. Because so many men in Company E were of German origin, they felt very comfortable with Van Allstyne.

One morning in early October, Captain Luther Hopkins announced to his Company that they and the entire Regiment would be moving to Baltimore. Sebastian immediately penned a letter to Elizabeth telling her of the imminent move, but had no other information to relay to her. He posted the letter at his

Company headquarters. The Company clerk assured Sebastian that the letter would be posted properly. The next day Sergeant Van Allstyne lined the men in columns of four and Company E and the whole Regiment marched all day until just after dark, when they settled in their new camp near the Baltimore city piers. Sebastian, and many of the other men, had never heard of Baltimore. After a few more days, the entire Regiment embarked on two large but slightly overloaded ships. The men were amazed when they saw the type of ships they were boarding. The ships had sails, but also had tall metal smoke stacks and side paddle wheels. Van Allstyne told the men that the ships were a new type called a "steamer". None of the immigrants had arrived on anything like this and most of the American born men had seen only smaller sailboats plying the Hutson River. No one had seen a "steamer". They were amazed that the paddle wheels could move the ship. The two ships departed early on the morning after they had been loaded with their human cargo.

Although no information was given the soldiers, after a few days they easily determined that they were sailing south, with the land they felt, just barely out of sight on their starboard side. Sebastian was glad that he had posted the letter to Elizabeth before embarking, for he knew not when he would again have an opportunity to write her.

After several days at sea the men were still not told of their destination but they knew that they were continuing southward. The ocean breezes were becoming warmer each day. Sebastian had counted the days since departure. Six days had now passed. The ship turned westward, with even warmer breezes wafting by, then northward. On the ninth day they sighted land. The Captain said that it was Louisiana. Again, many men, even most, had not heard of a place called Louisiana. All wondered, even the Captain and Sergeant Van Allstyne, why had they been sent here?

Back in Cheltam, Elizabeth received Sebastian's letter from Baltimore in early December, though she knew not that it would be a very long time before she would again hear from her dear Sebastian. With no man about the house, Elizabeth and Mrs. Huber were finding the necessary chores very difficult, especially gathering and chopping wood in preparation of winter. And Elizabeth was now sure, she was pregnant.

Christmas of 1862 was a somber time for Elizabeth and Paul, and Mrs. Huber too, for she felt their sadness. It was equally sad for Sebastian and the men of the 182nd Regiment. When enlisting, none had expected to be so far from home at Christmas. They foolishly had hoped that they might receive a leave of absence to visit home for the Holiday. They wondered, often aloud, why they were sent so far from their homes. Wasn't the war to be fought against the Confederates States? Would that not mean battling in Maryland, Delaware or Virginia? What are we doing way down here in this mosquito-ridden place, Louisiana?

After landing in New Orleans and encamping in swampland south of the city, the men learned that a naval officer named Admiral Farragut had captured this important port city a few months earlier after a very difficult sea battle. So now the Confederates could not receive needed supplies from Europe nor could they ship their precious cotton to Europe, to obtain the money that they needed to sustain the war. Captain Hopkins explained that it would be necessary that other cities along the Mississippi river had to also be taken. Control of the entire river was important to General Meade's war plan. After a brief encampment the Regiment embarked onto a great many small craft, and with a few gunboats along side, they sailed across a large bay, disembarking on the north shore. Soon they were engaged in a battle to capture a place with a strange name, Ponchatoula. Then other engagements took place at places called Barratara, and Gainsville. After taking these objectives the men marched back around the bay to New Orleans. With only a few days of rest they then soon marched northward to Port Hudson on the Mississippi River. By now it was March of 1863. Sebastian was ill. Not just in spirit, but physically as well. He and many of the men were in great pain with dysentery. But still they had to march and fight, for a minor condition such as bowel problems had plagued armies for centuries, but never stopped them. In the eyes of the officers, these maladies were not serious enough. The affected men were still soldiers, capable of performing their duties.

On May 28th of 1863 Elizabeth gave birth to a girl. She named her Mary, the American version of Maria. She did not feel that a child born in America should have a German given name. Following the terrible winter, she and Mrs. Huber began baking more than their needed supply of bread and pie. Their daily output was growing because many more of the women of the village were now fulfilling the chores of their husbands, and having no time to bake themselves. So they depended upon this purchased bread as the primary sustenance for their families. And an occasional pie lifted the spirits of their children and a few grandparents also residing with them.

After giving birth to Mary, and after only a few days of rest, Elizabeth joined Mrs. Huber again in the baking effort. Their reputation had spread beyond the village and now carriages were arriving from other villages as well, purchasing stocks of the delicious baked goods. It was very hard work for the two women in addition to their other chores, as well as tending to Paul and his new infant sister. But it was necessary labor, for with this income they were able to buy the other goods that they needed for themselves and the children. They were beginning to find that they even had excess profits, which they could secret away for their future.

About mid-August, a little more than a year since the local men had left, two men of the village returned from their Army duties. One had his left arm missing at the elbow and the other limped badly from a wound to his right leg. Johan had also returned, having been wounded in a battle in place called Gettysburg. His wound in the left leg would cause him to limp slightly for the rest of his life.

As they arrived by coach from Altady, the townsfolk swarmed around them, anxious to learn of Company E and other companies of the 182nd Regiment. Most of the news in the periodicals told only of battles taking place near the Mason-Dixon line. These men of the 182nd told of the Regiment's voyage to Louisiana, the early battle engagements, and then the siege of a large city on the Mississippi river. That city lay high on a bluff overlooking a double bend in the river. It was well fortified and from the bluff the enemy could see many miles around. The Union Army had been trying for many months to overcome the city's defenses and the battle was still raging when these men were wounded and evacuated. But what of the others? Everyone called out a name.

"What news of my Willy Blaine", or

"What can you tell me of Hans Haltenmeyer?"

After many, many minutes, hours it seemed to Elizabeth, she was able to speak with the men. Yes, they remembered a soldier named Sebastian, a man with a strong German accent that the men had nicknamed "Seb". They also remembered him because he was the shortest man in the Company, being three inches shorter than the average man of five feet, seven inches. They also remembered that whenever the Company had to march, which was very often, this man Sebastian had trouble keeping up and had to run a few steps periodically in order to stay in place in the line. Elizabeth thought,

'Oh! My poor Sebastian!' She asked, "What of his health? How are his spirits?"

One of the men replied,

"Last I knew he had dysentery like a lotta the men. But that don't get nobody outta the Army".

Elizabeth was distressed. Anxiously she asked,

"How can I write him? He now has a daughter that he does not even know about. Can I write him? Will the letter be sent through?"

The men looked doubtful. "Not likely, ma'am", said one.

Periodically other men would return to the village or villages nearby. Each of them had sustained a serious wound, so that they were incapable of any further duties. They told of other men that were also wounded but were returned to duty after treatment by the field doctors. The men also reported the activities of the 182nd Regiment. Battles had ensued in places with names of an unusual nature to the men, not like the English or Dutch names as in their area. They reported that the Louisiana campaign was going well, that Meade's strategy had worked well and had caused a separation of the Confederate States either side of the Mississippi. The men said that soon the whole XIX Corp, with its many Regiments, would be shifted more to the north. Mistakenly, many villagers then thought that their man would soon be coming home. Stories abounded about the Regiment and its battles. As the wounded returned they would tell of its exploits, and sometimes would report the death of certain men, even before the Army notified their families.

Almost another year passed. Elizabeth and Mrs. Huber continued their baking venture, tended to their chores of feeding and milking Gretel the cow, chopped wood for their bake oven, and tenderly cared for the two growing children. More of the wounded returned. They told of the Regiment sailing back to Baltimore, then of it being assigned to General Sherman's Army Of The Shenandoah. Then, just before Christmas of 1864, Sergeant Van Allstyne returned. He was the bearer of bad news for Elizabeth. He told of their Company performing picket duty one October night, down in Virginia. It was very foggy in the early morning. At dawn the Rebs, who had hidden in the nearby woods all night, were able to surprise the few men on guard. When the alarm was sounded, the entire Company ran for their muskets, but they were too late. Almost the entire Company was taken prisoners. They were marched down to Staunton by the Confederates, placed on rail cars and sent to

Richmond. They were imprisoned there for a few weeks then moved again by rail to a prison in North Carolina. Many of the men, Van Allstyne included, were ill with dysentery and some with even greater intestinal disorders. He reported to Elizabeth that because Sebastian was so frail, he had one of the worse conditions and that he died in late November. Van Allstyne explained that he did not actually see Sebastian die, that what usually occurred was that each morning the Confederate soldiers would enter the prison of the captured northerners, and would usually find that many men had died during the night. They would drag these bodies from the barracks and bury them in large pits that were dug by the northern soldiers, knowing sadly that they were to be the graves of many of their comrades. Van Allstyne said that he was quite sure that Sebastian was buried in one of these mass grave with hundreds of other men that died of either disease or untreated wounds. He told how shortly after the day that he found Sebastian missing, he and two other men escaped on a rainy night when the Confederate guards were attempting to shield themselves from the weather.

Elizabeth was devastated. She collapsed to the ground. Van Allstyne picked her up and helped her to her cottage door. Mrs. Huber met them and engulfed Elizabeth in her arms. Paul and Mary looked on, wondering why their mother was so ill. The two ladies cried hard. Seeing this the two children also began to cry, sensing that something was hurting their Mama and Mrs. Huber. For several days Elizabeth stayed in her room, not eating the meals that Mrs. Huber prepared for her. Occasionally she took the children to her bed, hugging them tightly, but most of the time they played in the living room with their home-made toys.

After almost a week of seclusion Elizabeth emerged from her bedroom. Mrs. Huber hurried to her, again enfolding her in her arms.

"I must not remain a recluse. I must tend the children and I must help you with the baking."
Elizabeth was resolute, mainly for her own reinforcement more than to Mrs. Huber. In motherly fashion Mrs. Huber silently agreed and the two ladies went into the kitchen. Now Elizabeth repeated to herself over and over,

'This is the way it is to be. Now I am a widow, but my life must go on without Sebastian. Now I must carry on for the children.'
And so life continued in this manner for another year. When the terrible war finally ended everyone was happy that the Union prevailed, but the village was a sorrowful place for a long time. Many young men, husbands, fathers, sons, never returned. Most of their bodies were brought home for burial, but many, like Sebastian, were buried in strange faraway places. In November of 1864 Lincoln was reelected by a large plurality. On April 9, 1865, General Robert E. Lee surrendered to General Ulysses S. Grant, essentially ending the war. But on the fourteenth of April President Abraham Lincoln was assassinated. The nation and the village of Cheltham, like all of the nation mourned but survived. The horrors of the tumultuous previous four years and the several years of confusion that followed were never to be forgotten by those who lived through them.

Because their baking business had grown so much, Mrs. Huber and Elizabeth rented a shop on Cheltham's Main Street. Paul began his schooling at the local one-room schoolhouse, and Mary tagged along at her mother or Mrs. Huber's side, as they prepared the bread dough and peeled the fruits for pie fillings. Now they expanded the line of goods being offered to include dinner rolls, cookies and on holiday occasions, struesel-filled cakes They named the shop Elizabeth's Kostlich Backerei, "Elizabeth's Delicious Bakery." Some of the locals referred to it as "Sweet Elizabeth's Bakery": their impression of this lovely young lady.

CHAPTER EIGHT

An Unusual Encounter

On one particularly moonless night in November a soldier in a prison camp returned from the latrine hole and told another prisoner with whom he had become friendly, that he noticed the Confederate guard was fast asleep at his post. He motioned for his friend to follow him, indicating that complete silence was necessary, so as not to awaken even their own comrades, for one of them might make an alarm-like noise, and alert the Confederates. Moving slowly and stealthily, the two friends slid out the door of the barracks, along the outside of the wall on the darkest side of the building, and towards the outer rim of the prison camp. Both knew that possible death awaited them, but they were desperate to end their terrible situation. When they believed that they were far enough past the outer rim, the "dead-line" marker of the camp, they crouched low then began to run towards the wooded area on the south side of the camp.

They moved as fast as possible all through the rest of the night, resting occasionally and listening hard for any indication that their escape was discovered. After a few minutes to catch their breath, they moved on again. By daybreak they were several miles from the camp, still surrounded by a thickly wooded forest. During the day they hid, stealing vegetable roots from gardens and at night they moved stealthily through the trees. After three days of this existence, they came to a large clear area. It appeared to both of these soldiers who had been experienced farmers, that it was an abandoned farm. A large dilapidated barn offered concealment and shelter. They crouched low and ran towards it. They slumped down in the back of an unoccupied stall, settled down and fell fast asleep.

They were awakened shortly after sunrise by the sounds of footsteps in the dirt of the barn floor. Bare black feet, feet of a youngster, appeared at the stall opening. The young black boy of about eight years age looked at the two men in surprise but made no attempt to alert anyone to their presence. When he realized that they were northern soldiers, not confederates, he smiled at them.

"You yanks got loose from da prison away up yonder? Land a'goshen, how'd ya'all do that?"

The first soldier, named Cyrus, answered the boy in low tones.

"Yep, we uns got loose from them rebs and got arselves down to here. Can ya help us? Can ya get us somethin' to eat?"

The boy nodded a "yes" signal and left. The other soldier asked Cyrus,

"Do yoo tink he'll help us, or turn us in?"

"I don't know, but we'll find out soon anuff, won't we."

In a few minutes the boy returned, this time with a black lady of about twenty years of age. The young lady had some food scraps in her apron. She dumped them on the ground in front of the two men, then quickly turned, pulled the boy by the hand, and left. The fugitives gobbled the food scraps, everything from stale bread to partial ears of corn, from bits of dried meat, to pieces of uncooked turnips, carrots and beans. Between gulps of the food scraps, Cyrus quipped,

"Looks like somebody ain't goin' to have the fixins fer their soup today."
The other man nodded agreement and kept eating.

The young lady returned with a well-worn old wooden bucket having a bullet hole in its side. It was about one-third filled with water, all that it could hold without spilling the contents out of the hole. Without a word the young woman turned away again. The men drank from the rim of the bucket, wiped their lips with their tattered sleeves and settled back against the wall of the stall.

"What ve doo now?", the man asked his friend.
Cyrus did not answer his friend. Neither man said another word, just sat and waited. After about a quarter-hour or so they both fell off to sleep again.

Nothing more happened all day long. A few hours after dark the young black woman returned. She came into the stall, knelt by the men, looking them over intently, then lay between them.

"I ain't had a man in a long, long time. How about ya'll. Been a long time since ya'll laid yer woman?"
Cyrus moved quickly, rolling on top of the woman while at the same time opening his clothing. The other soldier sat back in total amazement. He got up and left the stall for a while. After there was no more sound of movement from the stall, he went over and peered in. Cyrus had rolled onto his back and was appearing very happy.
The young black woman asked the other man,

"How 'bout ya'll honey. Iz ya'll ready?"
He made no movement so the young woman got up, smoothed her clothing a

little and said,

"That's alright honey. Maybe tomorra night ya'll be wantin' some. I'll be 'roun' honey." The reluctant soldier sat near the opening of the stall, still in a state of astonishment.

Cyrus addressed him,

"Hey, buddy. Didn't ya want some a that sweet gal. Oh, it was soooo goood."

The friend looked at the face of his friend.

"Ja. I can tell that yoo liked it."

In the morning the quiet soldier told Cyrus that he though that they should move on.

"Where to? We got no place to go, least wise not without getting' caught an' shot. I think we're good an' safe here. This young gal wants us ta stay. Ya can tell that. She ain't gonna squeal to nobody."

The uneasy soldier nodded that he agreed but was still apprehensive. He knew that Cyrus was right in his assessment of the situation, but he still felt very uncomfortable that the young black lady would be after him. He didn't feel that he wanted to avail himself of her charms. He tried to appease Cyrus.

"Alright. Vee just stay a few days. Den ven ve sure dat dere are no rebs around' den ve can start nort'….to home."

"Sure! Sure! That's a good idea." Cyrus replied, but inwardly he hoped that by then his friend would agree to stay for a longer period of time.

They did stay a few more days, then a few more. The black lady provided more scraps of food, and more water for them so that they did not have to leave the barn to forage. They went into the sunlight only once or twice a day, staying very close to the barn, being sure that they would not be detected. They felt the need to stretch and feel the sun. Cyrus and the black lady continued their romance, finding enjoyment each day. The other soldier always ambled to the other end of the barn at these times. The black lady had offered herself to him once more on the second day, but then left him alone after that. She was happy enough with Cyrus's daily attention.

Thus, many weeks went on. The barn and the part of the farm on which it was located was remote enough that no strangers came by, nor was there any indication that there were any other humans any where in the area; just the woman, the young boy, and the two escaped prisoners. After several more weeks, Cyrus' buddy became restless again. A new thought came to him. He worried out loud to Cyrus.

"Vaat if some Union army company come dis far sout'? Vaaat if the var is go zo good for the nort' dey take over dis part o' the country. Do yoo know vat dey will tink aboud us? Dey'll say vee be deserters. Dat's what! Den vee be shot by our own army. Ever tink 'bout dat Cyrus?"

Cyrus looked pensive for a moment then said,

"Yea, maybe yer right. But if we try to go north our chances a gettin' caught and shot by the rebs is a better chance a happenin' than the north getting' down here. We better stay put. We're doin' O K ain't we? The nice black gal is takin' good care a us ain't she?"

The other man nodded agreement, stating only a disgruntled, "Ja".

By 'takin' good care a us', he wasn't sure if Cyrus meant food wise or pleasure wise. But he decided that Cyrus's reasoning was probably better than his. So they stayed.

But soon he began wondering if they would ever get home again. Even when the war ended, how would they find a way to travel more than the thousand miles back north. Could they walk it? Would they get help to find food along the way? Would the southern people help them, knowing that they were former northern soldiers? And what if the south wins the war? What will happen to them then? Will they be shot or put back into prison for escaping? The soldier grew tired of his own questions. He resigned himself to the situation and prayed for God to help him get home someday.

After one particularly disturbing night of memories he asked Cyrus,

"Ain't yoo got no folks up nort', Cyrus? Ain't yoo got a family vaiting fer yoo?"

Cyrus's answer greatly surprised him.

"Yea, I got folks up north. But me an' my ole lady wasn't getting' along so good anyhows. This gal down here is treatin' me a lot better than my ol' hag did. Besides, by now my ol' lady an' the kids must think um dead. By now they must be adjusted to their new life without their ol' man. They'll be awright widout me."

The other soldier replied with determination in his voice,

"Vell, yoo may be happy here, but I ain't. I'm headin' out early t'mora mornin' and goin' back home."

CHAPTER NINE

An Encounter With Reality

While Sebastian was away fighting in the war, Elizabeth had missed him greatly and at first she had remained hopeful, with expectations that he would return when the fighting was done. She did not want to accept the possibility that Sebastian did die, as Sergeant Van Allstyne had surmised. Although the days during the next two years were terribly lonesome and the work load at Mrs. Huber's house and her bakery were often overwhelming, she still held to the dream of a future good life, either there in Cheltam with Sebastian and her children, on some vineyard near the lakes to the west. She tried not to accept that she might be a widow with two children at the age of twenty. As she prayed each night, she asked God to give her strength to carry on, and acknowledged that His will was to be accepted. After the first several months, and after crying each time that she thought of Sebastian, she finally accepted the reality of her situation. Life had to go on, and it did.

Several years passed. Little Mary started school in a strange town. By the time that she was going on age six her mother had moved to a new, larger place, Hutson City. Now she and her mother and brother Paul lived upstairs in a nice apartment and Mommy's bakery was right down stairs so she could go down to visit Mommy almost anytime that she liked.

After Elizabeth had finally accepted Sebastian's death, she determined to make a secure life for herself and her children, a life that would allow the children to become educated, so that they would not live their adult lives in menial occupations. She wanted that Paul not be a farm hand all of his life and Mary not be a maid until able to find a husband. And she determined that she herself would not spend the rest of her life as a maid, or laboring in front of a hot oven.

She and the children had continued to live with Mrs. Huber for four more years, but last year Mrs. Huber had died. Having no relatives in the United States, in her will she left her small house and its land to Elizabeth, who had become like a daughter to her. Elizabeth was saddened by her death and thankful for her generosity, but she did not wish to remain in the house, nor even the village of Cheltham anymore.

For the several years after the war had ended, each April most of the town folks would gather at the town square conducting a memorial service. Notables would give addresses acknowledging the great sacrifice that many had made, then most of the participants would march to the cemetery where widows and others would decorate the grave of their loved one that had sacrificed their life in the noble cause. But Elizabeth had no grave to visit, no headstone to decorate or pray at, for Sebastian's body never came home. And when she thought of his body being cast into a trench with hundreds of others, unidentified and callously treated, she would cry hard even after these many years. Henry Van Allstyne had described the horrible treatment that the prisoners had received and the terribly irreverent tossing of their bodies into a trench, layer upon layer. Van Allstyne had estimated that more than two thousand men had been disposed of in this most disrespectful manner, for the death rate was very high due to the lack of nourishment and the squalor of the prison camp.

After cousin Johan had returned home from the war, and after a respectable time had passed since the news of Sebastian's death, Johan pressed Elizabeth to become romantically involved with him. Elizabeth reminded him often that they were cousins and could not marry within the canons of the Catholic Church. He tried to convince her that since his father had married into Elizabeth's family, they were not blood relatives, and therefore had no restrictions on their ability to marry. Although Elizabeth inwardly agreed with his reasoning, she did not wish to become involved with any man at this time. Her whole interests were for her children and her bakery, which would provide the income for a better future life.

The town of Cheltham and Mr. Aldrich had both honored the payment owed to Sebastian, so that Elizabeth had come into the magnificent sum of five hundred dollars. As a commitment to Sebastian's memory, she determined that she would provide well for their children, just as if he had become a successful vintner, using the sum for which he had died. After Mrs. Huber's death, in addition to having the bounty money, and other funds from her bakery profits, she also owned a very successful bakery shop, and property near Cheltham's center that was reasonably valuable.

Elizabeth had learned of a bakery shop in Hutson City that was operated by a fine old man and a wonderful baker. Mr. Theodore Schoenfeldt had come to the United States around 1854, opening a bakery that became a very successful business. Over the years it grew into a much larger shop than

Elizabeth's shop in Cheltham. She visited his shop, introduced herself to Mr. Shoenfeldt, and asked if he was in need of an assistant. Whether he had intended to create such a position or not, he happily hired Elizabeth, for who could resist this petite, pleasant and pert young woman. Elizabeth quickly sold the house and the bakery shop in Cheltham and moved to Hutson City. After working at this new bakery for a short time, she convinced Mr. Schoenfeldt to retire and sell the bakery to her. Schoenfeldt was a widower of many years. His two sons had left him to find adventure in the western territories and had never returned. Elizabeth wondered why children are often so uncaring about their parents, but she never asked the reason that they might have had for leaving, for Mr. Schoenfeldt certainly seemed like a pleasant man. After a few days of thought, and after a few more suggestions by Elizabeth of the wonderful travel that he could enjoy, Mr. Schoenfeldt did indeed retire and sell his shop to Elizabeth.

As Elizabeth's new shop grew even larger than when Mr. Schoenfeldt owned it, she was able to buy the entire property, which included a very sizeable apartment above the shop. She was not only a good baker but also a shrewd business woman, as well as a loving, compassionate mother to Paul and Mary. Elizabeth was now finally adjusted to her new life well enough and the children were happy, too.

The new school that the children attended was a short walk for them. They soon became friends with other children who also walked along the same route that they did. Occasionally however, especially at first, Paul had to defend himself against the torments of other students. Elizabeth explained to him that soon he would be accepted by all the other boys and fighting would no longer be necessary. Paul had defended himself well against all tormenters, so he was not fearful. But seeing the fights frightened Mary, so Paul was more concerned for her than for himself.

After school, each of the children helped in the bakeshop. Elizabeth had created small chores for each to perform so as to instill proper attitudes of character and work ethic. The family now attended Sunday Mass at nearby St. John's Church. After the service many of the town folks introduced themselves to Elizabeth, since many were almost daily customers of her bakery. So the situation in Hutson City was developing into a very enjoyable lifestyle.

A few weeks after Elizabeth and the children moved to Hutson City, Johan had arrived at the bakery, seeking a position that would be of assistance to Elizabeth. She surmised that he wanted to continue his romantic illusions, but she employed him nevertheless, because she did need the help of a man to lift heavy barrels of flour and to prepare wood for the ovens. She was confident that she could deflect any advances that he may make.

After Elizabeth had the opportunity of meeting some of the ladies, she occasionally attended one of their afternoon tea parties. Although it was pleasant to have a broader circle of friends in Hutson City, her involvement as baker and shop manager was still keeping her so busy that she did not find much time to expand her social life as much as she would have liked. Arising well before dawn each morning, spending many hours at the kneading table and the ovens, then preparing a list of the baking materials that she needed was a full day job. And very shortly after dinner with the children, which often included Johan, she would retire to her bed. Each night, however, she remembered to pray for Sebastian, and to thank God for His many blessings.

As time went on, Elizabeth entrusted more and more of the bakery business to Johan, but she still maintained the monetary side of the business. Because of her generous nature, and having been raised herself in meager circumstances, Elizabeth often granted "credit" to many families who were with lack of sufficient funds to keep current in the cost of their purchases. Because of this, she herself sometimes found it difficult to promptly pay her suppliers. Many months she had to decide how her available funds would be distributed. She dared not ignore her creditors completely or she would not be able to obtain the necessary ingredients to keep going. Nor could she afford to not pay her monthly payment to the bank against her mortgage, nor taxes to the town. Sometimes she would ask Johan if he would forego his salary for a month. He always agreed to do so, and even offer to help by working more hours so that she could get more rest. She knew that she had a faithful friend in Johan, but she did not wish to become too indebted to him for his kindness.

After a few more years of such travails, and with her monetary situation becoming more stable she decided that it was time to move forward again. Because of her ebullient personality, Elizabeth made friends easily, and many enjoyed being her friend. Even though she was only a shop owner and not of the level of the wives of the professional men of Hutson City, several of these wives nevertheless invited Elizabeth to their afternoon teas and even occasional shopping ventures.

Elizabeth was thankful now that Johan had followed her to Hutson City as she could rely on him to run her shop as well as to oversee Paul and Mary after school. They called him "Uncle" Johan. Neither he nor Elizabeth disputed this title, for they felt that it was not an important distinction to make. Further, he was like a brother to her.

Even though Elizabeth had attended occasional gatherings of the ladies, she was still surprised and pleased one day when two of the ladies invited her to accompany them on a shopping trip to Altady, where the newest fashions were always available. Elizabeth eagerly joined them and although she bought no new clothing, she not only enjoyed this venture, but took advantage of her time in the city. Always a woman to be concerned with the future, as the three ladies walked the shopping areas, Elizabeth also looked down the side streets, streets where bakeries would be located. She made mental notes of several.

A few weeks later she boarded the stage to Altady, alone this time. When Johan had learned of her plan, he was very nervous and had warned that an attractive young woman of only twenty-three should not be walking the city streets alone. And when he was told by her that she would not return until tomorrow, he was aghast. He blurted out,

"For heavens sake, Elizabeth, are you going to stay in a public house alone. Do you know what difficulties you may encounter? Don't be so foolish!"

Elizabeth calmly explained to him that she was perfectly capable of protecting herself, for she carried the woman's best weapon, a long hat pin.

Upon arrival at Altady, Elizabeth knew exactly where she would proceed. She had her route planned already. She walked along State Street, viewing the displays in the ladies millinery stores, but kept walking. After reaching

Franklin Street she turned to walk down one of the side streets. Only a few shops from the corner there was a large bakeshop. She introduced herself to the owner and spoke of the possibility of buying his shop. He turned away with a shrug of his shoulders. Elizabeth visited several other bakeshops in the general area, but found no owner ready to remove himself from his enjoyable vocation.

Somewhat disappointed, she walked back to State Street, decided on a public house that looked respectable, and inquired for a room. The clerk in attendance asked about her companion and about baggage. Elizabeth replied that she had neither, that her personal needs were in her handbag. He seemed doubtful, but because of her confident manner, he agreed to provide a room on the second floor. Elizabeth signed the registration book and as she turned towards the stairway, a very handsome and distinguished looking man nodded and smiled pleasantly. To Elizabeth he did not appear to be more than forty years of age, and his manner was not disarming. She gave a slight nod towards him and continued up the staircase.

After a few hours of rest, Elizabeth came downstairs again. The handsome man was still loitering in the lobby. Elizabeth purposely did not acknowledge him but proceeded quickly to the public dining room. She ordered a glass of wine and her dinner. Soon after she had taken the first sip of wine the handsome man approached the area of her table. He obviously wished to start a conversation with Elizabeth. She thought a few moments, but then decided that conversation with him might be interesting. She nodded and smiled. He quickly accepted the cue and came to her table edge.

"Good evening madam. Did you find the facilities of this public house to be suitable?" Again Elizabeth smiled demurely and replied,

"Oh yes. Very fine."

The gentleman seized the opportunity and expanded the conversation, but continuing to stand. After a few more pleasantries Elizabeth felt that she could trust the gentleman and asked if he would like to join her for dinner.

"Oh yes", the man replied, "that would be most enjoyable."

He introduced himself.

"I am Schuyler Van Essen. I visit Altady often. I am a financier of trade. I am pleased to make your acquaintance."

Elizabeth was less forthcoming. She simply replied,

"My name is Elizabeth."

The man waited for her further explanation but she gave none. He seemed puzzled but nevertheless continued the conversation, now turning to the weather, the general activities of Altady, noting its strategic locale for the boat traffic on the river, the stage lines, then even the barge traffic on the canal just north of the city. Elizabeth listened politely, smiling often, but offering not much comment. Though she did not display it, she was very impressed with the man's knowledge of commercial activity. Would it someday be of benefit to her she wondered.

Following dinner they partook of glasses of brandy, then Elizabeth announced that she was going to retire. The man asked if he might join her for dinner the next night, but Elizabeth simply replied that she would not be here tomorrow. The man seemed to want to delve into her plans but she gave him no opportunity. She smiled, left the dining room and climbed the stairs to her room. Inside, she sat on a chair, loosened her blouse a few buttons and began to fan herself. She was exhilarated, even enthralled. She had not spoken to, nor dined with another man, other than Johan, for several years. And this man was so handsome, and so gentlemanly. Would she dare attempt to continue any liaison with him? She could, if she wished, attempt to meet him in the lobby in the morning. But no, she decided that she was still not ready for any involvement with a man, romantically or otherwise.

She had to take the mid-afternoon stage back to Cheltham so she rose early and after a cup of coffee and piece of toast, she paid for her lodgings and left on her mission. But before departing the Inn, she inquired about Mr. Van Essen. The desk clerk looked puzzled. She was surprised when he stated,

"I'm sorry, Madam, I do not know the gentleman."

She said nothing, turned and left, but wondered why Mr. Van Essen had been idling around the hotel lobby, while apparently not residing there. She put the matter out of her mind.

This day she went in a different direction from yesterday, taking the horse trolley towards neighborhoods near the many mills. She found a large bakeshop. The sign over the entry declared *Freshbread.* From the size of the shop, however, Elizabeth concluded that the owner must sell more than just fresh bread. She entered. he shop; it was crowded with customers, women of course, and each was buying loaves of bread, rolls, pies and other baked delicacies. There were several younger female clerks to service the many women. Elizabeth believed that an older man should most likely be at hand. He was standing back a little letting the clerks do the sales work. Elizabeth eased her way to him, even entering behind the counter. He looked surprised. Elizabeth quickly explained why she was here. He motioned for her to follow him to the rear of the bakery where he had small office. He was indeed ready to sell the bakery. He wanted to retire and return to Germany where he could act like an American millionaire. The man wanted cash. They settled on a price and Elizabeth promised payment very soon. Elizabeth made written notes of many details, including the property owners name, the address of the property, and asked to see his land deed. He gladly showed it. The merchant owned the entire building which housed his shop and baking operation. It also included many apartments on the upper three floors.

'My, what wonderful income', Elizabeth thought.

She left the shop, hurried back to State Street and looked for a window with an attorney's name gold-leafed on it. She passed several before finding one which seemed to her to be more elegant than the rest. She entered and asked to see the senior partner of the firm. After a very short wait a fine appearing gentleman invited her into his office. Elizabeth quickly outlined her legal needs. He agreed to take care of all matters pertaining to the property deed, and would draw up a sales agreement that would protect her from possible later litigation.

Next, she went immediately to a nearby bank, one that appeared to her to be the most successful in Altady. She repeated the information to a Vice President about the purchase of a business and all of its assets. He agreed to provide the finance for her endeavor, using her property in Hutson City as collateral.

Now it was time for her to return to Hutson City. She took another horse trolley towards the center of the city, then hurried down the hill to the stage depot. After it departed, and after settling herself into the lightly padded bench, she now realizing how much her body was quivering. She tried to relax herself. She was very proud of her accomplishments. And immediately she began to plan her next objectives.

CHAPTER TEN

An Encounter with Great Hopes

It was after dark when Elizabeth returned to her apartment. The children were already asleep. Johan was nervously awaiting her. With much exasperation in his voice he said,

"My God, Elizabeth, you gave me a terrible worry."

Intending to show consideration for Johan's concern, Elizabeth replied,

"Oh, I am so sorry Johan. My business in Altady took longer than I had expected. But I'm glad you waited. Thank you for minding the children, ... and the shop."

At hearing, 'I'm glad you waited', Johan smiled, anticipating that Elizabeth might be ready for his more friendly attention. But it very soon became apparent that such was not the case. Elizabeth was pent up about business only. She explained some of what she had accomplished during the two-day visit to Altady. Johan was amazed, but he was even more dumbfounded when she added,

"And I'm going to sell this shop".

Johan began to express objections to her plans. To appease Johan, Elizabeth offered possible alternates. One was to sell the shop but retain the building, (for she knew that she had just offered it as collateral on her new mortgage), the second was to keep the property and to keep the shop open with Johan as manager, and thirdly, to keep it open with another, as yet to be hired, trusted employee as manager. Johan quickly agreed to the second, for the time being at least. But once more he expressed his desire to be near her, wherever that might be. Elizabeth smiled and stated, "Again, I thank you Johan. I believe that your agreement to remain here and tend the shop and the property is a good solution. It probably would not be wise for me sell the property at this time."

Johan agreed with her final decision, then bid Elizabeth goodnight. He returned to the boarding house where he was renting a room. He knew that he must arise at four the next morning to begin his bakery duties.

The next day Elizabeth waited until the children returned from school before explaining to them that they would be moving to a larger city. At first they showed much excitement but soon they began to show anxiety about attending a different school. Elizabeth explained that they would be attending a very fine school where they would be taught by nuns. They asked for and received an explanation of what 'nuns' were.

Within a few weeks, all of their personal belongings and furniture were packed on a large wagon. When it departed, Elizabeth and the children made a tearful goodbye to Johan, and the transients boarded a horse-drawn carriage with driver, hired from the town livery, for their trip to their new home in Altady. After about a two-hour ride the children were delighted when Elizabeth showed them their new home in the distance. They had been told by their mother that they would no longer be living in a small apartment, but would have a real home of their own. But neither ever dreamed of this kind of a home. As the coach turned into the circular driveway they looked at each other with amazement, then looked at Elizabeth who was smiling broadly. Elizabeth had purchased a fine twelve-room house on Monroe Avenue, in an elegant part of town. During the past several weeks, and after having made a second and a third visit to the lawyer and banker, she decided that she could afford to be, and should be, a part of the more elegant social life of Altady. On the separate visits to the professional men, they had each agreed with her proposal for such a home, for they were most happy to expect that this charming and pretty young lady would attend the same social functions that they themselves would be attending. They also agreed that she could afford such a life style even though she had borrowed a great deal of money. Both men believed that the prospects for her profitable business were strong.

By the end of the second week of life in Altady, Elizabeth had taken over active management of the bakery, now named

"Elizabeth's Bakery & Merchandise Mart."

Elizabeth was now planning to also offer yard goods and other items needed by the working class ladies in that busy part of the city. She and the children had already begun attending their new parish church, St. Matthew, which was also the Cathedral for the Diocese of Altady. Following their attendance at the first Mass, Elizabeth made a point of introducing herself to the Rector, Father Timothy T. Tierney. Upon inquiry by Elizabeth, with a little laugh he offered,

"Oh, my dear, everyone asks me about my middle name when I first meet them. The 'T' is for Thomas, Timothy Thomas Tierney. My mother liked phonetic names. I'm just lucky that my father did not have his way. He wanted my middle name to be that of his mother's family, Nottingham. I would then have been known as Timothy Not Tierney!"

They both laughed and in a short time it was apparent that the good Father was a jovial person, one it seemed who would enjoy participation in the many social events hosted by the wealthy members of his parish. In fact, he introduced Elizabeth to a number of these parishioners that very first Sunday, and more on the second Sunday. Many began sending their servants to buy needed baked goods from her shop.

Within a couple of months, Elizabeth decided that she herself should host an event at her new home. She asked for the names of suggested invitees from her lawyer, her banker and Father Tierney. Then Elizabeth began interviewing potential maids, a cook and a liveryman as well as

dispatching invitations for the event to be held in about one month, Elizabeth also wrote to Johan. In her letter she requested that Johan be in attendance at her planned function, that he should arrive at her home a few days early so that he could be fitted for a tuxedo, and she indicated that most especially that he not arrive on a common horse-trolley. Upon reaching Altady by stage he was to hire a surrey and driver to deliver him to her home. He was to arrive at the front door, not at the rear like an employee entering for work. When Johan arrived on the appointed day, he was flabbergasted to be met at the door by a maid who took his outer coat and signaled to the liveryman to take Johan's baggage upstairs. After greeting Johan, Elizabeth escorted him to his room. He immediately chastised her severely.

"Elizabeth! Have you lost your senses. How in the world are you going to pay for this extravagance!"

Elizabeth replied in an almost casual manner,

"Johan, don't be such a worrier. I have ample amounts of credit available from my bank. After all, I have two very valuable pieces of property, which they have been happy to accept as collateral. And, my bakery and the new merchandise mart have already shown very active sales. I do not believe that I will have any difficulty in repaying the loans. And, if I do, I'll be no worse off than when I arrived from Germany almost ten years ago."

Johan just slumped on the side of the bed.

"Oh alright, alright. Then tell me, why am I here?"

Elizabeth quickly explained her reason to want him at her first social function. She needed a man to act as her co-host. Johan expressed his feelings of discomfort,

"I don't know Elizabeth! I have never been involved in social events, especially this kind. I don't think I will know what to do or what to say."

Elizabeth's confident reply was,

"Do not worry, Johan, we have three days in which to coach you and teach you all the social graces. You will do very fine."

On the evening of the affair, a modest one by the standards of the social life of Altady, every invitee seemed pleased and willing to accept Elizabeth, and Johan, into their elegant status. One very surprising event occurred however, which surprised Elizabeth. Schuyler Van Essen had arrived uninvited. Elizabeth did not mind because, had she known his whereabouts, she would have invited him. As they spied each other across the room, each smiled at the other. Schuyler came across the room somewhat hurriedly, took Elizabeth's hand and kissed it, then leaned forward and gave her a kiss on the cheek. For her part, Elizabeth did not show any resistance to this advance, for even though they had only met once before, Elizabeth seemed comfortable, even joyous, at his attention. Johan, however, just glared at Schuyler. When Elizabeth introduced them, Johan showed his irritation at the forwardness of Schuyler.

"I did not know it to be proper for a casual acquaintance to be so forward. You have embarrassed Elizabeth. She did not resist your brashness as she did not wish to cause an incident, but you must resist such impulses in the future." But Elizabeth quickly made it known that she did not feel the least bit imposed upon.

"It is quite alright, Johan. Schuyler and I have met socially before, and have even partaken of dinner together."

Now Johan showed even more agitation with Elizabeth.

"Nevertheless Elizabeth, a lady does not allow such shows of affection in a public manner."

Elizabeth laughed lightly,

"Oh, so Schuyler and I may show affection in private, then?"

Elizabeth was releasing the girlish excitement that she was feeling. This caused Johan to display both his jealousy and his indignation. Meanwhile Schuyler was clearly pleased at Elizabeth's acceptance of his forwardness. Many of the guests, including Father Tierney, observed the rapport of the three with some curiosity.

As the evening concluded and Elizabeth bade her guests goodbye, Schuyler lingered. When all had left and with Johan still nearby, Schuyler asked Elizabeth if he might soon call upon her. Grasping his hand she replied,

"Yes, that would please me, Schuyler."

With this, Johan stormed up the stairs. In the morning he was packed and ready to depart before taking breakfast.

Elizabeth had also arisen early, expecting just such a reaction by Johan. She reprimanded him lightly,

"Johan, I do appreciate that you are concerned for my reputation, but I must ask you not to interfere in my private affairs. I very much value your assistance, and your recommendations about business, but please do not feel that I am an indiscriminate woman. I know fully what restraints I must place on my conduct. I do find Schuyler attractive, but I do not intend to become romantically involved with any man. I have my business and my children to consider first. But I am young, and I believe Schuyler to be an honorable man. One with whom I can enjoy an occasional social engagement. Nothing more."

Johan seemed unimpressed by Elizabeth's attempt at justifying her overly warm acceptance of Schuyler's attention. As he parted he spoke too sternly,

"Very well, Elizabeth. I'll not interfere, but as you so stated, your children and your business are far too important to let any womanly impulses distract you. Let me know when you would again like to discuss business matters, or if I can help the children adjust to their new home, and new mother."

Johan stressed the 'and new mother'. As he left, Elizabeth had inner anger.

'Johan is not my father or my brother. I will not let him rule my life, or my emotions.'

In spite of Johan's warnings and concerns, Elizabeth continued to enjoy occasional social activities with Schuyler. Dinners in Altady's elegant restaurants, Sunday carriage rides in the park, occasional picnics in more secluded places, and his escorting of Elizabeth to the many social events to which she was invited. Within a few months they were considered by most of Altady's elite to be well suited, and possibly due to become engaged.

During this half-year or so of an apparent courtship however, Schuyler would leave town for several weeks at a time. He explained that his financial activities required his personal attention in other places. He spoke of visiting Riverford often, or Buffalo or Erie. These were important ports of the Erie Canal, and Schuyler stated that he had much involvement in the activities of these ports. When in Altady, however, and when escorting Elizabeth to dinners or operas or other events, he often explained that his available funds were inaccessible due to his investments in the goods being transported on the many barges that plied the canal. Elizabeth accepted these explanations without doubt and paid the bills of fare.

About two years passed in this way. Periodic visits by Schuyler and a swirl of social activities while he was in town. Elizabeth herself had to occasionally travel to Hutson City to confer with Johan about matters pertaining to that part of her business. She advised Johan that she was going to expand the bakery portion of the building so that she could add another Merchandise Mart to the Hutson City operation. Johan agreed since he knew of the success of the Altady merchandise mart. Elizabeth had hired a woman to be the overseer of the children. Her daughter Mary accepted this arrangement, and the woman, but Paul did not. He felt that he was now old enough that he required no "nursemaid" to watch over him. Paul was now in the eighth grade at St. Matthew School. He was an adequate scholar, but not as bright and interested in school as was Mary.

After finishing the eighth grade, Elizabeth wanted Paul to continue his studies at a Catholic Academy, but Paul objected. He stated that since he was now fifteen, he could first obtain a job for the summer and then seek a permanent job. Elizabeth had no objection to the summer job and she felt that by September she could convince Paul to return to school. Paul had no difficulty in obtaining a job as a hand on one of the many barges that plied the Erie Canal. He was overjoyed at the opportunity to see the world, or at least many New York State cities.

Several months after being employed in this occupation he came to realize that some of the bargemen were spending extra days at one end of their travel or the other. Several times he asked his boss Sean Murphy, why the men seemed to delay returning back to their original city. Murphy always gave an elusive answer. At the beginning of one trip from Riverford, Paul noticed one of the bargemen waving happily to a woman and several children as the barge departed. He commented to the bargeman about the children and was told that this was the man's family. But when the barge arrived in Buffalo, a woman and children were at the pier to meet the same bargeman. Paul thought it odd. When he later mentioned the matter to Murphy, he was told,

"The guy has two families. It's none of our business."

Soon Paul came to realize that many of the bargemen had a family at each end of the canal. Neither wife nor family knew of the other, for there was no reason to communicate with anyone in a far-off-city at the other end of the canal. When Paul had mentioned the situation to his mother she appeared surprised, but then took the same attitude as Murphy, it was none of their business. Still, Paul thought it odd, even dishonorable, for men to deceive their wife and family, whichever family it was. But he too reluctantly decided that it was none of his business.

CHAPTER ELEVEN

Another Unusual-Encounter

A thousand miles or more from Altady, a man sat by a rustic fireplace, holding two children on his lap. It was obvious that his appearance and culture was different from theirs. The older of the two, a girl of about ten years age asked,

"Pappy, tell me agin how y'all an' Mammy met. Tell me agin 'bout the piggy."

The man laughed.

"Oh, yoo mean aboud de race dat me an' de piggy had? How   you Mammy's piggy got away an' I caught ' er?"

The child laughed. "Yea, Pappy. That story."

The other child, a boy of about seven also laughed.

"Yep, Pappy. How'd y'all ketch that ole sow anyhows?"

The two children, both dark skinned and having black curly hair, listened intently. The father related again how he and the children's "Mammy" had met.

The man told of walking alone for many, many days, mostly at night and hiding during the days. He told the children that some bad men were looking for him and that he had to keep ahead of them. He told of how, after many days of walking and hiding, one morning just after sunup, an old sow was waddling in the mud. He told of how he was so hungry that he thought he could catch the old pig, cut it up, take the meat and cook it.

The children squirmed as they envisioned the cutting of the pig. The man continued. He told the children that after he did catch the old sow he wrestled with it trying to hold her. Just then a woman came from behind an old barn, hollering at him to leave her pig alone. The woman ran to him, hollering that she owned the sow and that her brother, owned a hog, and that they were going to mate them and divide the piglets between them. And they were going to raise crops and that was to be the start of a farm that they would own because they had a deed to some of the land given them by the former owner that was killed in the war.

The man then explained to the children that he and their Mammy had become good friends, that he stayed and he helped her do the farming and raising the pigs and a few goats that they got by trading some of their tobacco crop. The man said that after he and their Mammy got to know each other good, God gave them three children. He told them of how he built the cabin that they live in, like one that he had built long ago in a far off land, across the wide, wide ocean. The two children hugged their Pappy hard and the older one said,

"Pappy? Is that why y'all talks diff'rent than the other folks 'roun' here? Cause y'all came from way across the big ocean?"

"Ja. Dat's vhy I talk different. I vas born vay across dat ocean."
The children tightened their hug around the man. After a short time of silence, the girl said,

"Thank y'all Pappy, for makin' this nice cabin an for he'pin' Mammy to grow all them fine fixins that we'all ate. An' thank y'all for bein' so very good

112

Encounters Elizabeth's

to Mammy and our sister Rosella before they died last year."

CHAPTER TWELVE

An Encounter with Bewilderment

As the next several years rolled on, Elizabeth's bakeries and merchandise businesses continued to grow. She was having no difficulty in paying her mortgages, her suppliers, nor her payroll. She also had no difficulty in financing her expanding social life. Within the past year she had purchased another bakery and incorporated a merchandise mart into it. The new bakery was in Riverford, a town with many mills having many female employees. These she realized, were the women who had families to feed, but because of their long work-days, had no time for baking. They did however need to find the time to do much sewing for their own clothing and their children's clothes. Some of these women were like Elizabeth, widows of men that had died in the Civil War. Others had husbands that worked on the barges or the railroads. Men who were often away from their home for several weeks, and some were not dutiful breadwinners. The taverns along their routes may have seen as much of their paycheck as did their wives.

Elizabeth had intended that Paul would become the manager of this newly acquired business, for he had been familiar with Elizabeth's shops since he was a child. Elizabeth believed that he would be capable and wise manager, representing her interests well. Paul would soon turn twenty-one years of age.

When Paul had turned sixteen, he and Elizabeth had many discussions about his returning to school, but Paul was adamant about continuing to work rather than attend secondary school. Finally Elizabeth relented. She was disappointed that he would not become a professional man but she realized that Paul truly enjoyed his work on the barges. It was exciting work for a young man. Even after these several years as a bargeman, Paul found the many trips to be a new adventure each time. Elizabeth had tried to convince Paul that he was now older and should settle into an occupation more worthy of his stature in the community. Paul, on the other hand, felt that it would be several years more before he had to settle into a respectable vocation. He insisted that he would not become Elizabeth's shop manager. Fortunately, Elizabeth found one of the previous owner's employees to be trustworthy and sensible. Elizabeth reluctantly accepted Paul's decision to remain a bargeman.

In the meantime, Mary, who enjoyed school very much, had attended the St. Mary Academy For Girls in Philadelphia for the past several years. She loved the Academy and the larger city. She wrote her mother often about her studies, her many new friends and many visits to sites in the city. She was fortunate to have visited the Centennial Exhibit and she was the person who first advised her mother of the wonderful creation of so many new inventions.

Mary was indeed becoming a very literate young lady. During the summer months when she was at home, Elizabeth was extremely proud to escort Mary to museums, operas and the kind of social activities that a young woman should properly attend. On many such excursions, Schuyler also joined them. Mary did not seem to feel displeased with Schuyler's company.

Paul however did. Although Paul was working and away much of the time, he continued to live at home between trips. Elizabeth favored this, for she was still hopeful of developing Paul into a refined gentleman, like Schuyler. To Elizabeth, Schuyler was the perfect example of a courteous and genteel person. Oh how she had hoped that Paul would turn out to be as polished. Paul, however, was very happy to wear the clothes of a working class man and be among the common people. Indeed, many times upon returning from a long barge trip, often as long as several weeks, Paul would join other bargemen in their enjoyment of several drinks at the tavern near the pier in Riverford. But he never drank to the point of being obnoxious as some men did. And often these men, after too many drinks, would tell each other the stories of their visit to their *other* family, the family at the other end of the canal, 300 miles away. When they started to speak of these open secrets, Paul would excuse himself, not wanting to know of their other lives.

One early evening, after a couple of drinks of whiskey, as Paul was leaving the tavern, a barge was just setting out on its journey to the western end of the canal. Although he wasn't paying a great deal of attention to the barge or its crew, he did catch a brief glimpse of one of the bargemen. The man looked vaguely familiar, but Paul could not recall where he had seen the man. As he rode the horse trolley from Riverford to Altady, he suddenly realized why the man looked so familiar. He looked like Schuyler Van Essen! But could he be sure? After all, he had had several drinks of whiskey, the man was in a typical bargeman's clothing, and it was nearing darkness. Still, Paul could not convince himself that it was not Schuyler. My God! What if it was! What if Schuyler were not a financier! What if he were leading a double life like so many of the other bargemen? What was he to tell his mother? What would be her reaction? Would she even believe him? Paul decided that he should not yet bring this matter to his mother at this time. She did not need this added concern. But he resolved that somehow he had to determine if it was indeed Schuyler.

On one of Johan's visits to Elizabeth's home to discuss business, Paul found a moment to tell Johan that he wished to speak to him secretly. They agreed to meet at a tavern near the corner where Johan would be taking the horse trolley back to the stage office. Paul outlined to Johan his suspicions. At first Johan was disbelieving and extremely doubtful. Then Paul described the number of men that he had learned of, who had second families at the other end of the canal. Johan said that he had heard such stories but took them to be the exaggerations of many gossipers. But after some thought, and remembering the many weeks at a time that Schuyler would be away, he admitted to the possibility that Schuyler could be living such a double life. Then he cautioned Paul to say nothing to his mother, or anybody, until he had proof of this fact.

Paul had a few days before he had to return to Riverford for another barge trip. As was his usual custom, he just lingered about the house. But Elizabeth sensed that he was not as relaxed as usual. She asked him several times if he something on his mind. Had he met a girl that he liked? Did he have trouble with Sean Murphy, his boss? Was he tiring of the bargeman's life? To each of these questions Paul replied "No, Mama, I have no difficulty in life. I am as happy as I have been for these past several years. And I look forward to my next trip to Buffalo, maybe even Erie."

Reporting at the pier for his next trip, Paul made a point of engaging Sean

Murphy, the barge company's manager, in more friendly conversation. After feeling that he had gained a little closer relationship, Paul asked Murphy if he had a bargeman named Schuyler Van Essen working for him. Murphy was a little surprised at the question. He stated, "No, I don't know anybody by that name. I doubt that anybody with a fancy name like that would be working on a barge. Sounds more like he'd be an uptown banker or something."

Paul lied as he replied,

"Yea, I guess you're right!",

then laughed to make Murphy believe that he knew he was wrong. But he was determined that he would expose Schuyler if he found it to be true.

On the next several trips Paul kept a keen eye on the barges traversing in the opposite direction from his, whether traveling east or west. He believed that sooner or later he would again see the man that resembled Schuyler Van Essen. After all, Van Essen had a distinguished looking, well trimmed beard and mustache. Most bargemen were more unkempt in their appearance. Then on a barge trip to Buffalo some months later, as Paul's barge passed another traveling eastward, Paul spotted the man that he believed he had seen many months earlier. There existed a friendly fellowship among the bargemen, so as the barges passed each other, Paul called out in the usual manner,

"Hi there, fella, how ya doin' today".

The man on the other barge first looked towards Paul then quickly turned away, pretending Paul thought, to be busy coiling a rope. But Paul had gotten enough of a glimpse to feel that it was indeed Schuyler Van Essen, or someone who looked an awful lot like him. Paul made a mental note of the barge number, and the time and location at which they passed.

Two weeks later when Paul returned to the Riverford pier of his barge company, he sought out Sean Murphy. Paul gave the registry number of the barge on which he had seen the suspicious man. Murphy stated that that barge did not belong to the New York Barge Company, the one for which he and Paul worked. But at Paul's urging he did agree to look up the number on the registry of barges. But Murphy reminded Paul that it would take some time to obtain the information.

In the meantime a new opportunity arose for Paul. On his next trip to Erie he learned that a barge company that plied the Ohio and Mississippi Rivers was soliciting more experienced bargeman. Paul applied and was immediately hired. But he told his new employer that he needed a week to settle his matters back in Altady. The new agent agreed but asked that he hurry back to Erie. When Paul returned home and told his mother of his new commitment, she was furious. She stated that she did not feel that he was old enough or had enough experience in life to travel so far. But Paul explained that this was an ideal opportunity to travel the entire Mississippi river, and to get to see New Orleans. His excitement showed as he related to his mother that he would be gone for six months or possibly more. After feeling that his mother had accepted his required long absence, he left to travel to Erie, then a stage to Pittsburgh, to begin his new adventure. Elizabeth however, was still very irate.

There was much anticipation for the New Year of 1880, for it was the beginning of a new decade, one that most people felt would be a momentous period. Only a few years earlier, at the Centennial Exposition of 1876 in

Philadelphia, many astounding inventions had been displayed and demonstrated. The most talked about was Alexander Graham Bell's *telephone*, and another new machine that would print words on paper when one pressed keys on a devise called a *typewriter.* Mary had attended the Exhibition and wrote her mother about all that she had seen. Elizabeth and almost everyone realized the importance of these startling inventions. And now, only four years later, companies were already manufacturing these devices and had installed them in many offices and a few homes. Elizabeth herself eagerly awaited the time when the telephone would be available in the Altady area because she could join her three shops together by wire, and be able to speak to Johan or her other managers at any time. It would save Johan the trouble of coming to visit whenever it was necessary to discuss business decisions. But would she miss seeing Johan? She had not ever considered that she might not see him for long periods of time. Would speaking to him only through an impersonal machine satisfy the feeling that she always enjoyed with Johan's presence, even if he was sometimes antagonistic?

In May of the year Mary turned seventeen years of age. She was now a mature young woman, and an attractive one too. Like her mother, she was somewhat petite of stature, but handsomely developed in her womanly attributes. She was soon to finish her schooling at the academy in Philadelphia and would be returning home. Elizabeth looked forward to having Mary near her all of the time, or at least more of the time. She thought about the kind of a gala that she might arrange so that Mary could be presented to the Altady social set, including eligible young men. A party with a small orchestra would be pleasant, so that Mary would be asked to dance by many of the young men, thus become more acquainted with them. Elizabeth smiled each time that she thought about Mary's return home and about this wonderful affair.

In late June Mary did arrive home, having ridden on the steam railroad train that traveled from New York City to Altady and beyond. On the earlier part of the trip, Mary had also utilized the railroad as she traveled from Philadelphia to New York.

When Mary reached Altady, Elizabeth met her at the railroad station, using the new surrey that she had purchased at the time of hiring Martin, her liveryman. Mary looked disheveled and tired as she dismounted the train steps. Elizabeth showed motherly concern. Mary explained that although she enjoyed the travel by railroad very much, it was nevertheless tiring, and the stops at cities and villages along the way were not long enough for a lady to properly refresh herself.

Mary marveled at her mother's new surrey and soon became bubbly and began to chatter all the way home. She seemed to Elizabeth to be unusually happy and buoyant. Elizabeth allowed Mary several hours of rest before dinner. When Mary descended the stairs for dinner, one that Mary hoped would be simple and quiet, she found that her mother had invited Schuyler. Although she did not normally dislike Schuyler's presence, tonight she had hoped that only she and her mother would dine together. She had an important announcement to make to her mother. Elizabeth sensed that Mary was a little tense and not as jolly as earlier, and not entertained by Schuyler's usual banter. Elizabeth asked if there was anything troubling Mary. After first stating that there was nothing of concern, Mary then asked Elizabeth if she could speak with her privately. They adjourned to another room, leaving Schuyler wondering what of such importance Mary had to tell her mother.

In the adjoining room, Mary began to pace. Elizabeth became alarmed.

"What is it Mary? You seem to have a matter of importance on your mind."

"Yes, mother, I do," Mary nervously replied.

"I had hoped that you and I would dine alone tonight, but I can't delay speaking about what's on my mind just because Schuyler is here."

Elizabeth showed even more alarm.

"My God, Mary, you are not pregnant are you?"

Mary looked aghast at her mother.

"Of course not, mother. Have you no trust in me? Do you not believe that I am a chaste young woman? Don't you realize that my religious convictions would never allow me to be intimate with a man? Oh, mother! I am very angry that you could even suggest such a thing."

Elizabeth was showing her anxiety,

"I'm sorry, Mary! But what is it then? What in the name of heaven is it that you wish to tell me?"

Mary calmed herself and stated,

"Sit down mother! I want to tell you of a decision I have made. While attending the academy in Philadelphia many of us had an opportunity to meet a wonderful woman. This woman is wealthy, very wealthy. But she gives all of her annual endowment from her father's estate to the poor, to Negroes and others that are despised by some elements of society. This woman has received permission from the Cardinal to charter a new order of nuns. I want to join her in this wonderful work."

Elizabeth turned white and looked very, very dismayed.

"What do you mean? Join her."

It was obvious that Elizabeth was hoping not to hear the answer that she was about to receive. Mary's reply stunned her nevertheless.

"I have decided to become a nun in the new order. We will work among the Negroes, and soon many of us will travel west to work among the Indians. These two groups are mistreated by almost everyone. They need persons with empathy to render them physical and emotional support."

Elizabeth hurried to Mary, engulfing her in her arms.

"Oh, Mary, Mary. Have you really given this matter enough thought! Do you realize what this commitment means? It's for the rest of your life! You are too young to make such a decision!"

Mary hugged her mother tightly and replied,

"Yes, mother. I have given it a great amount of thought. I am old enough to know my own feelings, and I believe that God wants me to devote my life to this service to others.

I know I'll be happy as a nun."

The two hugged and then both cried a little.

A cough by Schuyler came from the other side of the door. Elizabeth called,

"Oh, Schuyler. Please excuse us. We'll join you in a just a minute."

The two ladies started to dry their tears, dabbling at each other's eyes. They returned to the dining room. Schuyler looked inquiringly at them.

"My, my, Elizabeth . . Mary. What can be so alarming that you both have shed tears. Should this not be a happy evening together?"

In spite of Mary's attempt to stop her, Elizabeth relayed to Schuyler the startling news of Mary's decision.

"What in the world is the matter with you Mary?" he almost shouted.

"Have you no regard for your mother's feelings. Don't you know how much she looked forward to your entry into her social world. What the hell do you think you can do for those people? They will never be anything but lower class parasites. You are just like your brother Paul. How ungrateful are you two to your mother!"

Elizabeth was surprised by Schuyler's derogatory words, but Mary was infuriated.

"How dare you speak to me and my mother in this manner. And such intolerance! I never would have believed that a man of your intelligence would be so prejudiced toward other misfortunate humans."

She ran from the room and up the stairway. Elizabeth chastised Schuyler also, but not quite as severally as had Mary.

"Well then, under the circumstances, I had better leave."

Schuyler started towards the front door. Elizabeth quickly followed and at the door she took his arm.

"Oh, Schuyler! Please, let's not depart in this state. Come by in a few days. Hopefully Mary will have changed her mind and will be sensible again."

With a bow and a slight kiss on Elizabeth's cheek, Schuyler departed.

Early the next morning Mary left the house. She returned in about an hour and a half. Elizabeth meekly asked where she had gone.

"I attended Mass, mother. I wanted to pray and to think again of my decision."

Elizabeth jumped to the conclusion that Mary now meant that she had changed her mind. She crossed the room and hugged her. But Mary disappointed Elizabeth.

"Oh no, mother, I am now even more convinced that I do want to become a nun. I spoke with Father Tierney after Mass and told him of my plan. He agreed wholeheartedly with my decision. I have invited him to lunch so that he might make you better understand the important work being done by sisters."

Father Tierney did take lunch with Elizabeth and Mary, and although each was cordial to the other, it was apparent that Elizabeth was still greatly upset with Mary's plan. Then Elizabeth became embarrassed when Mary related to the priest the comments that Schuyler had made. With a click of his lips, Father shook his head and said,

"Elizabeth, I would like to speak with you privately later."

Mary looked up in surprise, but the priest's glance told her that there was no change in his supportive position of her intentions.

After a respectable amount of time had occurred sipping tea, Mary excused herself. Quickly Elizabeth asked,

"What is it Father? What more did you want to say about this disheartening matter." Elizabeth was not going to relent in showing her disagreement with Mary's decision, and what she now believed to be the priest's interference. But what Father Tierney now stated caused Elizabeth to become even more incensed. The priest began slowly and deliberately.

"Elizabeth, I know that you have a high regard for Schuyler Van Essen and enjoy his company. He is a very handsome and cultured gentleman."
Now the priest leaned closer as if wanting no other than Elizabeth to hear. Elizabeth cocked her head to hear what Father was about to say regarding Schuyler. Father Tierney continued,

"It grieves me greatly to tell you this Elizabeth, but I have recently learned of distasteful situations in which Schuyler has been involved."
Elizabeth stood, showing much anger.

"No Father, I don't wish to hear this! I don't know what malicious gossip you may have heard and I am disappointed that you would even repeat what other jealous persons may have stated. For shame on you! If you are willing to become a gossip monger, you are not welcome in my house!"
Now the priest stood, showing great surprise and alarm at Elizabeth's dismissal of him.

"Oh, I am truly sorry, Elizabeth. I would not want to lose your friendship for the world. But I felt it my duty to try to protect you from a man who has apparently become involved in many serious deceptions."
Elizabeth became even more incensed.

"Oh, you men! First Johan, then Paul, and now you! Are you all so jealous of a refined gentleman that you must tarnish his image. You are all so petty! And so soon after I have been dreadfully disheartened by my dear

Encounters Elizabeth's

daughter's decision to become a slave to that righteous religion of yours!"

Now the priest looked astounded. He sheepishly moved to the door. Picking up the priest's hat, Elizabeth virtually threw it at him, then slammed the door behind him.

CHAPTER THIRTEEN

An Encounter with the Past

Elizabeth's telephone had been installed for almost a year now. She had one placed in each shop and in her home. She could now more easily oversee her businesses because she had reliable managers in charge of each shop. Johan remained in charge of the bakery and mercantile mart in Hutson City, while in Altady, Elizabeth had hired a man to run her bakery while she herself remained in direct charge of the mercantile mart. Her Altady bakery manager was a fine German immigrant that had arrived in the area a few years earlier. Otto Arnsmeyer had owned his own bakeshop in Germany and proved to be a great helper for Elizabeth. In Riverford, at her newest bakery and mart, Elizabeth appointed as manager a woman that had worked for the previous owner for several years. She was a Canadian immigrant named Antoinette Robillard. She and her husband Jacques had moved to the US in the 1850's when construction was booming in the Riverford area, as Jacques was a carpenter. But he too had accepted a bonus to enlist in the New York Volunteer Infantry, and had been killed at Gettysburg. Antoinette took employment so that she could support her six children who were very young at that time. They now were all grown and married.

One morning Johan arrived at Elizabeth's home unexpectedly. After being informed by the maid that Mrs. Mueller was in her study, Johan hurried to her.

"Elizabeth! Where in the world have you been? I've been trying for several days to reach you by the telephone, but each time your maid said that you were not at home. I even called your other shops. They had not heard from you either. Naturally I became alarmed that you were in some difficulty. It's not like you to be unavailable for so long a time."

Elizabeth tried to ease Johan's concern. She moved from her desk to a nearby settee and sat, motioning for Johan to join her .

She explained,

"Yes, Johan, I have not been unavailable for a few days, because I took a voyage to New York City."

She started to elaborate but was interrupted by Johan's startled inquiry.

"You went to New York? What business compelled you to do that? Why did you not mention this to me the last time that we spoke?"

Elizabeth's explanation startled Johan even more.

"Well, Johan, Schuyler could see how upset and sad that I have been because of Paul's absence and Mary's entry into the convent. He knew that I needed some emotional uplifting. He suggested that we take the overnight boat cruise to New York City as a sort of therapy. It was a hasty and rash decision by me, but for a time I did greatly enjoy the excursion. But soon sadness began to affect my feelings."

Again, as she tried to continue to elaborate, Johan interrupted.

"Ellliiizzzabeth! You didn't succumb to Schuyler's romantic charms, did you?"

Elizabeth was candid,

"No, Johan, I did not. But quite honestly, when we departed Altady, I was

129

prepared, even hopeful, that we might be intimate."

Johan showed shock,

"Oh Elizabeth! How could you feel that you could do such a thing?"

Elizabeth ignored Johan's fatherly attitude. She related how sad and lonely she had been feeling, alone in her large home. Schuyler came by often, taking her on surrey trips through the park, or visits to the museum, even one canoe venture on a large lake northeast of Riverford. But then he too would be gone for several weeks and she would spend many evenings weeping in her bedroom. Johan chided himself aloud,

"Oh my dear cousin! Why didn't you call me. And damned you, Johan. Why did you not have enough sense to realize Elizabeth's sorrowful state."

Elizabeth now looked sad and with a far away look in her eyes, she asked,

"Johan, do you ever think of home? Germany, I mean. Do you ever think about our families and our village?"

Before Johan could answer, Elizabeth continued,

"I said that I thought that I might become intimate with Schuyler on the boat trip. You see, we had only one stateroom, but as the trip developed, we never used it together. When I went to sleep, Schuyler slept on one of the deck lounges. When we left Altady, as we sailed down the river, the night lights and the views were so charming and so beautiful. We stood by the railing with our arms about each other's waists. But after a short time my thoughts strayed from Schuyler's embrace. My mind wandered to the barge trip that Sebastian and I had taken so long ago, with little Paul, on our way to Rotterdam. As I thought about that long ago past, I could not help but feel very melancholy. So I could not bring myself to enjoy Schuyler's charms. Oh Johan, I still miss my dear Sebastian. You will never know how much I came to love him."

She began to weep. Johan placed his arm around her shoulder. She placed her head against his chest. He very much wanted to caress her more intimately, even kiss her lips, but he was sensible enough to know that she wasn't seeking romance, just sympathy.

Elizabeth elaborated on the circumstances of her marriage to Sebastian. Johan had never asked, nor known why she married a man so much older than she. She told of her rape as she was returning from Johan's parent's home one evening, by one contemptible young man while two others held her. It had happened a few years after Johan had left home. The village priest wanted to know the culprit's name and wanted him to marry Elizabeth, but both Elizabeth and her parents would not agree to this. Her parents knew that the assailant would never be a dutiful husband to Elizabeth. They then considered the available men from the area who could expect to be a responsible husband. They thought of hard-working Sebastian. Even though Sebastian was much older, Elizabeth agreed it was best for her and her future child. Elizabeth then told Johan of the arrangement that her father had made with Sebastian. Johan was very understanding. He squeezed her hand as a way of stating this understanding. Then Elizabeth related how Sebastian remained celibate for more than a year, until they had moved into Frau Huber's house, before he very gently fulfilled their marriage. Johan was dumbfounded.

"Oh, Elizabeth. I am so glad that you told me. You must know how I disliked Sebastian at first. I was jealous! When I had written your father, I was naturally hoping that you would come to me. As soon as you became sixteen I was going to ask you to marry me. But I came to realize the love between you and Sebastian, and that he was a good husband to you and father to Paul. It is so sad that he never returned."

Elizabeth began to cry harder.

"Yes, it is sad. Paul was so young that he does not remember his father, and Mary never even knew him at all. Oh, Johan, please don't ever speak of this. You see, when Paul was quite young he came to realize that his father was much older than I. He had learned this from the Army records that he searched at Town Hall. He was curious about our age differences. I told him I would explain to him when he was older, but he never raised the matter again."

Johan confirmed that he would never discuss the circumstances of Paul's birth.

"You know, Johan, it's terrible to say, but as much as I loved my family, I have never written back to them. Isn't that dreadful?"

Johan agreed.

"I haven't either, Elizabeth. The only letters I wrote back were those to your father, to urge him to send you here and to tell him that I could help you find work. He likely expected that as soon as you were sixteen I was going to ask you to marry me."

Elizabeth gave a pleasant smile to Johan.

"Oh my, where have the years gone Johan?"

The two now sat close, but in total silence as they each felt remorse at the indifference to their families, thousands of miles across the sea.

The very next day Elizabeth did indeed write to her family. She knew that they surely must have been anxious and wondered all these years, wanting to know of Elizabeth's, Paul and Sebastian's life in the United States. Elizabeth first offered sincere apologies for not writing much sooner, explaining the urgencies of their new life and subsequent events. She related the sad circumstances of Sebastian's untimely death, of the birth of her second child Mary, of their growth and present conditions, and of her ownership of the bakeries. She told of the wonderful kindness of Johan. As she wrote this somewhat long missal she often had to stop to recompose herself, for tears often welled in her eyes. She was in a most reminiscent and regretful mood. As she posted the letter she wondered whether her family would even receive the communication. Many months later, she received a letter from the parish priest in which he told of the death of Elizabeth's parents many years earlier. He stated that they had often commented that they were happy that their daughter had gone to Amerika with a husband that they trusted completely, to make a good home for her and her baby. He related to her that one brother and one sister had died sometime after Elizabeth left home and that one brother had also gone to Amerika but he knew not where. Elizabeth then hoped that a remaining brother or sister would communicate with her but none did. Each must have believed that was done was done, nor could it be changed.

CHAPTER FOURTEEN

An Encounter with Discovery

Paul had been away for almost eight months. He returned home with numberless experiences to tell, of the wonderful views along the Allegheny, Ohio and Mississippi Rivers; of cities like Pittsburgh, Cincinnati, Memphis, Vicksburg, Natchez, Baton Rouge, and of course New Orleans. He told of the many new people that he had met. Colorful riverboat captains, crewmen that were a mixture of whites and blacks, ruffians and gentle folk, and of course, riverboat gamblers. Some of these he said reminded him of Schuyler. His mother did not like this comparison. He was also excited about a form of music that he had never heard. In New Orleans it was called "jazz", and seemed to be played everywhere, on street corners, in cafes, in theatres, and even on the boats of the river.

In November of the year, Elizabeth received the first letter from Mary since her departure to become a nun. In it Mary explained that during the months of their postulant and early novice training they were not allowed any contact with home, not even by mail. It was a test of their endurance to the oft-times lonesome life to which they were committing themselves.

In this letter Mary stated that would however, be allowed to visit home for a few days at the Christmas season, before making her final vows of commitment in the spring. Elizabeth was elated. She began immediately to enlarge the party that she had already been planning. The list of invitees was expanded and many more festive decorations added. She advised Matilda, her cook, to hire additional help for cooking and serving. She engaged a string orchestra and prescribed the Christmas songs that she wished them to play. A few would be the favorites that she remembered from her childhood days in Germany. Elizabeth was plainly elated, not just that her two children would be home for Christmas, but because she had had no opportunity for more than a year to host such a magnificent affair. How she loved it!

Although she had not spoken to Father Tierney since the "gossip incident", as she called it, he was invited, as well as the usual professional men and their wives. Johan, Antoinette and Otto Arnsmeyer were invited to attend, and Elizabeth hoped upon hope that Schuyler would be in Altady at that time. He did visit in early December but after only a few days in town, he advised Elizabeth that he had business dealings that would take him out of the city during the weeks before and after Christmas. Elizabeth was very disappointed.

While Schuyler was visiting their home however, Paul took advantage of the opportunity, and cleverly inveigled Schuyler into making statements that Paul might use to trap him. One evening Paul steered the conversation towards family lineage. He knew that Schuyler would claim to be of important heritage, since he was boastful about himself on almost all matters. Paul asked,

"So, Schuyler, were your family important settlers of Altady?"
Schuyler seemed evasive but knew that he must reply to Paul in some way.

"Well no, Paul" he replied, "actually my ancestors were among the founders of Regalston, down the river, you know. Through the generations they became quite wealthy and influential. But I came here to Altady because I knew that I could find ample opportunities for investment and the financing of trade along the canals."

Paul led Schuyler to think that he was convinced,

"My word, Schuyler, you certainly can take pride in your heritage, eh"

Schuyler quickly showed that he wished to change the subject. He immediately asked Paul questions about his travels. Soon thereafter Schuyler excused himself, moved to the side of Elizabeth and bade her and Paul goodbye. As Elizabeth walked to the door with him she commented,

"Oh I'm so sorry that you won't be spending the holidays with us, Schuyler. But I understand, your investments must take precedence."

As he kissed Elizabeth's cheek he replied,

"Yes, I'm afraid so my dear. I'll see you soon after the New Year. I hope that you will have a wonderful Christmas. Goodnight."

The next morning Paul called Johan and told him of last evening's conversation with Schuyler. He told Johan,

"Later today I'm taking the train down to Regalston to check on his story."

Indeed Paul did travel south to Regalston where he visited the city library. Upon inquiry to the archivist in the family history section, the librarian told Paul that she knew of no family by the name of Van Essen, that there were no records to indicate that they were founders of the town. Nor was any family of that name prominent in the history of the city. She elaborated,

"Of course, that name could have been that of a daughter of a founder that married a Van Essen, but I have never noted that name in any of our early records. And I believe that it surely would have been mentioned in some document."

As Paul rode the train back to Altady he wondered if he should tell his mother of his inquiry and its result. He decided to wait for further proof of Schuyler's lies.

The next day he went to Riverford to learn whether his boss Sean Murphy had been able to trace the records of the barge that he had noted almost a year ago. Murphy said,

"Oh yea, Paul. I did check into that. But it was so long ago I forgot where I put the note."

Paul anxiously asked him to search further. After scrounging in the drawer of his old desk, Murphy finally withdrew a piece of scrap paper.

"Here it is. I jotted the information down on this paper. It's all I had at hand when Big Mike O'Brien called me with the information. The barge is registered in his company's name. He looked up the list of men that usually work that barge. There is no Schuyler Van Essen. But he gave me the names of the seven guys that were on that run you inquired about. They're on here."

Paul quickly seized the paper and scanned the list. Matthews, Seligman, Clement, Menard, O'Toole, Frazier, (his mind wandered for a second, 'that's the young guy with the beautiful wife'), McKesson. No, there is no Van Essen.

'But wait', Paul thought to himself.

'This guy McKesson. His first name is Shamus. Shamus McKesson, Schuyler Van Essen. Could they be aliases of each other?'

Paul asked Murphy where he might find Big Mike O'Brien.

"Most likely in his office, on pier 17."

Paul hurried there. Finding Mike in his office, Paul asked if he could tell him anything about his man McKesson. Mike eyed Paul suspiciously.

"Why, whadda ya wanna know fer?"

Paul sounded indifferent,

"Oh, I ain't a cop or nothin'. I'm just curious. I once knew a guy with that same name. I was wonderin' if it was him, that's all."

O'Brien seemed more relaxed.

"Well, what d'ya wanna know?"

Paul then gave a description of Schuyler's unique appearance, of his well-trimmed beard and mustache, of his haughty gait and stature. O'Brien said,

"Yea, that sounds like 'im alright."

Paul tried to sound casual. He asked where this fellow McKesson lived. O'Brien said that McKesson lived in Buffalo, and that Riverford was his turnaround station. Again Paul wanted to sound casual.

"Oh I suppose he's married by now. Probably got a lot a kids too. I ain't seen the guy in years. We used to work together when they built the new rail spur up to Rockledge."

"Yea. I understand he has a family. I don't know how many kids", Mike replied.

Paul spoke a casual 'thanks' for the help and left Mike's office. Outside, he wanted to jump and sing. He couldn't wait to tell Johan, and then decide how to tell his mother of Van Essen's double life. The next day when Paul called Johan and related the new proof, Johan was far more cautious.

"You can't jump to that conclusion Paul, you need a lot more proof than just your assumptions. There's more than one guy in the world with a beard and mustache",

was Johan's sensible reply. Paul began to explain that he didn't believe that any two men would have the kind of well trimmed beard that Schuyler had, but again Johan cautioned him to obtain more proof.

"Okay" , Paul answered, "Then I'm going to sign on with Murphy again, so I can get a trip to Buffalo. That way I'll be able to check on this guy McKesson."

Ten days later Paul was indeed in Buffalo. He again went to the city library. The most recent Buffalo city directory listed one Shamus McKesson, occupation, barge-man. It listed a wife, but the directory did not list children. Paul wrote down the address of the McKesson home. He walked there, as it wasn't too far from the piers. For two days he loitered about, trying not to arouse anyone's suspicion. On the third day, a policeman arrived at the McKesson house and rapped. Mrs. McKesson answered the door. Paul could not hear the conversation, but Mrs. McKesson just kept shaking her head 'no'.

Paul waited several hours, then went to the police station. He inquired if they were seeking a man named McKesson. The sergeant on duty called another man. A detective came to Paul and introduced himself. Paul tried to ask questions about McKesson, but the detective instead asked Paul many questions. Did he know McKesson? How well? How long? Did he work with him? What did McKesson usually do in Riverford? In Altady? Did he have lady friends in those places? Paul was as evasive as possible.

"Why, I don't really know him that well. I thought it might be a guy that I once worked with. I haven't seen him in years. I didn't know you was lookin' for 'im. I just came in to ask if you guys knew an easy way for me to find the guy, in case it was my friend. That's all."

The detective seemed to accept Paul's explanations.

"OK, we don't need ya no more. But in case we do, are ya stayin' in town?"

Paul replied, "No, I'll be leaving on my barge early tomorrow morning', back to Riverford."

The detective rose, and without saying another word, he returned to his office.

A few days passed in Paul's travel back to Riverford. He immediately took the stagecoach directly to Hutson City to seek out Johan. Johan was in the bakery's basement. When Paul stepped down there, Johan greeted him.

"Hello Paul. What are you doing here?"

Paul returned the greeting then said,

"Johan, I have important news about Schuyler."

Johan stopped his work abruptly.

"Alright Paul. I want to know. But first I have to finish setting these rat traps. They're beginning to be a real problem."

After baiting another five or six traps, the two went upstairs to Johan's office at the rear of the bakery.

Paul related all that he had learned in Buffalo. He was convinced that McKesson and Van Essen were the same man. He said that he felt he must now warn his mother of the situation. Again, Johan was more cautious.

"Paul, you're jumping to conclusions again. You didn't really find any proof that they were the same man. So maybe this fella McKesson looks like Van Essen. And maybe he is in some kind of trouble with the law. That don't make him automatically be Schuyler. Please don't upset your mother with this. Especially now. She's looking' forward to having Mary home for a few days, and to this big Christmas affair that she's been planning."

Paul conceded,

"You're right, Johan. I'll wait until after Christmas. But by God, I'm going to find out the truth about Schuyler. If he's the two-faced four-flusher I think he is, I'll kill the bastard!" Paul was now showing how pent up he had become about his 'detective' work. Johan again calmed him.

"After Christmas we'll figure out some way to find out the truth. But wait until then, will you Paul?"

Paul nodded, "Yea, OK Johan. I'll wait till then."

Unknown to either, Sonya, one of the clerks, had returned to the bakeshop to retrieve some article that she had left behind. She was within earshot when Paul stated,

'I'll kill the bastard.' She quickly placed her fist into her mouth to muffle her astonished gasp. She wondered why Paul was so vehement, 'though she knew not of whom he spoke. She quickly and quietly exited the bakery.

Paul began to leave but suddenly stopped short and asked Johan,

"Are these rats giving you a lot of trouble, Johan?"

With a nod 'yes', but with a glance that told Paul not to speak too loudly, he softly replied,

"Yes. They are. I've tried several times to drown them, but I don't seem to get them all." Paul looked surprised,

"Drown them? How in the hell do you do that?"

Johan related how he had several times used the method that was used in many nearby mills. A barrel is placed in the middle of the basement, then half-filled with water. A layer of flour is then placed on the top of the water, and a board placed from the floor to the barrel's edge. The rats naturally run up the board, jump down to obtain the flour and of course fall right through the thin layer. The barrel is deep enough that they are unable to scramble to the top.

"We've drowned several barrels of them but more seem to keep coming back.", Johan commented. Paul was amazed.

"Then what do you do with the little bastards?" Johan answered,

"I found a guy that was willing to take the barrel down to the river for a couple of bucks, and dump them there. That's what the mills do, too."

Paul showed his astonishment,

"Wow! I wonder how many of those little varmints have floated down the river?"

Paul again turned to leave, and as he did so, he whispered to Johan,

"My mother must be having trouble with the little bastards in her Altady shop too." Johan's reply was casual,

"I'd be surprised if she wasn't."

On the stage ride home Paul could not help but make the comparison of Schuyler and the rats. He wryly smiled and thought,

'Mama may have more trouble than she realizes.'

It was late afternoon when he arrived home. Elizabeth showed anxiety.

"Paul, thank goodness you are home. I was beginning to think that you signed on for another trip and would be gone when I will be having my party."

Again Paul intended to sound casual.

"Oh no, Mama. I wouldn't do that. I want to be here with you and Mary. Are Johan and Schuyler coming to this big shindig?"

Mary showed indignation as she reprimanded him,

"Please Paul, call me 'Mother'. And for goodness sake, try not to use the common language of the barge crews. We are to hold a gala on Saturday evening, do you understand?"

Paul nodded with a light laugh,

"Alright Mother. I'm going up to wash now. I'll see ya at dinner."

But as he rose up the first few steps he repeated his question,

"Is Schuyler coming to this shind…gala?"

In her reply, Elizabeth sounded unhappy,

"No he is not! Business matters will keep him out of the city until after the holidays."

Without replying, Paul turned to continue his ascent. As he did so, he smiled to himself as he was thinking,

'Maybe he's going to spend it in jail.'

When Johan arrived for the festive party the day before Christmas, he was immediately invited by Elizabeth to remain until after Christmas. He expressed concern that his absence from the bakery might cause a problem during this very busy season, but Elizabeth assured him of her faith in the ability of

Johan's assistant. Johan conceded and remained for several days.

All too soon for Elizabeth and Mary, the Christmas holidays passed. The party was a lavish affair and a great success. Each of the guests, especially Father Tierney, wished Mary good fortunes and blessings in her forthcoming religious life, and in her endeavors in whatever mission her Mother Superior might assign her. As each guest expressed their good wishes to Mary, Elizabeth silently prayed that Mary might not be sent to the far west, or any place too distant from home. Elizabeth kept saying to herself,

'Please God, spare her. She is too young to be given such abhorrent tasks.'

The party and the Christmas day events pleased Elizabeth greatly. She expressed her happiness that all of her family, her children and her cousin, were together. Once or twice during the day, she made comments about her family in Germany, and remarked how pleasing it would be if Sebastian were still alive. Except for these few moments of reverie, and the thought of Mary's departure, the season was generally pleasing to Elizabeth.

Immediately after Christmas, Paul announced that he was signing on for a trip down river to New York City and would be leaving in a few says. When Elizabeth expressed surprise and disappointment at his intent to leave again, he said,

"In New Orleans I got a taste for the big cities, Mama. I ain't never been to New York, so this is a good chance for me to see the sights."

A few days later Mary left, returning to her convent school in Philadelphia. Elizabeth showed her sadness, but resigned herself to the fate that Mary had chosen. Johan too, left for his home city. Elizabeth was sometimes tearful, alone in her large house. Very often she thought of Schuyler. When would he return? she wondered.

Shortly after the start of the New Year Schuyler did arrive unexpectedly. As the maid escorted him into the sitting room, Elizabeth jumped up quickly, showing her joy at Schuyler's arrival, even if without prior notification. Elizabeth had become accustomed to Schuyler's surprise appearances. After greeting each other with warm embraces and light kisses on each other's cheek, Elizabeth expressed her pleasure at seeing him again, and at her disappointment at his absence at Christmas and New Year's Day. Schuyler seemed indifferent as he simply explained,

"Sorry, Elizabeth, but I had other matters that needed my attention."

Schuyler remained in Altady for several weeks, visiting Elizabeth often and sometimes escorting her to a restaurant or local social affair. Then one day he came to visit Elizabeth in the afternoon. He advised her that he again must leave the city for several weeks. He would be leaving early the next morning. By several of his comments however, he appeared to Elizabeth to be in a romantic mood. In her mind Elizabeth wondered,

'Should I invite him to stay overnight?'
She had almost convinced herself to say 'Yes', when Paul unexpectedly, and unannounced, arrived in the room.

"My God, Paul, you startled Schuyler and I. Do you not have enough social grace to know that you should knock before entering. And I suppose that you arrived by the servant's door again. Will I ever be pleased that you have finally learned proper manners?"

Paul just laughed, than taunting his mother a little, he said,

"Well, yes Mama, I did have a good trip. Thanks for asking." He continued,

"Don't you know that I'm happy to see you again Mama . Oh, hello Schuyler. How come you missed mother's big party before Christmas."

Paul seemed to have a tone of derision in his question. Schuyler seemed annoyed that he must explain his absence to Paul.

"It was necessary that I be out of the city for business reasons, regrettably.", Schuyler replied. Then he added,

"Because of business concerns I had to spend a few days in New York City, on urgent matters."

Paul immediately seized the opportunity to try to trap Schuyler.

"No fooling, Schuyler. I just returned from there myself."

Schuyler now appeared uneasy. Then Paul continued setting his trap. He lied,

"That's really big news down there, eh? About the Columbian Centennial exhibit people reconsidering the Chicago site. They are looking' into having it in New York instead. Wow! What a shock that'll be to Chicago!"

Schuyler did not wish to converse with Paul, but he felt that he had better answer him in some manner.

"Ah, oh I don't remember reading about that. I was very busy with my business transactions."

Paul again lied,

"Gosh Schuyler, I don't know how you missed it. It was in all the papers, the Sun, the Times, the Gazette, the Dispatch, you know, all the big papers."

Paul had purposely lied about the names of the latter two papers. Again Schuyler reluctantly replied,

"Oh yes, now I recall. Yes there was quite a stir. Many newspapers did carry the story." Schuyler appeared nervous. He began to move towards the front door. As he did so he called to Elizabeth,

"Well, my dear. I must be running now. I have much to do before my departure very early tomorrow."

Elizabeth quickly moved to the front hall.

"Why Schuyler, you've just arrived and now you're already leaving? I thought that we might have dinner together tonight. Must you really leave so soon?"

With only a slight hesitation at the door he replied,

"I am so sorry Elizabeth, but I really must leave now."

"But Schuyler", Elizabeth pursued him, "will you call me from your hotel. At which hotel are you staying? Is it the place where we first met?"

Schuyler did not reply. Elizabeth again showed her anxiety,

"Schuyler! What is the hotel's ring, in case I wanted to reach you?"

Schuyler glanced at Paul. Elizabeth saw the glance.

"Are you upset with Paul's very discourteous interruption of our conversation?"

Now Paul also moved to the hall. He wanted to observe Schuyler's reaction to that question.

"Well, no Elizabeth".

Then glancing at Paul again he said,

"Although Paul's attitude and manners could both be improved upon."

With that he moved through the door and with a slight nod to Elizabeth and a quick,

"Good night my dear", he was gone.

Elizabeth whirled around to Paul. With obvious displeasure she blurted,

"See what you've done Paul. You have alienated the only true friend I have in Altady. I am very upset with you!"

She appeared about to cry. Paul was visibly shaken.

"Oh I am sorry Mama. I didn't mean to upset you. It's just that Schuyler - - -" He decided not to press the matter any further, at least not at this time.

CHAPTER FIFTEEN

An Encounter with Contradictions

In 1893 the World Columbian Exposition was indeed held in Chicago as it had always been planned. But Paul's ruse to entrap Schuyler had convinced him more than ever that Schuyler was indeed a liar, and perhaps much worse, a scurrilous scoundrel. If not, why would he have lied about his heritage and about his visit to New York City. And what of his physical likeness to Shamus McKesson? And what of the Buffalo police wanting to interview McKesson? Paul had discussed these suspicions with Johan many more times but Johan continued to caution Paul that he had not enough evidence to convince his mother of Schuyler's possible deceit. He further pointed out that whether he was right or wrong, his mother's life would be irreparably damaged. Johan argued, what if Schuyler is a deceitful knave, so long as he did not try to convince Elizabeth to marry him nor to inveigle her money, why should she not continue to enjoy Schuyler's company? If his only interest was in Elizabeth's social status, thus allowing himself to be self-pretentious, what harm would that cause to Elizabeth? Paul reluctantly agreed with Johan's assessment, but he was nevertheless continually troubled.

This matter had been going on in Paul's mind for several years now. Each time that he traveled the length of the canal, his mind was continually occupied with the matter of Schuyler. He was feeling confused. He was naturally concerned that his mother would feel distressed by any scandal involving

Schuyler, or worse, that she might become enamored by Schuyler's attractiveness and worldly charms. But he certainly did not want to be the one that disheartened his mother by false or misleading accusations. He was determined to find the real truth and determine whether Schuyler Van Essen and Shamus McKesson were indeed the same person.

Paul decided to sign on for another barge trip to Buffalo. He was determined that this time he would unravel the mystery of the aliases of the suspicious man or men. It had been a year since he had spoken to the Buffalo police and he wondered if he could learn anything more of why they were interested in the man Shamus McKesson. Upon arrival in Buffalo, and having a few days before he had to return to Riverford, he first lingered about the neighborhood of McKesson's home. In the local bars and cafes he tried to casually inquire of anyone's knowledge of McKesson. Almost no one knew of his activities, or perhaps they just did not want to speak of them.

Paul continued his surveillance. On the third day in late morning, he was leaning against a building across from, and down the street a bit from the McKesson house. Suddenly he came erect, his attention focusing on the McKesson front door.

'Sure as the devil, there he is!', Paul mentally remarked.

Yes, indeed it was Schuyler Van Essen entering the house, but in workman's garb. There was no mistaking his appearance. Paul was ready to run to the police station.

'But what will I tell them? What crime will I accuse him of? What can I prove?'

He decided to wait until Schuyler would leave, then follow him to determine whether he was returning to Altady and whether he would visit Elizabeth immediately.

But Paul reconsidered his plan. He did go to the police station. He found the same detective that he had spoken with before. He decided that the only way that he could gain the confidence of the detective was to divulge to him what were his suspicions. After relating his story the detective did speak more openly about McKesson. He said that they actually were anxious to speak with McKesson at the request of the Syrica police. The police there wanted to question him about the possible murder of a local man. It seems that a Syrica businessman, one who was quite wealthy, was an avid fisherman. He was found one morning floating in a lake, with his fishing gear still in his boat. At first the police assumed it was an accidental drowning, but later learned that a man had been seen earlier in the day with the businessman at the boat launch site. In order to close the case to their satisfaction they needed to interview that mystery man. Paul asked,

"But why did they feel suspicious of McKesson. He lives here doesn't he? Not in Syrica" The detective explained. Yes, McKesson was a local resident, but as a bargeman he traveled to many of the cities along the canal. When the Syrica police investigated further, they learned that the businessman's wife had been having an affair with a man friend who enticed her to give him some of her jewelry. From the description of the man, and from other testimony of the lady's maids, the Syrica police thought that McKesson might be the mystery man. They naturally wondered if this secret lover had purposely drowned the businessman. The detective told Paul that the Buffalo police did find McKesson some time ago and interviewed him, but found no reason to believe that he was involved in the matter.

Paul asked,

"When did this interview with McKesson take place?"

The detective replied,

"Oh, that was almost a year ago. The reason that I remember it so well is because it was few days before Christmas, and I felt bad that I was keeping McKesson from enjoying the holidays with his wife and kids."

"Oh," asked Paul, "how many kids does the guy have?"

Very indifferently the detective said,

"At the time he had six kids. I understand that his wife has had another since then."

Paul asked if the detective had any more concerns about McKesson's behavior.

"No", he replied, "We don't. But I understand that the Syrica police are still watchful because people there report that this McKesson guy resembles another uptown dude that calls himself Sylvester Von Ekter. This dandy Von Ekter preys on the socialite ladies too, but so far they got no evidence of any wrongdoing. It's just that he's always takin' the ladies to the opera or restaurants, but never pays a bill. Nice life if ya can get away with it, eh?"

Paul was ecstatic! Now he was sure that Van Essen and McKesson and Von Ekter were the same man! He couldn't wait to get home to tell his mother. All the way back to Riverford he reviewed in his mind how he would relate all that he knew to his mother. At the same time he was watchful of the other barges, in case he might see McKesson passing. As soon as he landed in Riverford and attended to his concluding duties at the barge pier, he ran to the new electric trolley that was now running between the two cities. Arriving at Altady he ran all the way to his home.

It was late afternoon. As soon as he was in the house he began to call,

"Mama! Mama! Are you home? Where are you?"

There was no reply from his mother, but a maid entered the room and told Paul that Madame Mueller was out for the afternoon, that she was in the company of Mr. Van Essen. By now Paul was full of anxiety. When he heard that his mother was out with Schuyler he first whirled in several directions, wondering what he should do. He thought that he might go to his room and get the pistol that he had recently purchased. He did not do so because he would like to have to used it on Schuyler the moment that he entered the house. He must have appeared ferocious because the maid quickly excused herself and almost ran from the room.

Just then Paul heard a most unusual noise in front of the house. It almost sounded like a railroad train starting. He ran out the front door. Coming along the circular driveway was an astonishing machine. Perched upon the seat of this devise were his mother and Schuyler. The very strange looking machine had four wheels like a large wagon and a chimney that was belching black smoke and white steam at the same time. It looked a bit like the horse-drawn fire apparatus that Altady had purchased a few years ago, but it was smaller and there were no horses. With a gush of steam, the vehicle stopped at the front steps. On the seat beside Schuyler, Paul's mother was almost screaming with merriment. As soon as she spied Paul she called to him. She was laughing and trying to talk at the same time. Finally she was able to gush out some words.

"Oh Paul! I am so glad that you are home! Look! Schuyler has just taken me for a tour with this very latest device. It's called a Stanley Steamer Automobile! Is that the correct name Schuyler?"

It was difficult to hear voices above the roar of the machine. Schuyler just smiled broadly and nodded a very exaggerated 'yes'.

After pulling on a large lever that operated clamps on the wheels, Schuyler descended and ran to the other side of the machine. He helped Elizabeth descend the step. Schuyler then took Elizabeth's hand and kissed it. With that he gave a tantalizing nod to Paul, and then said to Elizabeth,

"I hope that you enjoyed this excursion Elizabeth. Someday I shall give Paul a ride also. For now, good day to you both. I must return this devise to the newly appointed dealer." He ascended the machine and with another great puff of smoke and steam the vehicle began to roll out of the driveway. When it reached the street, and after causing two horses to bolt wildly, the noise and the smoke slowly departed the area.

Elizabeth was still in a state of great exhilaration.

"Oh, Paul! What a wonderful drive we have just taken. What an exciting machine. Imagine! It's the first one in Altady and Schuyler has already driven it! My! He is so extraordinary! He's always ahead of everyone! He brings me so much enjoyment! He believes that I should buy this machine. He and I could make use of it around the city."

Paul immediately decided that he had better delay the intended report to his mother and instead visit the new Stanley Steamer dealer, the one from which Schuyler had borrowed the machine. The next day he did so. When hearing the dealer's lively comment on what he believed would be a certain sale, Paul asked why he felt so positive. The dealer explained that the man to whom he had loaned the machine the day earlier stated that he knew of a wealthy lady, one with whom the eminent borrower had much influence, and that he could persuade her to buy the Stanley Steamer even though she herself could not operate it. He believed this because she was vain and always wanted to be the first to impress high society in Altady. When the lady would buy the machine, the dealer promised to pay a handsome commission to the distinguished gentleman. How sure was the gentleman that the lady would buy?

"Oh, he sounded very sure. He said that he had the control of the lady's emotions, and even her purse-strings."

Paul was furious at learning of another deception by Van Essen, and even more so that Schuyler thought Elizabeth was of such weak character. Now Paul was sure that the time had come to advise his mother of Schuyler's manipulative intentions.

For the next two days Elizabeth continued to display here pleasure and excitement when reminiscing about the Stanley Steamer excursion with Schuyler. Because of his mother's exhilaration, Paul once again decided not to relate his knowledge and his suspicions at this time. He simply made minimal comment about the machine and his mother's excitement. He advised his mother that he would like to take a nap and after a few more words he went upstairs, with this question,

"Are we dining here tonight, Mama?"

Elizabeth was now somewhat unwound from her excitement. She answered,

"Yes we are Paul. And there is something that I wish to speak to you about later."

Paul began to fret. Was she to tell of an impending marriage?

'Oh God I hope not!' he thought to himself.

During dinner Elizabeth made it very obvious that she was glad that Paul was at home, that she missed him, that with Mary gone, her life was often lonely. Paul thought for sure that the next statement would be her of decision to marry Schuyler. Instead, Elizabeth changed the conversation to business. She explained to Paul that she was in negotiations to purchase another bakery, this one in Shelby, a nearby city. She said that she had discussed the matter with Johan, whose business judgment she greatly valued, and he had agreed that it would be wise investment. She stated that Schuyler also agreed that it would be a profitable acquisition. Then she hit Paul with the bombshell.

"I would like you to manage this bakery for me Paul."
Paul immediately showed his displeasure with her desires.

"Oh no, Mama! I'm no businessman. I'm not a manager like Johan or Antoinette, or Mr. Arnsmeyer, and certainly not like yourself for that matter."
Elizabeth acted as if she had expected that reply.

"But Paul, you cannot remain a common bargeman all of your life. My business and estate are now quite valuable. If anything should happen to me, you and Mary will inherit quite a great fortune. I would feel much more comfortable if you became directly involved in the business. Someday you could be the manager of the entire enterprise. And when that time comes, Schuyler has made it clear that he will be happy to assist you with the financial aspects."

Paul ignored the statement about Schuyler. He retorted,

"Gosh Mama. You're still a young woman. Why you're barely in your forties, right? Nothings going to happen to you for a long time yet!"

Elizabeth looked saddened.

"No Paul, I have just turned fifty. Why of course it is possible that something can happen to me. I would feel much more comfortable if you were around all of the time and involved in the business with me. And when I think about Mary being part of that church mission in wild Montana, I am terribly afraid for her safety. It's so far away, and it still has many thousands of wild Indians."

Paul recognized that his mother was feeling very terrified. He wanted to calm her but instead he upset her more.

"Who told you such a thing Mama? I'm sure that those Indians are well tamed by now. They wouldn't send nuns into a place where their lives would be in danger."

Elizabeth retorted,

"Schuyler told me about Montana and the other western territories. They're still full of untamed savages. The Army has to keep peace out there! There is no law and order! Why in the world does the Church allow young women to go out there among those people?"

Encounters Elizabeth's

Paul spoke with bitterness,

"Damn it Mama! You listen to Schuyler too much. Why do you let him upset you so much. He's nothing but a scalawag. If you knew as much about him as I do, you'd probably want to kill him, just like I do."

Elizabeth was flabbergasted.

"Paul! What are you saying?"

The maid listening just outside the door was frightened, not for herself, but for Schuyler.

CHAPTER SIXTEEN

An Encounter with Shock

At about this time in Hutson City, Johan was walking from the bank to the bakeshop, briskly as usual, partly because of the chilly November weather, but also because it was his nature to hurry. As he neared the shop, a man that Johan knew as a person that was always informed of town activities, and gossip, stopped him.

"Good afternoon, Johan. How are you today? Well, I hope."
Johan nodded to indicate his day was going well, but wondered why this man seemed so pointed in wanting to engage him. After a few more pleasantries about the approaching winter, the man asked,

"Say, Johan, did you know that there's a fellow, a stranger in town, asking about you?" Johan showed surprise.

"No, I didn't know this. How do you know?"

"Well", the man replied, "you see, I sit in the park across from the bakery many hours of the day, enjoying the sunshine you know. I started noticing this fellow a couple a' days   ago. I knew he was from outta town. He was dressed different than folks around here, ya know. And he had a beard y'know. And the strange thing was that he lingered in the park until you left the bakery. And when you left, he always seemed to be starin' after you. Then he'd go inside the bakery. He did that a couple a times. After his second visit I went in later to ask about the man. Your clerk said that the guy was askin' what time

159

the baker had to start work in the mornin' You're the early mornin' baker ain't ya Johan?"

Johan did not reply to the man directly but began immediately to wonder who this stranger was and why did he want to know of Johan's schedule.

Johan thanked the man for his concern then continued to the bakeshop. When he entered the bakery he immediately asked Sonya the clerk, if a man, a stranger, had been in the day before asking questions.

"Why, yes," she replied.

"Well, what about?"

Johan was getting impatient that he had to prod the answers from Sonya. The clerk elaborated. "Well, he was askin' if the owner of the shop was named Johan Bleier. I didn't know the man so I pretended that I knew nothing about you. Somethin' about him didn't seem right, ya know. Really strange. An' his clothes was different, too. A little old, I'd say."

"Oh, that was wise Sonya. Thank you!"

Johan spoke with relief in his voice. But inwardly he was extremely anxious about the stranger.

'Who is he, and what's he up to?' Johan wondered 'I don't know why, but from what Sonya and the man told me, I wonder if it could have been Schuyler? But why would he be here trailing me? And why would he be wearing common clothing, not his usual fancy coat and trousers.' It was not long before Johan had reason to become even more concerned and even much more curious of the stranger.

Sonya had been away from the bakery for several days with a bad cold.

Johan had told her to stay home for he did not want a sneezing clerk in his store. But just a few days later as Johan was traipsing along the street he was approached by a youngster and handed a note. Its contents gave Johan much surprise. It stated,

"Johan, I need to see you as soon as I can. I have information about that stranger that was in town. I live at 31 Elm Street. Please come here quick."
It was signed, "Sonya, your clerk."

Being fully familiar with the city, Johan walked briskly to Elm Street. Number thirty-one was the second block from the corner of Main. He approached the front door with no idea of where to look for Sonya but he didn't have to wait long. He heard a window on the second floor being opened. Johan immediately recognized Sonya's head projecting out of the window. She called him with a loud enough voice for him to hear, but with a tone that seemed to imply secrecy was intended.

"Up here Johan. Come up here."
Johan bounded up the steps to an open doorway where Sonya now stood half peering out.

"Johan! You won't believe this but that man, the one that was hangin' around the park, the one who came in the bakery askin' about you. He's still around. He still hangs around the park, but doesn't talk to anyone...an' he seems lost...kinda crazy."
Johan was listening intently while his mind was trying to assess the situation.

'Who is this man?...what's he up to...why was he askin' about me?'
The questions reeled through Johan's head.

"Tell me again Sonya, did he ask about me again. Is there anything about him you forgot to tell me?"

Sonya was twirling her apron front in her hands.

"Well no. But only before like I told ya he was askin' about a Johan Bleier. An' he mentioned, as best I could understand 'im, a woman named Elizabeth, and someone named Paul."

Johan was anxious,

"You say that you had trouble understanding him? Why so, did he have an accent?"

"Well yea", Sonya replied, "didn't I tell ya that before?"

Johan did not answer her, but he knew that she had not previously made any statement about having trouble to understand the man.

The very next morning, as he was hurrying to begin his duties at the bakeshop, he smelled smoke in the street. Just then, the fire apparatus with its snorting horses, came swirling around the corner. Johan ran to follow. As he turned the next corner he stopped short and was awestruck, for he saw his bakeshop fully engulfed in flames. Luckily, no one was in the building, for the former apartment above the shop had long ago become Johan's office and a storage area. By now, the firemen were beginning to pump water from their wagon onto the flames. Another wagon of water arrived but in spite of the efforts of all of the firemen, in just over an hour the building was a collapsed pile of charred wood, with everything burned except the iron ovens.

The fire chief interviewed Johan about the possibility that an oven was left untended last evening and became overheated.

"I suppose that could have happened",

Johan agreed, but inwardly he connected the stranger in town and the fire. He was sure that he had shaken-down the wood burning in the ovens before leaving last evening. He then suddenly shook with the realization that he had accidentally slept over almost an hour this morning. Normally he would have been in the bakery by the time of the fire outbreak.

'My God', Johan became alarmed, 'was this fire set deliberately and was I suppose to be in the fire?'

He could not dismiss thoughts about the inquisitive stranger in town. And of the possibility that he himself might have been burned to death.

Johan knew that he must call Elizabeth to report to her the disastrous news. But he felt it more imperative that he first locate the local park-loiterer so that he could obtain a better description of that stranger. Would the description be one that resembled Schuyler Van Essen? Johan put the idea out of his head. That possibility would be too preposterous. Why would Schuyler want him dead?

But Johan could not find the loiterer to obtain a description of the stranger, so now he was even more confused. Johan could not be sure if it was Schuyler at all. Through the description of the physique of the stranger could fit many, and the loiterer did previously describe the stranger as being commonly dressed. Johan thought a moment then convinced himself that if Schuyler were up to some nefarious scheme he wouldn't wear natty apparel anyway and perhaps would talk in a fake accent. He wondered,

'But who else would be asking about me, and about my cousin Elizabeth and about Paul?'

Johan went into a nearby merchant's shop and asked to use his telephone. The man quickly obliged, since he knew Johan and recognized Johan's state of anxiety.

Johan telephoned Elizabeth to tell her of the bad news, but not of his suspicions about the stranger, only of the fire. Elizabeth's reaction was one of shock and great concern, not just for the bakeshop, but more so for Johan and the other employees. Johan explained the details of the disastrous event and described how lucky he had been, due to his fortunate sleepiness and his resultant tardiness this morning. He then inquired of Elizabeth whether Schuyler had visited her recently.

"Why no. He told me that he would be out of town for several days so I did not expect him to call."

Johan hesitated for a moment then decided to reveal to Elizabeth his suspicions. He told of the stranger, of the park-loiterer's observations. He stated that he believed that the stranger in town could well be Schuyler, and further, that he suspected Schuyler of being the arsonist. He did not go so far as to state his belief that Schuyler intended to murder him in the fire. Elizabeth was astounded. But then her attitude turned to fury.

"What in the world is wrong with you and Paul. Why are you both so damned determined to turn me away from Schuyler? You are both being ridiculous with your accusations."

Johan gave a determined reply.

"I've come to agree with that Paul, that he is correct in his belief of Schuyler's double life. And when I am a little more positive of that, and that he started the fire with intentions of murdering me, I'll be the one doing the murdering."

Elizabeth tried to calm him.

"For godsake Johan! Calm down! Come visit me here immediately. We have much to discuss, both about business and our personal lives as well. But before you come here, contact each of your employees to assure them that they will be paid until we make other arrangements. Then come here! Do you understand?"

"Alright Elizabeth. I'll be there by mid-afternoon."

Before Johan arrived, Elizabeth decided that it was time for her to speak with both Paul and Johan simultaneously. When Johan did arrive, she called Paul to come to the drawing room so that he would hear Johan's report of the fire loss directly from him. As Johan described the conditions of the blaze and stated that he was quite certain that it was caused by arson, Paul looked very expectantly into Johan's face, awaiting the next words. When Johan related the story of the stranger, his actions in town before the fire, and Johan's own suspicions, Paul jumped from his chair.

"There, didn't I tell you Mama? Didn't I tell you that Schuyler was a contriving sonovabitch? Didn't I tell you! I just know that he has some diabolical plot in mind. No doubt he intends to finagle you out of your money!"

Elizabeth showed disappointment. Not just at the suspicions of Paul and Johan, but also because of her knowledge of an event that had occurred a few days previous. She decided that she must relate to Paul and Johan the details of a conversation with Schuyler.

"Listen Paul, Johan. I'm not saying that I agree with your suspicions, but I must tell you both of a conversation that Schuyler and I had a few days ago." The two men leaned closer to Elizabeth. They had never seen her so somber before. Trying to sound sympathetic, Paul asked,

"What is it Mama? What happened?"

Then Johan interjected,

"Wait Paul. Let your mother tell her story. Don't jump at her. Don't upset her any more that she is already".

But it was obvious that both men could not wait for Elizabeth to get the first word out of her mouth. She seemed very distressed.

"My Lord! I can't believe that you two have caused me to become suspicious of a man that I truly admire. Oh! I hope that I am not making myself unworthy of Schuyler's loyalty and fondness for me!"

Now the men were both ready to explode at Elizabeth.

"Well! What is it?" Johan almost screamed.

Elizabeth forced herself to settle down. She also began to cry a little.

'Oh God! Is she ever going to tell us?' Paul wondered.

Elizabeth began.

"Last Sunday afternoon as Schuyler and I strolled along in the park along the river, Schuyler asked me about my arrangements for my business and other assets. It was the first time that he had ever asked such personal questions and I was a bit surprised by his inquiry".

Paul immediately thought,

'So that's why Mama brought up the matter of me taking an active roll in the business?'

Elizabeth continued.

"Schuyler did point out to me several matters about which I have been procrastinating. Such as, who would inherit my shops, and what would be the distribution of my other funds. He felt that since Mary was a nun, bound by an oath of poverty, she would not even care to inherit any of my money. He also pointed out your indifference, Paul. He said that you would probably fail at running the shops if you tried, and that you would likely squander any cash that I would leave you."

Both men were leaning back in their chairs, throwing their heads back and raising their hands in utter astonishment. Paul spoke with vengeance.

"Why that sonovabitch. So he *is* trying to finagle your money Mama! He's trying to be sure that Mary and I are cut out of your will."

Looking directly at his mother, he stated,

"Next, he'll start to convince you that *he* should take over the shops and the handling of your money! What a sneaky bastard. Now I'm sure I want to kill him!"

Elizabeth shook her head, ignoring Paul's statement but she reluctantly concurred with the possibilities that he suggested. Crying a bit more, she gasped,

"I believe that you may be right Paul. Oh I can't tell you how disappointed I am. Not just at Schuyler, but at myself too, for admitting to myself that you may be correct in your accusations."

Now Johan spoke. Quietly he asked,

"Did my name come into the conversation Elizabeth?"

She answered, again showing dismay.

"Yes, it did Johan. I told Schuyler that in the event that Paul would not wish to take over the management of my shops and business funds, I would ask you to perform that duty. I told Schuyler that I was completely confident in your business ability, and fully trustworthy of your loyalty."

Now Johan began to nod his head up and down.

"Thanks for your trust Elizabeth. But now I see why he wanted me out of the way. I was the last obstacle to his scheme. I had to be put out of the way."

Now Elizabeth sobbed loudly, seeming to nod her agreement with Johan's statement. The three now just sat motionless, each in total dismay. There was silence for quite some time. Finally Paul arose.

"Well, I have to leave now. I'll see you both later. Or maybe tomorrow at breakfast. You staying here tonight Johan?"

Elizabeth looked up.

"Oh, Yes! Please do stay Johan. And Paul, please do not go out tonight. Both Johan and I need comforting assurance tonight."

Looking at Paul, Johan asked,

"You got something to do tonight Paul? You going someplace? You not going to get in any trouble are you?"

Elizabeth looked perplexed.

"Paul! Should you not remain at home tonight? After all, we have all had a very unnerving evening. We had better not make any rash decisions."

Not wanting to cause further anguish to his mother, Paul nodded and shrugged.

"OK Mama. I'll wait on my business until tomorrow."

But Paul went out to stroll the street in front of the house, to get some air while reviewing the latest events in his mind. He was just turning into the front walkway when he was sure that he saw a man loitering across the street, a little distance from the house. He dismissed the suspicion as being caused by his nervousness.

In the morning Elizabeth, Paul and Johan each kept busy on individual matters, or were they just avoiding each other. At noon the three enjoyed a delicious, but not comfortable luncheon. Each was still uneasy. Just as the three were rising from their chairs, the maid entered and said,

"Pardon me, Missus Mueller, but Mr. Arnsmeyer wishes to speak with you on the telephone".

Elizabeth excused herself and left the room for a few minutes. Showing some concern when she returned, she spoke to Paul,

"Paul dear. Mr. Arnsmeyer called to say that he is not feeling well. He is leaving for home now and does not feel that he will be able to open the shop tomorrow morning. Would you be a dear and open the shop. Will you do that for me?"

She had chosen to ask Paul rather than Johan because she saw this as an opportunity to involve Paul, hoping that he might acquiesce to become involved in the operation of the bakeries. Paul immediately realized his mother's motives but agreed to comply with her request so as to relieve some of her tenseness.

That night each slept fitfully. From their separate bedrooms Paul and Johan could each hear Elizabeth crying, but neither intruded into her bed room. Both Paul and Johan arose during the night at different times, but each returned to their beds. From their separate rooms each wondered why the other was moving about. Each wondered, or did they imagine, that the front door of the house was opened, then quietly closed.

At breakfast Paul arrived late. Elizabeth did not ask why. She had fully expected that Paul was at the bakery earlier until one of the clerks arrived.. After nodding to Paul, all were silent for quite some time. Then Elizabeth spoke.

"Paul. Johan. I have been thinking. There is a least one matter in which Schuyler is correct."

Both men looked up quickly, waiting to learn in what matter Elizabeth agreed with Schuyler.

"Schuyler had urged me to see my attorney to revise my will. He is correct. So I made an appointment with Attorney Hodges"

Seeing the anxiety in the faces of the two men, she continued.

"Schuyler told me that he would gladly accompany me, to give me support in the decision that I must make with regard to my finances and business. Schuyler said that he felt it would be wise to assign him as the executor, and perhaps even include a statement in the will, of my intentions for him to become the active manager of my business. He tried to assure me that he would be a much more prudent manager than you Paul, if you should decide to take my place. Or even you, Johan!"

Johan looked disdainful, thinking but not saying,

'That sonofabitch. He's always angling.'

Rising from the table Elizabeth announced,

"I want both of you to accompany tomorrow at my appointment with Attorney

Hodges. But I'll leave Schuyler out of this for now."

CHAPTER SEVENTEEN

An Encounter with Indecision

The next morning all were silent at breakfast. Then Elizabeth broke the silence by asking,

"Paul, did you open the bakery again this morning? Mr. Arnsmeyer called to advise that he was still not feeling well."

"Yes, Mama, he called me too. I took care of it."

"I hope that you were on time. Mr. Arnsmeyer is always on the job by four a.m. Did you arise early?"

Paul replied to the affirmative, but qualified his conduct with,

"I opened the bakery, Mama, but I must confess that I was a few minutes late."

Elizabeth accepted his reply without comment.

Then Johan spoke,

"Oh, by the way, Paul. Are you having as much trouble here with the rats as I was having in Hutson City, ah, before the fire that is."

Elizabeth looked quickly in back of her to be sure that no maid was nearby. Her motions indicated that she wanted no one to hear such comment. But Paul spoke up anyway.

"Oh, I would say yes. When I went to the basement these two mornings I could hear them scrambling around. I noticed that Mr. Arnsmeyer had a tin of poison powder down there. If he doesn't get in today, I'll go over after closing and spread some. OK, Mama?"

Elizabeth smiled at Paul.

"Why yes, Paul, that would be sensible."

She looked back again to be sure no one heard Paul, and she smiled to herself at the thought that Paul was showing some concern for the bakery's operation.

Shortly after lunch the three visited Elizabeth's attorney As the weather was very pleasant she and the two men walked to Attorney Hodges' office on Monroe Street. Upon entering the office the receptionist greeted Elizabeth very warmly and nodded to the two men as she quickly went to the attorney's door. By the actions of the receptionist, the men knew that Elizabeth was a very important client. Standing at the open door the receptionist announced the three. Mr. Hodges came bubbling from his office.

"Oh, good afternoon, Elizabeth. How nice to see you again".

He called her by her first name because they both often attended many of the same social events of the city. He greeted the men with,

"Nice to see you also gentlemen. It's been quite some time since I have had the pleasure of meeting you."

With the formalities concluded, the four seated themselves and began to conduct the business of Elizabeth's will and choice of executor. Elizabeth instructed that both Paul and Johan were to be co-inheritors of her assets, co-executors, and to have joint power of attorney, should she become incapacitated. She also made provisions for a generous donation to Mary's religious order, the Sisters Of Charity, for her parish, for Father Tierney and a few other charities. She did not specify it as a codicil, but she instructed Paul and Johan to make generous bonus payments to each of her employees.

"There!" She stated, "I believe that we have covered all of the necessary requirements." Mr. Hodges did not ask, but Elizabeth sensed his curiosity.

"I have decided to make provisions only for my family and employees. I am leaving Schuyler free of any responsibilities."

Then, appearing wistful, she said,

"Perhaps I will include him later."

Mr. Hodges only nodded that he understood. Paul and Johan looked at each other with quizzical glances. Was Schuyler in or out, they wondered.

Attorney Hodges spoke to Elizabeth.

"I wonder if I might have a few words in private with you Elizabeth."

"Of course, Robert", was Elizabeth's calm reply.

Without comment, Paul and Johan left the office, going to sit in the reception room.

"Elizabeth, I hope that I am not speaking inappropriately", Hodges began.

"I was pleased, if not a little surprised, that you omitted Schuyler Van Essen from your financial arrangements."

Elizabeth looked up quickly. Hodges continued.

"A few evenings ago I was attending an affair at Mrs. Stanton's home, you know the widow lady. It was a charming affair. I was surprised that you were not there. Well, anyway, as I chatted with Mrs. Stanton, she motioned for a young lady to come to her. She stated that she would like to introduce the lady to me.

She was from a leading family of Troyton. As I looked in the direction of the young lady I observed that she was in the company of a distinguished looking gentleman. When he saw me looking in their direction he quickly turned away. When the young lady came to us, and after being introduced, I asked if she had an escort.

"Why yes", she replied. "He has just gone to the gentlemen's lounge. He's a delightful man. His name is Simon Von Rathbone."

Elizabeth, I am sure that it was Schuyler Van Essen. I have seen him many times at other social events, acting as your escort. I now believe that he may be a charlatan, even a gigolo."

Elizabeth made no reply. She nodded to Hodges, turned and left the room.

'It seems that I may have been the only person who did not see the deceit in Schuyler Van Essen', she thought to herself.

That evening Paul suggested that the three dine out, in celebration that such an important matter had been finalized. Elizabeth declined however, so the two men left for dinner, and no doubt a few drinks after. Although she did not regret her actions of the day, Elizabeth was still dejected when she thought of her decisions to omit Schuyler.

'But what was I to do, in view of all the evidence that Schuyler is just a charlatan'.

After the men left she sat in the library in a pensive mood. But since the day had been stressful she decided to retire earlier than usual. She started to ascend the staircase but as she did so the front doorbell rang. She hesitated until the maid opened the door. From the stairs she could see Schuyler. In spite of her surprise, she immediately descended and greeted Schuyler cordially.

"Oh, good evening Schuyler. I am happy that you called. We have matters to discuss." Schuyler seemed a bit nervous, but surprised and greatly pleased at such an amiable greeting.

"Elizabeth. Please excuse my arriving without notice, but I have just returned to town and I wondered if you might join me for a quiet dinner?" Elizabeth gave a polite smile,

"Why yes Schuyler, I am quite hungry."
Upon receiving Schuyler's invitation she decided to accept it as this would give her the opportunity to speak to him about what was on her mind.

"I'm very glad that you arrived because I intended to call you tomorrow. There is something that I must tell you."

As Elizabeth motioned for the maid to bring her a shawl, Schuyler looked very curious.

Meanwhile, Paul and Johan had dined at one of Altady's finest restaurants, then retired to the bar of a nearby hotel. By their conversation and through their quaffs, they complimented each other on finally convincing Elizabeth of the dastardly intentions of that devil, Schuyler, or McKesson, or whoever he is. The two left the bar intending to return home, but as they turned a corner in their walk, Paul said,

"You go ahead Johan. I've got to go to the bakery and set out the you-know-what for our little friends with the long tails."
He laughed a little. Johan offered to help him but Paul declined, urging Johan to go home to bed. Paul weaved only slightly on his way toward the bakery. As they parted, Johan said,

"Oh, Paul! I may not see you tomorrow. I am leaving early to return to Hutson City, on an errand that your mother asked me to perform."

Johan too, weaved a bit as he went on his way, but he appeared to be going straight to the Mueller mansion.

Elizabeth had indeed asked Johan to perform a task for her. A few days earlier she had asked him to return to Hutson City to determine whether to purchase a building for another bakery, construct her own building, or not open another bakery there at all. Johan did as he was asked and returned to Hutson City. On the second day he was there, a stranger began to follow him. Yes, he was sure that someone was following him. But why? He decided to confront the man.

After turning a corner and going out of view of the other man's sight, Johan abruptly stayed at the corner so as to surprise the man. When the man came around the corner, and upon being surprised by Johan's presence, he suddenly stopped. Then both men were stunned.

Johan almost screamed,

"Forgodsake, is that you? I can't believe it!"

The man spoke equally surprised,

"Ach du lieber, iss dat yoo Johan? Ja! Yoo do be Johan? I haf not seed yoo for a long time, so I don't know if it be yoo.

Johan responded vigorously,

"Yes! I am Johan! My God! The last thing that I expected was to see you alive! I can't believe this! How in the world did you come back from the dead? Oh! There must be an explanation! No one returns from the grave. But my

Encounters Elizabeth's

God! How can this be?"

The man started to explain how it was that he returned after supposedly being in the grave but Johan began to lead him by the arm. As he pulled the man, Johan exclaimed again,

"My God! Sebastian! How in the world are you alive? Where have you been all these years?"

Johan was anxious to know, but was also anxious to decide how to break the news to Elizabeth and Paul. And he was anxious to tell Sebastian of Elizabeth's status in life, Paul's manhood, and about his yet unknown daughter Mary. Sebastian did not even know of his daughter's existence.

While all these thoughts whirled through Johan's head, he was also mentally trying to determine where he would bring Sebastian to get him bathed and re-appareled, for Sebastian indeed looked, and smelled, like a vagrant. Johan could certainly not let Elizabeth reunite with him in such a condition. And as all of these thoughts transpired, Johan was also trying to explain to Sebastian what was Elizabeth's present situation. He did not want to reveal too much however, for he felt that Elizabeth should be the first to relate to Sebastian the story of her life during the past thirty years. All that he did was to assure Sebastian that both Elizabeth and Paul were well, and that he would soon be reunited with them. He did not even mention Altady yet, as their ultimate destination, nor Mary, the daughter of whom Sebastian is still unaware.

Johan led Sebastian to a nearby hotel. As they walked, Johan briskly, and Sebastian falteringly, Sebastian was trying to talk to Johan.

"Johan, after der fire, vhen der bakery burn, ya know, I vas not know vat to doo. I did not yet found yoo und I vas not aple to ask no vun ver to find yoo. I vas stay at da Stadte hotel, I tink dey call it. Yoo know, der gasthaus ofver un da udder sidt of town yoo know. But I waz almos' out uff money, I only haf a leetle bit. I vas get wery vorried about vat to doo. Vun day I follow yoo to Altady. I take the stagecoach rite after yoo doo. In Altady I follow yoo to a big red-brick house. I vait for yoo but yoo no come oud. Oh, I vas zo worry. I decide to come back to Hutson City. I know dis place better. All of mine money iz gone. I vorry much! Den I see yoo today! I am be so happy!"

Now Sebastian was gasping from trying to talk and at the same time to keep up with Johan. Suddenly Johan realized Sebastian's breathless condition. He stopped,

'Why am I running? Poor Sebastian can't keep up. He's gotten so old! I wonder what Elizabeth will think when she learns that her husband is alive, and when she sees how old and weary he looks. And what will Paul think, having such an old man as a father?'

Now he remembered that over the years since the end of the war, occasionally he would read of a man that was thought to be dead but would suddenly appear in his hometown. In almost every case, he had been a deserter and was afraid to come home, but the urge to do so finally overcame his worry about being sent to jail. Was Sebastian a deserter?

'Oh I hope not! If he is, what will happen to him? A long prison sentence, or worse?'

Now Johan and Sebastian reached the Embassy Hotel, a fine

establishment, not like the 'flea bag' hotel where Sebastian had stayed. Johan obtained a room, then after allowing Sebastian some time to regain more of his breath and to collect himself, Johan went across the hall to the bathroom and began to fill the bathtub with warm water. This hotel, being one of the more modern in Hutson City, had running hot water, as well as the other modern indoor conveniences.

As Johan waited nervously in their rented room, Sebastian soaked himself in the tub for sometime. It was obvious that he not only had not bathed in a long time, he had never had the opportunity to enjoy such a restful indoor bath. In fact, the bath made Sebastian drowsy, so after he returned to their room wrapped in towels, Johan urged him to get into the bed and take a well-needed nap. This would give Johan the time that he needed to purchase an outfit of clothing for Sebastian.

By the time that all of this had occurred it was mid-afternoon. Johan had to help Sebastian get into the new clothing. The fit was not well, but Johan felt that it would suffice. The trousers and the sleeves were a bit long but here was no time to tailor them. They rolled up the pants cuffs. It was obvious that Sebastian was very nervous. And it was also obvious that Sebastian wanted to get going and to meet Elizabeth. But Johan felt that one more step was necessary, to get Sebastian's unkempt beard shaved. The barber did a fine job of shaving all of the beard off and trimming his hair. Sebastian now looked presentable and nearly like himself except for the age wrinkles on his face.

The two men were anxious to see Elizabeth. Johan led by hurriedly walking to the stage depot with Sebastian again gasping as he tried to keep up with Johan's pace. The two boarded the next stage to Altady. Although Altady had trolleys which began operating a few years earlier, there was still no tracks connecting Hutson City and Altady. Upon reaching Altady, Johan again led Sebastian at a fast rate as they walked to Elizabeth's house. Although Sebastian would falter, Johan just kept walking and urged Sebastian to keep up with him.

At the front door of the mansion, which Johan had not yet told Sebastian whose home it was, the maid opened the door, greeted Johan, glanced at the stranger, then went into the drawing room to announce Johan's arrival. Johan did not wait for an invitation from Elizabeth nor an indication from the maid to enter, he just briskly did so, leading Sebastian by the arm. Elizabeth was just rising from her chair.

Johan spoke quickly.

"Elizabeth, prepare yourself for a shock, a very pleasant shock!"

Elizabeth looked up, first at Johan then at the stranger. She started to smile, to receive Johan's new friend with pleasantness. But as she stepped towards them, she looked harder at the stranger. She opened he mouth as if to speak, but instead, fainted to the floor.

Johan moved first, Sebastian immediately beside him, and the maid came quickly across the room to Elizabeth also. The maid was aghast that the stranger had obviously caused her mistress great distress. Johan quickly lifted Elizabeth into his arms, crossed a few steps to the settee, and placed Elizabeth upon it. Sebastian moved just as fast as Johan did. After Elizabeth was in place and Johan stepped back, Sebastian lifted her shoulders, embraced her in his arms, and rocking to and fro, he began to weep. The maid stood frozen, not knowing if she should notify the police, seek a doctor, or begin pummeling the stranger. She looked to Johan for an indication of which to do. By his look, and a wave of the hand, Johan quickly assured her that her mistress would be alright and that the stranger would do her no harm. The maid backed away, but it was obvious that she was not so sure that Johan's explanations satisfied the matter.

After a few minutes, Elizabeth began to awaken from her senseless state. She saw Johan standing near by and could feel that someone was holding her. Without being fully conscious, she must have believed that they were the same person.

"Oh, Johan. I just had the most amazing dream. I dreamed that Sebastian had come back and was standing beside you. Oh my! It seemed so real!"
Johan came to her side quickly, knelt down and took her hand. He knew that he had to be careful about how to explain the truth, or she might faint again.

"Elizabeth, dear cousin, what if I tell you that it was no dream, that Sebastian is here, with you right now."
Elizabeth smiled, nodded her head and answered,

"Oh, wouldn't that be wonderful Johan. To see Sebastian again. To believe that he never had died."
Now Sebastian was unsure of what to do. He continued to hold Elizabeth, then whispered to her in German,

"Ick bin es Sebastian mein schatz! Ick bin mein! Es tut leid! Ja leid, sehr leid. I be trooly zorry Elizabeth"
He did not know if spoken words at this time would ease Elizabeth or confuse

her again. But he could hold back no longer.

"Oh mein sehr Elizabeth. How I haf vant to hauld yoo in mein arms like dis. How I haf vant to let yoo know dat I really be alife, dat after all dese years, vee are again togeder now."

Elizabeth stirred, looking at Johan, wondering why he had said such words. Then her mind began to clear. She suddenly realized that it was not Johan that was holding her or had spoken to her. She looked at the man whose face was close to hers. She shook her head side to side, stared hard at that face, then looked as though she would faint again, but did not.

"Oh my God! Is that really you Sebastian?"

Johan could not distinguish whether she was questioning Sebastian's looks, for he obviously appeared much older, or was she showing doubt that Sebastian was really here, not just in her dream.

Just at that time, Paul entered the room. When he had entered the front door, everyone was so intent on the matter in the drawing room that no one even noticed his arrival. Then when he saw a stranger holding his mother, he too was confused and greatly concerned. He could see the ashen color of his mother's face, so he mistakenly believed that the stranger was a doctor.

"What's the matter, Mama? What's wrong? Have you had a spell. You look very peeked. How is she doctor?"

At that, Johan knew that he must quickly explain to Paul the unbelievable, and do so in a calm, rational way, or Paul might be the next person to faint. Johan motioned for Paul to come closer to him, away from his mother and the man holding her.

"Paul. Perhaps you had better sit."

Paul looked even more apprehensive.

"Why? What is it? What's wrong with Mama? Is she seriously ill?"

It took a lot of skill by Johan and quite a bit of time to make Paul understand, and to accept the unbelievable and incredible story that Johan related. At first Paul thought that Johan was playing a very morose trick on him, but Johan repeated the story several times, each time reiterating the details of the events of the past day. And then added that he too, did not yet know the entire story of how Sebastian escaped the prison camp and survived all these years, and why his father had never returned home until now.

For the next several minutes nothing was spoken by anyone. Each person sat pensive, in self-doubt at what they had learned. But gradually they seemed to realize, even if not understand, what was occurring. They began to more readily accept the fact that it was not a dream, not a fantasy, but an actuality.

Elizabeth was slowly coming back to her usual, calm manner. She began to respond to Sebastian's loving hold. She nestled into his arms and finally found her voice to express her great happiness that Sebastian was with her once more.

"Sebastian, oh my dear husband. What a great joy to know that you are alive! And here with us now! What better gift could God have given us. Oh, you poor dear! You look so old..."

She corrected herself,

"You look so tired."

Then, finally realizing Paul's presence she called,

"Paul! Oh my darling Paul! Come over here and greet your long lost father. Poor boy! You were only a tiny tot, not more than an infant when your father left for the war."

As Paul began to move very slowly towards her and his father, Elizabeth came to another realization.

"Oh my God! Mary! Mary will be astonished! Oh, my God, Sebastian! You don't even know that you have a daughter!"

With that, Sebastian seemed to suddenly awaken from his euphoria.

"A dauter? I haf a dauter? Oh mein sweet Elizabeth, vere iss mein dauter? Ven vill I meet her?"

Paul had hardly started to cross the room. He suddenly stopped. Did his father want to meet him, or was his unknown daughter the only child that mattered to him in his new unbelievable state of ecstasy.

Throughout this time the maid had remained nearby, in wonderment that what she had overheard could possibly be true. She had sat on a chair in the corner of the drawing room, unnoticed. Now Elizabeth stirred a little and upon noticing the maid sitting, Elizabeth called,

"Oh! Amelia! Would you be so kind as to prepare coffee for us? I think that we may be in or a long evening. I don't believe that any one of us is thinking of sleeping tonight."

"Yes, mum." The maid responded and quickly left the room.

CHAPTER EIGHTEEN

An Encounter with Remorse

When the maid returned to the drawing room with a tray of coffee, cups and saucers, everyone was now repositioned. Elizabeth had finally fully aroused herself and had asked Sebastian to assist her to her feet. She slowly paced a few steps across the room with Sebastian holding his arm about her waist and with Johan standing tensely nearby to also assist if he were needed. Paul was the only one now seated. But he now stood and moved towards his father. After he timidly reached his father, Sebastian extended his arms to Paul. With this gesture, Paul reacted a little more warmly to his newly acquired father.

"Paul, mein sohn Paul. Oh, how are yoo Paul? Ven last I see yoo, yoo vere jus' a baby in yoo mutter's arms. It be hard to tink dat all dese years be past; dat yoo be a bik grown boy, .., Oh! I mean, a bik mann."
The two embraced for a few seconds, then Paul seemed to be the one that wanted to end the hug. Both Elizabeth and Johan sensed Paul's seeming coolness to his father. Sebastian too looked disappointed at Paul's terseness. Paul turned away and returned to the chair that he had been occupying.

Now the others seated themselves also and Amelia poured a cup of coffee for each person, serving it to them at their place of seating. Elizabeth and Johan appeared to be balancing their cups in their hand but Paul and Sebastian held their cups awkwardly and shakingly, glancing about to see where they might place it.

After a few more seconds of what seemed like endless minutes, Sebastian spoke.

"Yoo know, I vant to hear all 'bout yoo folks during de past t'irty years, but I tink I be the one that better do de first talkin'."

Sebastian then rose and began pacing. He began to relate his long story of escaping the prison with his friend Cyrus. He told of how Cyrus had helped him while they were prisoners, that Cyrus brought him food, swill actually, when Sebastian was too weak to go for himself, of how Cyrus always made sure that Sebastian was not overlooked by their fellow prisoners, because each man was so constantly concerned at keeping themselves warm and alive they sometimes overlooked the needs of others.

At this point Elizabeth realized that Amelia was still in the room, listening just as intently as they were. By way of politely dismissing her, Elizabeth offered,

"Thank you very much Amelia. That will be all for now."
Amelia obeyed her mistress' order and left the room, but remained within earshot just outside the doorway.

Sebastian continued his pacing He related the details of how they evaded the guards, of their plodding through the woods and of their first few days of hiding. Then he explained about Cyrus' delight with the young black woman that had helped them. He told of his own desire to get back home, but he had to depart alone, because Cyrus made it obvious that he was going to stay with the young woman and the boy, her son. When Sebastian told of the black woman's explanation of the reason that she was such a young mother, of being raped at a young age, he stopped, looked at Elizabeth, then realized the embarrassment that he must be causing her, remembering her own distasteful assault. He looked at Paul, and wondered if he was ever told anything about his own conception. Then he thought to himself,

'Vy did I even tink to talk about dat part of mein story?'

He explained that after he had walked a few days northward, only at night, which made it slower, he was hiding in a barn one night, when he was discovered by two black men. They signaled that they would be quiet. They left, but came back soon with a small amount of food. Sebastian told of how he garbled it down, then fell asleep, a bit more at ease than on previous nights, because the black men seemed friendly and protective.

In the morning the two men talked to Sebastian about his plans to get home in the north. They said that it was far too dangerous to travel, that it would be safer to stay there for a while. Sebastian reluctantly agreed. But after a few weeks he thanked them and began to walk again, only at night. After many, many nights of walking and hiding in the woods, or in dilapidated houses or barns, he was completely exhausted, not just from the physical effort of walking, but by the stress that he felt, caused the by tenseness because of the fear of being caught.

On one bright morning, after what seemed like a lifetime of walking, Sebastian came out of the woods where he had slept, looked over the rich farmland and the expansive fields before him. Of course the land showed evidence of neglect, and even in some areas, signs of a battle having been fought there, but he loved the view, and the land. He slumped against a tree and wondered to himself,

'Am I efer goin' ta get home? Vill I be kilt afore I get der? An' maybe Cyrus vas right, dat all of my folks tink I be dead anywayzs.'

For the first time Sebastian realized that he was beginning to give up hope of seeing Elizabeth and Paul again. He told of deciding to stay in that woods a few days, to restore himself to better health, he convinced himself. Then he explained how each morning as he sat against thetree, looking over the fields, he fantasized that he was the farmer, the owner of this wonderful land.

One morning he decided to venture across the field to an old barn. When he entered the barn he discovered that it was occupied by a number of black people. At first they looked surprised at seeing him, but then almost immediately seemed to disregard him. After a time he asked them,

"Ain't you folks goin' ta turn me in? Ain't yoo goin' ta tell da rebs that yoo foun' a union solyer?"

None moved at all, but all let out a weak laugh. An older man spoke,

"Us turn y'all in? Why if we'un saw a reb solyer, weed wanna kill him arself, not turns y'all ober ta him. We's jus' as bad off as y'all, we got no place ta go, no one ta find, an nuttin' ta do, no how."

Sebastian related to Elizabeth and the others that at hearing these comments, he slumped down with them and chuckled himself. He told them that he remembered something that his father used to say,

"Vee all be fishes in der same pond."

At that all of the black people chuckled and nodded 'yes' in agreement.

So Sebastian stayed with this small group of people. But after a few weeks of doing nothing, he suggested that they begin to work the field, to grow crops. They all looked doubtful. To prove that it was a possibility, Sebastian gleaned the field, digging here and there, and returned with a few small vegetables, or roots of plants that had somehow survived the lack of normal cultivation. He planted these vegetables and roots, found a stream nearby to obtain water with an old bucket that lay in the barn, and began to farm again. For the first time in years he felt good about life again. Now the other folks began to show signs of hope too. They all went out gleaning, searched the area in a wider circle, found other abandoned barns still holding remnants of useable farm gear. Everything they brought back needed fixing but everyone worked at the common effort and soon all were in a much more cheerful mood.

Before Sebastian had arrived the group had sustained themselves by catching a scarce rabbit or squirrel, and by eating the gleanings of the same kind of vegetables that Sebastian had found. This method of survival had now to be continued, but because the group had more interest in 'the farm', they worked harder and found more vegetables than before. They planted more of their 'surplus', tended it carefully, and in a few weeks, evidence of their efforts began to show in the soil-breaking of the new growth.

All during the time that this effort was going on, Sebastian was the accepted leader. One day he thought about the way that they had readily accepted his supervision. He asked why. The older man explained. They had all been slave servants to the estate owner. The man talking had been the household butler, two of the men had been livery stable workers, two others were the drudgery-hands that had to keep the out-houses and barn stalls clean. Two of the ladies had been maids in the household and one had been a kitchen helper to old Aggie, the cook, who was now dead. At the outbreak of the war, the estate owner, Master Burlingame had been appointed a Brigadier in the Confederate Army and was told to organize a cavalry troop, because everyone in the County was a horse breeder and expert rider.

" The master was dun gone quite a spell. Den one day the Missus was told by another occifer who comes by dat da Master, he wuz kilt at a place up nort' called Pennsa.. sumt'in'. The Missus and her daughter, first dey crys hard, we all do, den dey left da estate an' went to stay wid her sister ober in sout' carlina. Before she goed, she told alla us we'se free now, we'se can go do what we'se want. But we'se don't know what else ta do, we'se got no udder place ta go. Den da yankee solyers come an burn down da whole house, take da two cows dat was lef, an moved on to da Holgate place an burn it too. Da yanks burnt alla da stables an ebryting. Da onliest ting lef is dis barn, way out here. So we'all came out here to dis barn. Dat's all we knows what ta do."

Sebastian shook his head several times during his narration. because he had seen the same kinds of senseless rages by his own army company when they were in Louisiana and West Virginia, he was not surprised to hear it from the old man.

Sebastian paced and continued his story. Elizabeth and Johan were enraptured. Even Paul, who had at first feigned disinterest, was now very obviously engrossed. Outside the door, Amelia had pulled up a chair and was also intently listening to the amazing tale. It was now well past eleven o'clock, but no one was even thinking about leaving the room. Sebastian went on. He related that the group survived the winter, still living in the barn, and barely subsisting with the small cache of food that they wisely preserved. In the late fall they had seen an old heifer that had somehow survived, foraging at the far edge of the field. They captured her, reinvigorated her some during the next few months, but in mid-winter, they were near starvation so they had to slaughter her, cook some of her parts and preserve others, so that they might survive.

In the spring they began their farming efforts anew, with early, but minimal results. Sebastian organized the four younger men into two search parties, with himself as a lone third party. He assigned each a parcel of land further away than their last summer's grounds, in an effort to obtain more starter vegetables or other useful items. He told them to be very careful, that they did not have to return each night for the time coming and going was too valuable to repeat the walk every day. Sebastian headed northward, walked through some more woodland, then again came to a vast field with a forest at one end. He slept at the edge of the forest, planning to start in the early morning to continue the hunt. When he awoke, just after sunrise, he heard a strange, yet familiar sound. He was sure that it was the grunting of a pig or a hog. He lay quietly to determine if he was correct in his interpretation, and to determine from where the sound originated. After determining which way to go, he stealthily crept toward the sound. Yes, it was a pig, rustling in a small mud hole, among the woodland foliage. He pounced on the startled animal, held to it tightly, and finally was able to grasp its forelegs. He rolled it to the ground and looked for something with which to tie its legs.

Just then a strong female voice yelled fiercely,

"Hey yo'all der, wat's ya'all doin' wid my pig. She's mine, I ben searchin fer her fer two days."

When Sebastian looked up he saw a somewhat stout black woman, standing with her hands on her hips. It brought back the memory his school marm, as she stood years ago, when not satisfied with a slow response to her question.

"Oh I ban jus' holdin' her fer yoo. I vasn't goin' ta steal her, or nothin' like dat." Sebastian knew that he was lying, for he fully intended to take the pig back to his awaiting group. The lady came forward, and although the pig was squirming strongly, she grasped the pig and held it strongly in her powerful arms. Sebastian tried to make light of the whole matter, laughed a bit and said that he knew the pig must belong to someone nearby, that he was only trying to help the unknown owner.

Just then a black man arrived.

"So ya'all cawt the ol' sow. Dat's good. Les get her on back to da sty and make sure she's lock up good dis time."

Now that the excitement of recapturing the pig subsided the lady asked,

"Say, what y'all doin' 'roun' here anyhowz? Where y'all comes from?"

The black man too, suddenly realized that they had never seen the man in front of him.

"Yea! Where y'all cumes from, anyhowze? Hey! Y'all one ob dem yankee solyers?

Sebastian acknowledged that he was, told of his recent experiences with the group of black people a short distance to the south.

"Dey be from da Burlingame place, dey sayd."

With this explanation the two became more relaxed and friendly. They explained their own situation. They were brother and sister. They too had been indentured slaves but before their master had left for the war, he said that they were free. In fact he wrote a deed to them for a large parcel of his land. The next statement totally surprised Sebastian. They explained that they needed more help to cultivate their lands, that they would be very pleased if he, and his group would come to work for them. Before he even thought about his long-range objective of returning north, he gladly accepted the offer given him. Speaking for the others, he assured the couple that his friends would gladly come to work for them, at reasonable wages and board and food, of course. The three smiled, placed their fists together in a three-handed grip, and each agreed to the terms laid out by Sebastian. Then another statement by the black man surprised Sebastian,

"Yezzir, we'ze gonna hab da larges' tabacca growin farm in da state a Kentuck'!"

"Tabacca?", Sebastian repeated.

"Yep, good ole' Kentuck' tabacca. Ain't none better in da whole wide worl'!"

Back in Elizabeth's study, Sebastian paused, both to take a short rest from the extremely long time that he'd been talking, and to determine if the growing of the 'tabacca' product impressed any of his listeners. He had thought that some might be surprised at this information, but no one reacted strongly.

Sebastian then went on relating his additional ventures while on the farm in Kentucky. He said that he led all of his other friends to this new farm location, introduced them to the land-owning couple and everyone began to settle into their new life.

Sebastian told of how the stout black woman was especially kind to him, so much so that he became very friendly with her. He stopped to await the reaction of the three listeners, especially Elizabeth. All three sensed what he meant by *"very friendly"*. Elizabeth lowered her head and did not seem to want to face Sebastian. He went to her, placed his hand under her chin, lifting her face. She looked up and when their eyes met, their eyes spoke, hers' saying

'I understand how you must have needed love';

his saying , 'I'm sorry that I did not remain true to you'.

Outside the doorway Amelia had been dozing of and on in spite of her desire to know all that had occurred in this stranger's life. She sensed that he must have had some kind of intimacy with her employer in her earlier life and she wanted to know all about it. She had just reawakened herself and again became intense with the stranger's story.

Sebastian continued his saga. He explained that as Cyrus had said, by now my family must think I'm dead, and how can I go back and interfere with the new lives that they must have created. He admitted that perhaps he had only made these excuses to himself for his failure to try to return home. He related that although they were unmarried, he and the black woman had several children during the next fifteen years. Two had died as infants, and three grew older. Then several years ago the black woman and one of the children became ill with terrible chills and fever one winter. He and everyone tried to help the lady and the child, but they had only a few homemade remedies to apply. There was no doctor any where near the area from whom to seek aid. The woman and the child died, leaving Sebastian with the other two children, a girl and a boy, neither one yet beyond their tenth year of age. So he remained on that farm, raising the two children and working hard to grow the crop that was now providing him and the black group a moderately good life.

Sebastian continued; there was more to his story. When the oldest of his two children neared her twentieth years of age, she and her brother told Sebastian that they had decided to seek a new life in the expanding west. They urged him to join them in one of the many wagon trains leaving from Cumberland, one of the staging areas. But Sebastian did not wish to go westward so he bade them farewell, expressing his love for them and wishing them good fortunes in their future lives. He could not reproach them, for he himself had done the same thing when he was younger, when he and Elizabeth and Paul had left their homeland for the new country across the Atlantic. He gave his two children most of the small sum of money that he had managed to accrue, keeping only a few dollars to last him the next few months.

The two 'pioneering' children had left in the spring. Sebastian worked for the whole summer and into the fall. After the tobacco harvest, curing and auctions, he told his friends that he was leaving for 'home'. None seemed too surprised, as Sebastian had been commenting on this possibility all summer. The group of co-workers wished Sebastian good fortune and waved him goodbye.

The trip 'home' was long and arduous. Although Sebastian had the money to buy train fare part way back to the New York area, he preferred to save his money. He therefore traveled by seeking rides on farm wagons traveling towards northern destinations. Some times the farmer gave Sebastian an all day ride, but more often he was given assistance by farmers who were traveling only a few hours to their marketplace, or returning home to their own farm, so he accepted the kindness of many strangers.

When winter weather eliminated the possibility of wagon rides, Sebastian did buy fare on a stagecoach from city to city. It was less costly than the very expensive train fare. There were times however, when the stagecoach could not travel through the heavy snow, so he was stranded in some cities or towns for days, several sometimes even for a week. He wondered if he would survive long enough to reach 'home'. He traveled several months in this manner and it was spring when he finally reached Hutson City.

During the telling of his story Sebastian had continued pacing to and fro across the room. Now he sat, slumping into a chair as if he had no more life within him. There was silence for a few minutes. Elizabeth was the first to rise. She went to Sebastian's side, kneeling on the floor beside his chair. She took his hand into hers and said,

"Oh Sebastian my love. We are so grateful to God for your safe return after all these years. Let us pray that there will be many years that remain and they will be years of joy and happiness."

She hoped that Sebastian understood that she was forgiving him for what had happened while away from her. She decided that she should say no more at this time, as all were now too tired to become involved in conversations that might lead to recriminations.

"Let's all retire", Elizabeth directed.

Paul and Johan raised themselves from their chairs slowly, accepting Elizabeth's order, but still seeming to not fully absolve Sebastian. All started to walk towards the stairway. Elizabeth spoke,

"Amelia, you had better retire too." Amelia gave out a startled

"Yes, maam", and went up the back stairway.

At the top of the stairs Paul and Johan walked towards their individual bedroom doors, then suddenly each stopped. They realized that Sebastian needed to be told where he would sleep. Paul and Johan waited for Elizabeth's decision. Elizabeth took Sebastian by the arm and led him into her own bedroom. Paul and Johan looked at each other, turned and proceeded to their bedrooms. Paul realized that life with his "Mama" would now be different and Johan wondered what the future would bring to his life.

CHAPTER NINETEEN

An Encounter With Contradictions

The next day at breakfast, Elizabeth was bubbly with excitement thinking of all the places she wanted to show to Sebastian. In her mind she had determined the order of visiting each of her bakeshops. First would be Altady, then Riverford, then Shelby and finally to Hutson City to view a building that Johan found and recommended to Elizabeth as the location for her new bakery and merchandise mart. The complete tour occupied the entire day and by the time of return all were very tired. After taking a very light supper, Elizabeth and Sebastian excused themselves and went to their bedroom. Johan followed a few minutes later. He had hesitated to see if he could learn of Paul's whereabouts, but none of the household staff had noticed at what time master Paul had left, nor did he indicate his itinerary.

The following morning Paul was still not at home for breakfast, so Elizabeth, Sebastian and Johan ate together. Each of them loitered somewhat for the rest of the morning, having no particular place to go. Sebastian began to read a German book. Johan appeared anxious to be doing something but Elizabeth wanted him to remain with her. She was plainly disturbed by Paul's overnight absence. She spoke of a few business matters to Johan then glanced at several papers on her desk. She appeared to be nervous and preoccupied in thought. As usual however, Elizabeth was formulating her next plan in her mind. Also, she must contact Schuyler and advise him of Sebastian's return, so as to end the relationship that she and Schuyler had. She knew what she would say to Schuyler when they met again.

It did not take long for Elizabeth to have her opportunity to inform Schuyler of the new, disconnected, life that they both would lead. Unexpectedly as usual, Schuyler arrived at Elizabeth's in late afternoon. When Amelia announced his arrival, she seemed embarrassed to say Schuyler's name. Nonetheless, Elizabeth told her to escort Schuyler into the drawing room. Sebastian had been reading but had dozed off.

When Schuyler entered, Sebastian stirred. As he did so, he saw Schuyler kiss Elizabeth on her cheek. Sebastian rose quickly, looking to Elizabeth to receive an explanation of her visitor's action. Elizabeth immediately introduced the two men. They made an insincere hand shake.

When she told Schuyler of Sebastian's return after all these years he was flabbergasted and unbelieving. He gave Elizabeth an inquiring look, asking silently, 'Are you sure this is not an imposter?' Elizabeth recognized Schuyler's inquiring look. By way of explanation, and without a word, she moved closer to Sebastian and clung to his arm. Schuyler recognized Elizabeth's response to his non-verbal question. Schuyler himself now realized that the situation with Elizabeth would be different than in the past, but he still did not want lose the contact with one of his wealthy sponsors. He tried to be diplomatic. He expressed to Sebastian the hope that they would become good friends and that Elizabeth would hopefully continue her friendship with him.

Being as diplomatic as she could, she told Sebastian that she and Schuyler had business dealings that must be continued for a time. Schuyler smiled at that comment. Sebastian glowered a little but he knew that he must not intrude on Elizabeth's life and friendships, for isn't that exactly what Cyrus had warned of many years ago.

Elizabeth walked to the front hall with Schuyler and quietly arranged for a meeting later that evening so that they might dine together. It was her intention to tell Schuyler that their friendship must be finally and completely terminated. She knew that she would miss Schuyler's gentlemanly accompaniment, but under the new circumstances it would be improper for her to have social contacts with another man.

Schuyler sensed her intention to dismiss him from her life, but stated that he would indeed enjoy having dinner with Elizabeth, perhaps for the last time. For his part, he knew that he had to formulate a plan so that their relationship could continue, and that he might still be able to partake of Elizabeth's wealth. And he had to have his justification for his statement of continued involvement readily prepared by this evening. Schuyler departed, giving the appearance of his usual dapper, self-assured manner.

When Elizabeth returned to the drawing room, it was very evident that Sebastian did not like the visitor, nor did he like it when she told him of her need to dine out tonight. She explained to Sebastian that she felt that she owed a deeper explanation to Schuyler of why they could no longer be friends. Sebastian looked very angry, not at Elizabeth but about Schuyler.

"I am not like dat man. I am not happy dat yoo see him efer again. But I mind mein own business, because I haf stolen many years of yoor life. I am not tell yoo how to live. But for me, I would kill dat man iff I know he efer hurt yoo."

Elizabeth, believing that Sebastian was just showing bravado, just nodded, showing Sebastian that she understood.

Later that evening Schuyler escorted Elizabeth to a very chic, secluded restaurant, but one featuring the finest seafood menu in the city. It was located very nearby Schuyler's hotel, the Regency. After dinner Elizabeth began to release her pent up emotions. She revealed to Schuyler that she had revised her will, but would have to do so again now that Sebastian was to be included. Then she immediately promised Schuyler that she would make some sort of monetary provisions to allow him to continue his customary lifestyle. At this moment, she really meant to do so, but at the same time, she wanted to observe Schuyler's reactions to her offer.

"Elizabeth, my darling. The wonderful pleasure of your company is all that I ever desired."

His words seemed sincere enough to Elizabeth, so now she wondered once more, was he really the cad that others believed him to be, or an affectionate friend to her for all these years. She still felt confused, and at the same time she felt anger within herself at her doubts about his possible good intentions.

After another glass of fine wine they departed the restaurant and had only taken a few steps towards Elizabeth's home when she suddenly stated,

"Oh, Schuyler. I just remembered. Paul was to have checked the bakery tonight after closing. I'm not sure if he did take care of a matter of importance. Will you accompany me there?"

"I will certainly do so my dear, because I will then have more moments of your pleasurable company."

Oh, he is so charming Elizabeth thought. But then with a wry smile, she thought again,

'How clever is this man with his retorts. If I could only feel that he is sincere!'

To reach the bake shop it was necessary to walk a short distance in the opposite direction from Elizabeth's house. After completing Elizabeth's errand they would have to retrace their steps past the restaurant and Schuyler's hotel, then on to Elizabeth's home. Since it was a beautiful evening weather-wise, they enjoyed the stroll to the bakery. Soon they reached the bakery and Elizabeth opened the door stating,

"Schuyler, I have to go to the basement for a few moments. Please wait here for me."

She snapped on the switch of the newly installed electric basement light and descended the stairs, then walked to a far corner. She was gone only a few moments but when she returned to the base of the staircase, Schuyler was at the bottom. He asked,

"To what did you need attend Elizabeth? Could I not have done that for you?"

Elizabeth did not want to tell him of the need to spread rat poison in the basement. She ignored his question about the basement and without an answer she ascended the staircase. Schuyler followed. Elizabeth now noticed that Schuyler was eating something.

"What are you eating Schuyler? Some stale cookie or cake that was left from today's goodies."

Schuyler responded,

"Yes, Elizabeth. It was a chocolate cookie from a batch left on this counter, but it had a different, kind of bitter taste."

As he chuckled he added,

"Must have been baked with some extra bitter chocolate in the recipe." Elizabeth laughed as she locked the door. They retraced their steps towards Elizabeth's home again. But as they passed the front door of Schuyler's hotel, he suddenly hesitated and stated,

"You know Elizabeth, I am suddenly feeling slightly nauseous. Would you mind terribly if you assisted me to my room? It's just at the top of the stairs?"

Elizabeth was totally surprised but immediately realized the reason for Schuyler's request, as he did suddenly look somewhat ill. Holding his stomach, Schuyler mumbled,

"Perhaps it was the shellfish that I ate at dinner that was inadequately cooked."

"Oh, I am so sorry Schuyler! Let me help you into the hotel. I'll request the desk-clerk to assist you up the stairs and to your bed.", she stated, with her concern showing.

At the desk across the lobby, the clerk was seated with his hanging head down. He appeared to be sleeping. Elizabeth called to him but he did not move. She called louder and still received no response. Acting against her better judgment, she decided that she must assist Schuyler up the stairs herself. As they crossed the hotel lobby Elizabeth felt that thousands of eyes were observing her, but actually only the lone, apparently asleep clerk was present.

Elizabeth held Schuyler's arm as they ascended the stairs and moved to the door of his room. Schuyler fumbled for his door key and gave it to Elizabeth. She opened the door, allowing Schuyler to enter first. She was nervous.

"I'll help you to your bed, but then you must tend yourself. I must leave you Schuyler, but I'll send someone to assist you."

Schuyler moved more easily now and by his smile, she quickly realized he had a nefarious reason for enticing her to his room. She turned to leave but he moved in front of the door.

"Oh my dear Elizabeth! I am suddenly feeling much better! Forgive me for deceiving you this way! I earnestly wished to have you join me here! You certainly must know that I love you sincerely. And I believe that you are attracted to me. So before we part forever, would it not provide a pleasant memory for us both if we embraced in one final act of lo…?"

Elizabeth was aghast. She drew a small pistol from her purse and pointed it at Schuyler.

"Please Schuyler! Let me leave! It will be best if do not intrude into my life again! You know fully of my new life circumstances."

Schuyler did not move from the door. Elizabeth fired a bullet towards him. He grabbed his upper arm and quickly moved from blocking her exit.

"My dear Elizabeth! I never believed that you feared me so much that you would resort to…"

Elizabeth ran from the room and turned quickly towards the grand staircase while replacing her small pistol into her purse. Just as she took her first step downward she thought that someone was behind her. She turned abruptly. It was not Schuyler, but she could not determine who the person was. She descended the staircase quickly and as she passed by the desk she hoped that the clerk was still nodding. It appeared to her that he was. Apparently he must not have heard the sound of her pistol firing. She passed through the hotel front entrance and walked hastily to the street corner. She crossed the street because she did not wish to walk home alone and she believed that she could more readily hail a hansom cab from that side. She waited nervously for a cab to approach the area.

But as she glanced across the street again, she saw Johan departing the hotel's front entrance. Without any hesitation or question in her mind as to why his presence there, she called him. Johan quickly came to her. He did not explain why he was at Schuyler's hotel, but Elizabeth realized that it must have been Johan that she saw in the corridor behind her.

"Why! It is you Johan! My! You scared me half to death!"

"Yes, Elizabeth, It's me. But why in the world are you out alone?"

"I was out with Schuyler…",

Elizabeth started to reply. Johan interrupted her.

"Well, where is the bastard now? Why'd he leave you out here at this time of night? Is he daft?"

Elizabeth did not answer that question but quickly had one of her own,

"Well, Johan, while we are asking questions, why are you out at this late hour? Did you not have dinner with Sebastian?"

Johan stammered a bit, then finally half mumbled his reply.

"Ah, yes Elizabeth. Sebastian and I had a delicious dinner. Then I remembered that I needed some shaving soap, so I walked down to the all-night drug store, at the corner of Oak St. On the way back I stopped by this hotel to use the gentlemen's lounge"

Elizabeth looked doubtful.

'Has he been watching Schuyler and I all evening?' she wondered. But she did not question him about the matter. In a few more minutes a hansom cab approached and Johan hailed it. During the somewhat brief ride to Elizabeth's home neither said anything. But Elizabeth thought of Schuyler's sudden discomfort. Was it real or feigned? Now a very disturbing thought came to her. She remembered Schuyler's tasting of a 'bitter' cookie at the bakery a few minutes before he complained of his illness.

'Ohmygod! I hope that Paul did not place a cookie on the sales counter after he applied pois....' But she dismissed the possibility of Schuyler being infected when she remembered that he admitted that his illness was a ruse.

The hansom cab arrived at Elizabeth's mansion and left the two at the end of the long entry walk. As they reached the mansion, they suddenly saw Paul approaching from the street. Johan spoke first,

"Paul! Where have you been all day? What the hell are you doin' out here at this time of night?"

Paul seemed to want to be nonchalant in his reply.

"Oh, I had to go to the bake shop and take care of that matter, you know…And what are you two doing out so late?"

Elizabeth was surprised at Paul's first response,

"Why Paul! Schuyler and I have been to the bake shop and I saw that you had already prepared the poi…took care of the matter, before I got there. Why did you return there?"

It was Paul's turn to stammer. "Uh, well ah, oh, I forget to take care of a spot. Ya know, behind the old flour bin in the corner. I forget to do anything there earlier."

They continued the walk to the home's entry door in silence. Upon entering the house each commented about how tired they were and each immediately went to their bedroom.

Elizabeth had a fitful night and in the morning she and Sebastian, as well as Paul and Johan all slept a little later than was customary. At her first awakening by her maid, Elizabeth told the maid notify the cook to delay breakfast for an hour. By the end of the additional hour, Elizabeth was first to arrive at the breakfast table. Sebastian ambled down the stairs soon after, followed by Johan.

"Good morning Sebastian dear, good morning Johan. I trust that you had a good shave this morning with your newly acquired soap."

Elizabeth motioned to the maid for coffee. She poured for all. After a few sips Johan answered Elizabeth tersely.

"Yes, it was fine."

He returned his attention to the coffee cup. Sebastian seemed not to know what the conversation was about.

Paul arrived in the room and repeated the actions of Johan. Elizabeth allowed him to take a few sips of the hot coffee then was about to speak, but Paul spoke first.

"Mama, I know what you're going to ask."

He feared the maid might overhear him. He lowered his voice.

"Like I told you last night, I went to the bakery and took care of the matter."

Elizabeth nodded that she understood. She was happy that although Paul was apparently involved in a personal matter last evening, he remembered his managerial responsibility. Again, Sebastian only looked on, not saying a word. But then Elizabeth suddenly remembered another matter,

"Paul, did you check to see if Mr. Arnsmeyer opened the bakery this morning? Did you check to see if he was feeling well enough? The poor man has been ailing lately. I hope that there is nothing seriously wrong with him!"

"Yes, mother. I did that", Paul explained. "I got up this morning at five AM and called the bakery. Arnsmeyer was there already. I told him", he softened his voice, "about what to clean up. He said he'd be careful and would take care of it."

Elizabeth looked relieved, All turned to their breakfast, but suddenly Elizabeth remembered another matter, the possibility that Schuyler's ruse last evening was more than a ruse. She tried to sound casual with her question.

"Paul, did you happen to leave a few cookies on the counter last evening...some that you had sprinkled with....."

She leaned forward to say the word, but Paul anticipated it.

"No Mama. I didn't do anything that stupid."

The quietness of the room was suddenly broken by the sound of the front doorbell in the distance. They heard the maid open the door. Then a male voice spoke to her but they could not understand the words. Soon the maid came into the room looking ashen white. Elizabeth jumped up.

"What is it Amelia? What's the matter? Paul, help her. She looks as though she might faint!"

The maid managed to speak a few words.

"It's a policeman, ma'am. He said to tell you that Mr. Van Essen was found dead in his hotel room." Then the maid did faint. Paul rushed to the maid's side, sat her in a chair and then ran to the kitchen to get the other maid's help. Sebastian and Johan simultaneously started towards Elizabeth because it was obvious that she too was about to faint.

Elizabeth blurted,

"Oh my God! My pistol! Maybe I *did* kill poor Schyler…" Then she did go completely limp.

Doctor Newsome had been called from his nearby residence by the livery man after Paul had shouted to him from the kitchen. The doctor attended to both Elizabeth and the maid. Margaret, the other maid, now took the first, still ashen maid, to her room. In the drawing room, the doctor advised Paul and Johan that Elizabeth would certainly recover but needed a few hours of rest. Both helped her to her room and laid her on the bed. Sebastian followed but only looked on in disbelief, with doubt as to what he should do. Paul and Johan removed Elizabeth's shoes then placed a light blanket over her. They left as quietly as possible, leaving Sebastian alone with her. He sat on a nearby chair. He wondered,

'Vat did my dear Elizabeth do las' nighd? Did she shooted dat bad man?'

Paul and Johan descended the stairs together. Dr. Newsome had already left. Johan motioned to Paul to again retire to the drawing room where they would not be overheard by any of the household staff. But before either could speak they realized that the policeman, a plainclothes detective, had patiently remained in the reception hall during the fifteen minutes that all of the commotion was happening. Paul and Johan went quickly to the police detective.

The police detective was Sergeant Moran. He was a middle aged man with too much girth, the result of too much eating and imbibing, and not enough exercise since he had been promoted from being a cop on the beat. After introducing himself and Johan to the policeman Paul asked,

"What the hell happened? What happened to Van Essen?"

"Well we don't know a' course, except that he was shot. But we're gonna find out about the whole thing." the detective responded.

Johan also showed bewilderment. He looked towards Paul,

"I can't imagine what happened. Last time we saw him he seemed to be in good spirits." With that the policeman said,

"Well, I'll let ya alone fer t'day, but I'll be back tomorra. I'll have a few questions for ya, and your mother"

Paul escorted him to the front door. When he returned he told Johan,

Encounters Elizabeth's

"Maybe Schuyler had more enemies than we knew of" Johan nodded that Paul may be correct in his assumption. Thoughtfully, he then added,

"If we're right in our suspicions of Schuyler's double life, there's a widow and seven fatherless kids in Buffalo right now."

CHAPTER TWENTY

An Encounter with Authority.

As he had promised, Sergeant Moran did return the next morning. He did not request the maid to summon 'Mrs. Miller', but only Paul and Johan. He began to immediately grill his "suspects, perhaps to confirm facts that he already discovered.

First he addressed Paul,

"So, how well did you know this guy? Has he been a friend of yours for a long time? The desk clerk at this guy's hotel says that you been there a couple a times askin' about 'im."

The detective acted as though the two men would naturally know who 'this guy' was. The detective then stared at Johan,

"You from outta town? I ain't seen you around before."

Paul and Johan both thought, 'Does this cop know everybody in town?'

The detective next answered the question that Paul and Johan had on their minds before they could ask it.

"I came here first thing yestaday mornin' as soon as I was told about this guys death 'cause it's common knowledge that Mrs. Miller and this guy wuz pretty cozy."

At that, Paul became upset,

"What do you mean, 'cozy'? My mother and Van Essen were social friends, nothing more."

The policeman relented,

"OK, OK, so they wuz just friends. Now back to my first question. How well did ya know this guy anywayz?"

Then again looking at Johan he stated,

"Ya never did answer my question. Are ya from outta town?"

Before either Paul or Johan could answer, Moran threw out another questions,

"By the way, do either a you two guys own a gun?"

Now Paul and Johan looked at each other but neither acknowledge owning a gun.

Paul asked the detective,

"Why? What about a gun? Do you know for sure that that's what killed him?"

Both had expected that the police would believe that Schuyler had died because of the accidental poisoning, but not by gun-fire.

Moran elaborated,

"We think he maybe wuz killed by a second gunshot, from a gun with a bigger caliber than the first shot. He had a bullet hole in his chest, kinda near his heart, an' another in his upper arm. Duz either one a ya know about the shots? A gun wuz on the floor near 'im. We're getting' it checked out ta see if some local gun shop sold it to Van Essen himself. Summa the guys keep records, but not all a 'em. An' there was another pistol on the floor, an old Civil War piece."

Knowing that he was lying and looking sheepish, Paul quickly replied,

"No, I never owned a gun. We kinda thought that Schuyler had a heart problem or something. We don't know nobody that would wanna kill him."

Johan agreed,

"We've know Schuyler for quite a long time, and we didn't like him much, but we wouldn't shoot him!"

Johan suddenly realized that he had spoken too much. He thought that he had better explain.

"Truth is, we thought he was a gigolo, just chasing Paul's mother for her money. So we didn't like that idea, but we didn't want him dead, just wanted him out of Mrs. Mueller's life, that's all!"

The cop looked at the two men, then said,

"You mean Mrs. Miller?"

Paul explained,

"Yes, my mother. Her real name is Mueller, but when she came to America it got changed to Miller. Johan is her cousin, from Germany, so he still calls her by her German name."

"Oh", the detective answered, seeming now to not care about the name. He continued,

"Well, we gotta wait for the coraner to tell us what killed him. The bullet was near his heart so that coulda been it, but I seen a lotta guys get shot in the chest and still live. It's only a matter of a small part of an inch that can make the difference ya know. But there was one other strange thing. There wuz a trace a some white powder in his mouth, an' it also looked like he ate som'thin' chocolaty "

Paul immediately thought about the poison, and his mother's half statement, before she fainted.

Now the policeman again became interested in Paul's association with Van Essen.

"Ya didn't tell me why ya went ta this guy's hotel and asked so many questions about 'im from the desk clerk What'd ya wanna know about 'im, other than he was chasin' yer mother."

Paul hesitated for a minute, wondering if he should divulge all that he knew about Schuyler. He decided that he would tell the detective what he had learned about Schuyler's double life.

"I went to Schuyler's hotel to confront him. I was suspicious of his motives. A few years ago, when Schuyler first became acquainted with my mother, somehow I got suspicious of him. I don't remember how. Oh, yea, I saw him working on a barge. That seemed out of place for a dandy like Schuyler. So I started checking on him."

Then Paul revealed all that he had learned, of Schuyler's Buffalo family, his supposed escapades in Syrica, his lying about being in New York City, and his often long absences from Altady. He concluded by stating,

"When I accused him, Van Essen just scoffed at my accusations and told me that his relationship with my mother was none of my business. Can you imagine him saying that? I get angry every time I think of it"

All the while that Paul was talking, Johan was thinking,

'Mygod, Could Paul have done this? He was missing for quite sometime last night. Did he go to the bakery twice to spread the rat poison like he said, or was that story about the second visit a cover up? Did he really go to Schuyler's hotel to kill him? And I know that he purchased a pistol recently.

Johan concluded his own questions at about the same time that Paul finished his long list of insinuations about Schuyler. Now both were totally surprised when Moran said,

"Oh, we been watchin' this guy for quite a while, We knew about his chasin' after wimmin to live a grand life. We was just waitin' for one a 'em to turn him in, or worse yet, him to knock off one a these ladies to get her money. We figured somethin' was gonna happen sooner er later. Hey, maybe one a 'em did knock 'im off."

Looking at Paul he spoke a taunt,

"Maybe it was yer own ol' lady. From what I know, she had some reasons!"

Paul and Johan both simultaneously protested,

"That's ridiculous! My mother wouldn't hurt anybody, for any reason!"

"Of course not, Mrs. Mueller would never do such a thing. What the hell are you thinking?"

Moran snickered a little, then lying he said,

"Ok, Ok, I was just testin' ya. I don't suspect her,...yet"

Moran started for the front door.

"You guys stay around, get me! We ain't done with ya yet! Understand? An' by the way," he looked at Johan, "Where did ya say yer from?"

With intentional disgust in his voice Johan answered,

"Hutson City. Don't worry. I'm not going nowhere until we find out what happened to that bastard."

With a grin, the detective looked back at Johan.

"So ya really liked the guy, eh? Alright, I'll be in touch with ya again."

Just as Moran was about to leave, Elizabeth and Sebastian came to the entry hall, having heard voices after they had descended the stairs.

Moran spoke kindly to Elizabeth,

"Good mornin' Mrs. Miller. I was talkin' to the gentlemen here about Van Essen's death. They can fill ya in the details."

The detective now looked at Sebastian. Before he could ask who he was, Elizabeth quickly introduced him and explained that he was her husband, Mr. Mueller, who had recently returned home after being away for several years. Now the detective showed his own surprise,

"Well, Mrs. Miller. All the time I thought ya waz a widow. All the while ya waz bein' courted by Van Essen, you was a married…"

He stopped short, realizing that he was speaking too much. He picked up his derby hat, stuffed the cigar butt back into his mouth and searched for a match in his vest pocket. He slammed the door as he went out.

Paul spoke first,

"What do you make of that Mama? You see, Moran says Schuyler was shot. He must of had a lot enemies that we didn't even know about. What do you think about that? The scoundrel was shot!"

At the word 'scoundrel', Elizabeth looked at Paul as if to say, 'Please don't call him that.'

Paul tried to soften his accusation,

"Well, Mother, during these last few days we were all thinking bad about Schuyler. Maybe he was kind of a scoundrel, but he was a gentleman."

In her heart Elizabeth knew that she had affection for Schuyler, even after learning that he may have had a devious plan to inveigle money from her, and very possibly had deceived other women. But now that Sebastian was home, Schuyler's death eliminated a possible confrontation between Elizabeth, Sebastian and Schuyler. Elizabeth then chided herself for even thinking that Schuyler's death was a good development.

The rest of the day all waited quietly, but each separately. Elizabeth and Sebastian remained in their bedroom. Johan retired to his room and paced for sometime, occasionally lying on the bed, with his mind in an inquisitive mood. Paul was doing the same in his room. All declined the maid's offer to partake of lunch.

Johan repeatedly reviewed in his mind, the actions of others on the evening that Schuyler died.

'When I saw Elizabeth coming from Schuyler's room the other night, she didn't offer to explain her presence there. And I thought that I heard a muffled gunshot. After she went down stairs and I burst into Schuyler's room, he was wrapping a hand towel around his bicep. As much of a cad a Schuyler was, it's not likely that Elizabeth shot him. If not, who did?. But perhaps they had had an argument at dinner and it continued later in Schuyler's room. Maybe they argued about Sebastian's return. Maybe she told Schuyler about the changes to her will and him being left out of it. Maybe he was incensed enough to argue and then attack her. Yes! If Elizabeth did shoot him, it would have been in self-defense. Elizabeth would not intentionally hurt Schuyler, even if she had come to hate him. What am I thinking? Elizabeth would not hurt anyone. And she didn't own a gun! Well, at least I don't think she did!'

He tried to expel these notions from his head. But soon his mind was speculating on Paul's actions that same night.

'Paul said that he went back to the bakery the second time to place more poison in a place that he had forgotten before. But is that like Paul, to forget such a detail? Is he the one that went to Schuyler's hotel room and shot him? I didn't see Paul anywhere around Schuyler's hotel when I went there to ...' Johan kept tossing previous events in his mind. 'Oh yes, another thing! Paul said that he arose at five a.m. to open the bakery. Or did he get up much earlier than that and go to Schuyler's hotel and shoot him? But I didn't know that Paul had bought a gun, like I did. After returning from Schuyler's hotel, he could have then called Arnsmeyer to cover for himself. 'Oh for God's sake, Johan!' he chided himself again. 'Forget your damn suspicions and go for a walk or something. You have to put all this nonsense out of your head'.

In the other bedroom Sebastian was pacing and thinking,

'Did mein sweed Elizabeth shood dat awvil man before I got der? An mine ol' war pistol, the poliz must be find it der! He vas so upzet because I camed home agin. He push me an' I shooted it an' den I drop it and run oudt!'

As Elizabeth lay on her bed staring at the lace canopy over the top of the tall bedposts, she too kept mulling over the events of the fateful evening.

'Why was Johan out so late that evening? He said that he went all the way down to Oak Street to the all-night pharmacy. But would he go all the way there just to buy shaving soap! Now that I think about it, I don't even remember that he carried anything in his hand when he met me after coming out of Schuyler's hotel. And why was he at Schuyler's hotel? Perhaps not really to use the gentlemen's lounge. Could he have just run out of Schuyler's room, after shooting him?'

She too, chided herself,

'What in the world are you thinking Elizabeth? Suspecting your own cousin! He never gave me any reason to believe that he hated Schuyler enough that he would kill him. And I never knew him to own a gun!'

Then she again remembered that Schuyler said that he had eaten a chocolate cookie at the bakery. Could it have had poison on it? Or it possible that Schuyler was so despondent because I did not succumb to him? And he also knew that I had cut him out of my will? Was he so upset that he would take his own life?'

The maid knocked lightly and entered Elizabeth's room bringing two cool lemonade drinks.

"Oh, thank you Margaret! And how are you and Amelia doing?"

Margaret answered,

"We're alright Ma'am. Amelia's doing well. But we both feel terrible about Mr. Van Essen! What a terrible shock! We all feel so bad about poor Mr. Van Essen. He was such a fine gentleman. I can't imagine how anyone could hate him enough to shoot him."

With that she looked towards Sebastian.

"Will there be anything else, Ma'am?"

"Yes Margaret. Please wake us an hour before dinner time and thank you for thinking kindly about Mr. Van Essen, and for tending to poor Amelia."

As Margaret left the room she was beginning to weep, causing Elizabeth to think,

'My! I did not know how keenly my maids thought of Schuyler'.

Now another suspicion arose in Elizabeth's mind,

'There were some unfortunate bits of gossip around town about Schuyler and some of the maids in other households. Is it possible that something was going on here under my own nose and I didn't realize it? I'll have to ask Paul in some innocent appearing way. He would surely have noticed if any illicit events were occurring. And if he knew, he would not have told me of them, so as to spare my feelings. But that would be even more reason for Paul to hate Schuyler. But hate him enough to kill him? Or did my small pistol injure him so much that he died from the bullet wound? Oh, my head is hurting again. Oh, I've got to get some rest! Elizabeth! Clear your mind of these terrible thoughts!'

Then one more very disturbing thought came to her.

'Was my dear Sebastian so jealous and angered about Schuyler, angry enough to shoot him? When could he have done this? Neither Johan or I saw him near Schuyler's hotel. Did he bring a pistol home with him from the war?'

Finally, Elizabeth drifted off to sleep as Sebastian sat in a nearby chair, looking very angry. At this same time Paul, like Johan, had paced and rested and paced and rested and paced. His thoughts of the eventful evening also brought conflict to his mind.

'When I was returning from the bakery after that second trip, Mother and Johan were just returning in a hansom cab. Is it possible that either or both of them did the deed. Could they have been in cahoots without me realizing it? Oh, for God sake Paul! Use your head! Your mother would not kill anyone, no matter how badly they had hurt her. But on the other hand, I believe Johan could do such a thing, with enough provocation. And he did hate Schuyler as much as I did! But could he have gotten a gun without me sensing something was up? Ohmygod! Could my father have done it? Let's see.. Did he leave the house that night? None of us know because we were all out. How can I quiz the maids without raising any suspicions about Papa's movements that night?'

Paul rolled over on the bed, placing his face to the pillow, as if wanting to hide from these many terrible suspicions. But the thoughts continued.

'Think about it Paul. Schuyler must have had enough enemies to fill a train-load. Maybe that stranger I saw loitering the other night in Schuyler's hotel lobby was one a them husbands, trying to see if Schuyler was there. Maybe to follow and kill him. Think of all those wives and widows that he cultivated romances with. Maybe one of their husbands, or sons like me, would love to have done him in! Why should I believe that my own mother, father, or cousin Johan, would have done the murder. And now that I think about it! Was it a murder? Maybe Schuyler owned the gun and accidentally shot himself. That happens often enough!'

Paul, too, almost fell of to sleep. Then suddenly he remembered the words that his mother had said upon hearing of Schuyler's death. Something about a cookie, and she sounded as if she was about to say 'poison'.

Paul slid quietly out of his room, being careful not to make any noise on closing the door. He slipped down the staircase to the reading room where the telephone was located. He quietly lifted the hook and asked the operator to connect him with 'number 116, please'. Otto Arnsmeyer's gruff voice answered, "Elizabeth's Delicious Bakery".

Speaking very low, Paul asked Arnsmeyer several questions that were on his mind. When Arnsmeyer had finished answering, Paul whispered, 'Thanks, Otto", then replaced the telephone listening piece to its cradle.

'Oh, thank God for that!' Paul thought to himself. Then he stealthily returned to his bedroom. He fell onto the bed without even removing his shoes and finally fell off to sleep.

CHAPTER TWENTY-ONE

An Encounter with Truth

All the next day Elizabeth, Sebastian, Paul and Johan remained in the house, taking meals together and making conversation about the weather, seasonal activities, civic events, but none cared to bring up the matter that was most on their minds, Schuyler's death. Nor did they speak about their suspicions of each other of the possible cause of Schuyler's death, or whether it was an accident, suicide or murder. All through the day, without speaking of it, each expected Detective Moran to bring news that the authorities had definitely determined the cause of Schuyler's death. They all hoped that it was accidental but each thought surely that it was not.

But Moran did not appear for two more days. When he did, it was to ask Paul more questions, about the "white powder". Moran said that the coroner stated that it was confectionary sugar, but still, they did also find traces of poison at the bakery when they went there to check Paul's statement of his whereabouts the night of Schuyler's death.

The morning after Schuyler's death however, Moran had already called Otto Arnsmeyer to be sure that the white powder on the cookie could not have been any of the poison powder that they found in Schuyler's mouth and in the bakery's basement. Arnsmeyer assured Moran that no poison had been used in the upper floors of the bakery itself, only in the basement. When Moran told Arnsmeyer about the trace of chocolate and white powder found in Van Essen's mouth, Arnsmeyer chuckled a little.

"Oh, I can explain that. You see Detective, we made a batch a chocolate cookies that day and we forgot to put sugar in the mixture. They came out tasting terribly bitter. Then we put extra confectionary sugar on top of them to cover up, but they still came out tasting terrible. So I told Helga my clerk to throw the whole batch out. She must have missed a cookie or two that got left on the serving counter. I'm sure that it didn't have no 'powder' in it, if you know what I mean."

"Oh, thanks", Moran said, " that explains that. At least it explains one of our mysteries."

Moran finally did appear at the Mueller house again. On this visit he told the maid, Amelia, that he needed to speak with Mrs. Miller. Amelia said that she would immediately inform Mrs. Mueller of the detective's request. As she started to leave, Moran realized that it was the same maid that had fainted several days ago upon hearing the news of Schuyler's death. Moran spoke to her uncharacteristically gently,

"I see yer feelin' a bit better, ma'am. That's good."

Amelia turned slightly to him, made a curtsy, but without speaking another word, left the entry hall.

Elizabeth came quickly to greet Moran.

"Come in, Sergeant Moran, come in". She led him to the sitting room.

"Please sit. What can I do for you?"

Elizabeth sounded too anxious. Moran replied,

"Well, ma'am. The coroner's finished with the corpse, ..oh, I'm sorry

Mrs. Miller. The coroner has completed his work and we wuz wonderin' what to do with the body, you know, Mr. Van Essen's remains. We didn't know if we should notify you…to take care of it, y' know".

Moran's comments caught Elizabeth off-guard. She suddenly realized that for the past several days she had not even considered what was to become of poor Schuyler.

"Oh", she said. "Oh, I had not thought about that matter. I certainly should have, should I not? I believe that I am most likely the closest person to Schuyler. I suppose that I should take responsibility for arranging for his proper burial."

She paused, then spoke earnestly,

"Oh, yes, Sergeant. I'll take care of the matter today. I'll contact a mortuary service immediately."

At Moran's next remarks, Elizabeth was again caught totally off-guard.

"Well, fact a' the matter, Mrs. Miller we do know that Van Essen had some family. But they ain't been in touch with each other fer a long time, I guess. We notified 'em, but we ain't heard nothin' back. If we didn't think you'd take care a the matter, what to do with the remains I mean, they'd be put away in the potter's field up in Metands"

Elizabeth's concerned reaction showed very visibly.

"Ohmygod, no! Don't do that. I'll take responsibility. I'll arrange for the proper disposition of poor Schuyler."

She immediately wondered to herself if she should contact Monsignor Tierney to conduct a memorial Mass and to say prayers at the grave. But first she had to find out from Moran about the family that he spoke of.

"You said that Mr. Van Essen had a family? I never knew that. So you have been in contact with them? Where are they?"

Again Moran's reply surprised Elizabeth totally.

"Yeah." Moran elaborated, "we knew about Van Essen and his family for some time. He's from Buffalo. We been keepin' an eye on this guy…er, I mean Mr. Van Essen for quite a while. Always expectin somethin' wuz gonna happen."

By Elizabeth's reaction, Moran knew immediately that he was upsetting her. He just as quickly realized that he had better not divulge anymore of what he knew about the person he called 'this guy'. He changed his tact.

"Well, Mrs. Miller. That's real nice a' ya' ta' take care a' Mr. Van Essen." Moran paused a short time then asked, "Say, is yer son Paul around?"

"Why yes", Elizabeth replied. "I'll have Amelia find him for you. Please wait here."

She excused herself with a slight bow and went to the doorway which had a cord hanging nearby. She pulled the cord then left the room.

Amelia came into the room quickly.

"Can I help you, sir?"

Moran had never been treated like such an important person. His surprise showed as he asked,

"Can ya' ask Mr. Miller, Paul that is, to come speak with me?"

Again, Amelia curtsied as she left and said, "Certainly sir"

Now Moran felt as if he were the police chief or the mayor, or somebody important. My, how nice everyone was being to him.

Paul showed himself into the room quickly.

"Hello, Sergeant Moran. What's on your mind?"

Moran motioned for him to come closer. As Paul did so, he wondered what secret Moran was about to impart. They both sat close by each other. Moran spoke,

"We know a lot about this guy Van Essen, but I didn't wanna tell yer Ma. She's too nice a lady to know what I'm gonna tell ya".

For the next fifteen minutes Moran told Paul all that the Altady police knew of Schuyler's origination and activities. Much of it was just as Paul had suspected, the enticement of the ladies, several at the same time to utilize their fortunes, and the deceitful explanations to each for his absence while he was away romancing another woman. But Paul was surprised that Schuyler had been performing his deceptions for so many years without being prosecuted. Moran's explanation did not really surprise Paul, for he knew that his own mother would have reacted in the same way. When Schuyler's dastardly conduct became known to a lady, she invariably would dismiss him from her life but would not press charges against him. The police were helpless in the matter of seeking 'justice'.

But Moran's next comments completely surprised Paul. It cleared much of the suspicion that Paul had about the man that he often had seen on the barges, and that he had traced to Buffalo. Moran told of Van Essen's origination. He was born in Buffalo. His real name was Sean McKesson. He was born a twin and his brother's name is Shamus McKesson, who still lives in Buffalo with his wife and seven kids.

"We had the Buffalo police notify 'em about Van Essen, his twin brother that is, but we got no reply. I don't think they even wanna be known as related to the bum."

"Well I'll be damned!" was Paul's only response.

'So I was at least half right about the situation. I knew damn well that Schuyler was a double dealing bastard. But I really did think that he had that family in Buffalo. Boy, I'm glad that I didn't go talk to that man's wife. I would have messed up their lives terrible!' Thinking further he said to himself,

'Oh, they probably knew about the life that he was leading. They must have had inquiries, maybe many times, by the police.'

Paul's further curiosity caused him to ask Moran,

"So what did you find out about who killed the bast ...... Schuyler?"

Moran was very responsive,

"Well, first we suspected he was poisoned. Lotsa people would a done that when they found out about the bum. But the coroner said that it definitely was confectionary sugar in his mouth, and yer guy Arnsmeyer explained about the cookie. So we had ta check out the shootin' angle. He had a bullet wound in his left arm, and the gun that Van Essen owned was a 22. It had one shot fired. But yer ma owned a 22 too. She's the one that put the bullet in Van Essen's arm, in self defense um sure. We found another bullet in the wall. Turned out to match a gun that yer cousin turned in the day after the killin'. He wanted ta clear himself and knew that we could identify the bullet that kilt Van Essen. It wasn't from his gun."

Paul shook his head in disbelief. He did not know of Johan's gun.

Moran continued,

"The bullet that the coroner gouged outa Van Essen was a 38, so we knew that he was shot by somebody else's gun. An we found a Civil War piece on the floor too. It had been fired recently, one shot, but we found that in the wall too, so we knew that wasn't the pistol that killed Van Essen. Did ya know that yer father came home wid a pistol from the war?"

Then teasing Paul he said,

"Ya sure ya don't own a 38 revolver?"

Paul looked annoyed, both at the suggestion of his father being involved and the accusation that he owned a gun himself.

Moran continued,

"We knew he was romancin' several ladies at the same time. Anyone a them could a shot 'im. But he had a lady friend up in Riverford whose husband was an important business man that traveled a lot. Van Essen and this lady waz havin' a real hot romance every time this poor stupid husband lef' town, sometimes for a whole week."

Paul was listening more intently,

"Yea! And what happened?"

Moran continued.

"Somehow the husband got suspicious and started trailin' Van Essen. In fact, several guys were seen trailin' Van Essen. We had a lotta reports about that, after Van Essen was dead a' course. The description a one of the guys would fit yer father, yer father that just came home an' learned about yer mother's man friend, ..Van Essen.!"

Paul immediately thought of the stranger that he was sure he had seen lurking near their house. Could it have been his own father, or the suspicious husband?

Moran went on,

"Well, the other night yer mother left Van Essen's room near midnight. The desk clerk was pretendin' to be asleep 'cause he's supposed to stop a man from bringin' a unregistered lady to his room. He admitted that Van Essen paid 'im to not see any ladies. He knew it waz yer mother 'cause her picture's been in the paper once or twice. Anywayz, then the clerk saw a man lookin like yer cousin Johan go inta Van Esen's room, then come out quick. But now, listen ta this! Yer own father went there after Johan left. He even left a old Civil War pistol on the floor. The clerk's description a the man fits yer Pa ezac'ly. An' he said he heard three gun shots, but not all at a same time But dat ain't all. The clerk see another guy sneak in about two AM and boom! He hears a shot. Da guy runs out an' the clerk goes ta Van Essen's room and finds 'im dead in a pool a blood. The guy shot Van Essen right through the chest. Goodbye Van Essen!"

Even though Paul felt sure that Schuyler would come to a bad end someday, he was nevertheless surprised at Moran's explanation of Schuyler's fate. Moran kept talking,

"We found out about a Riverford lady 'cause the cops up there heard about our case, and they had a suicide on their hands. Turned out the lady's husband shot himself with a 38 the mornin' after Van Essen was found. Once the Riverford guys got workin' on the case, they picked up the gun an' got the dead guy's wife ta open up about her romance with Van Essen. After she spilled the beans she left town. I don't blame 'er fer hidin'. Boy, what some people will do ta mess up their lives jus'ta get some kicks. Anyways, the gun that the Riverford police sent down ta us matched the bullet from Van Essen's chest. It killed 'im alright."

Paul drew a quick conclusion,

"So, you kinda knew that somethin' like this would happen, eh?"

"Well, no, as a matter a fact, after I checked on yer cousin from Hutson City, an' learned about the fire, an' the suspected arson, and knowin' that yer cousin was jealous of Van Essen, he was really our prime suspect. We thought he had no alibi, but yer mother told us about him bein' wid her that night."

Paul was disbelieving.

"What! You actually suspected Johan. I can't believe that."

"Oh, He wuz high on the list. But so wuz you an yer mom, too! And yer father." Moran divulged.

"What! You suspected my mother and father?"

Paul didn't care that he was a suspect, but he resented that his mother and father were.

"Yea. Well, after all, when yer ma found out what a bastard that guy was, why wouldn't she think 'bout killin' 'im. An' what da ya think yer father thought, when he got home an' found out about yer Ma and Van Essen. An' they all went to Van Essen's room that night, yer Mom first, Johan next and yer

Pa later."

It was obvious that each of these conclusions seemed reasonable to Moran. He continued,

"An' you too. When you found out about the two-faced bastard, didn't you think 'bout killin' 'im? Admit it! Didn't ya? One a yer own maids said she heard ya tell yer cousin that you'd kill 'im, and a lady that usta be a clerk over in yer Hutson City bakery also said she heard ya make a threat ta kill somebody. Believe me, you wuz high up on our list for a while too!"

Though Paul would not admit it, yes, there were times when he would like to have seen Schuyler dead. But he would not confirm the detective's statements. He changed the subject.

"Oh, listen!" Paul pleaded, "Don't tell my mother any of this. Please don't! She'll be heartbroken. Poor Mama! She really had high regard for the bastard. Well, he was a charming guy, wasn't he?"

Moran agreed with Paul's assessment and also agreed that Elizabeth should not be told the full truth about Schuyler's lifestyle nor the reason for his murder.

"I'll stall a while, then I'll tell yer Mom it was an accidental shootin' by Van Essen himself. I think I can be convincin' enough."

As Moran rose to leave Paul concluded,

"Thanks a lot for all your help, Sergeant."

He walked to the door with Moran.

"That's OK", Moran replied, tipped his temple with his fingers, then placing his hat on his head, he went down the steps.

Paul immediately went to Johan's room and related all that he was told by

234

Moran. Both then just slumped into chairs in Johan's room. Then they both admitted to the other that they had threatened Van Essen with a gun; Paul a few hours earlier in the day and Johan during the visit right after Elizabeth's hasty departure from Van Essen's room.

They both had the same feeling of relief at the conclusion of their concerns after these many years. They agreed that Elizabeth needed to be comforted until she adjusted to Schuyler's absence. They nodded to each other that they would not fail to consider her feelings at all times.

A few days later Schuyler was buried in the old cemetery in Altady. Although Monsignor Tierney had told Elizabeth that he could not celebrate a memorial Mass for Schuyler, since he was not known to be Catholic, he did offer eloquent prayers at the gravesite, which included appeals to God for forgiveness of Schuyler's worldly transgressions, transgressions which Elizabeth did not want to believe to be true, many that she was never made aware of, and transgressions which were only suspected by Monsignor Tierney.

Throughout the graveside ceremony, Paul and Johan stood beside Elizabeth, supporting her as she openly wept. Sebastian remained behind Elizabeth. Some distance from the gravesite, under a large elm tree, two other women were seen to be weeping. They were Amelia and Margaret, the two Mueller household maids.

CHAPTER TWENTY TWO

An Encounter with Renewal.

The next morning Paul and Johan were already downstairs in the breakfast room when Elizabeth and Sebastian descended the staircase. They entered the room arm in arm looking very happy. Paul and Johan did not dare look at each other, but each knew what the other was thinking. Paul thought,

'Well, it looks like Mama and my once forgotten Papa have made up for all the missing years.'
Johan thought the same to himself.

Elizabeth broke the silence with a very cheerful "good morning" to all, took her seat and waited for the others to seat themselves. She rang the bell for the servant to begin the serving. Margaret entered with a tray of orange juice and coffee. Elizabeth inquired of Amelia's health and Margaret replied,

"Oh she's fine Ma'am. She has the day off today. It's just as well because she seemed very tired this morning."
Elizabeth laughed a little but the others remained silent during this few minutes. After Margaret finished the round of servings and left the room, Elizabeth spoke. She did not relate any of the events that may have taken place in her bedroom last evening but rather she announced,

"Tomorrow morning right after breakfast Sebastian and I are going over to the Rectory to see Father Tierney. Oh, by the way, he's a Monsignor now, elevated last month. We wish to arrange for a special Mass of celebration, to thank God for His wonderful blessings, and to make a renewal of our marriage vows."

That caused Paul and Johan to look at each other with nodding of their heads, indicating that they thought that that was a good idea. What a wonderful way for the long separated married couple to begin their future again.

Elizabeth next made a joyous announcement.

"It seems unbelievable, but just two months ago was the thirty-sixth anniversary of our marriage. What a lovely coincidence that Sebastian has returned at this time. It must be God's guidance that brought us together again. And in two weeks it will be Mary's birthday. She'll be thirty one years old. Can you imagine that! Oh, how I wish that she could be here with us to meet her father."

Now Sebastian spoke.

"You know, I didn't efen know vat yar dis vas. Elizabeth tol' me and den figure' out how old I be. She sayz I be sixty-tree. Dat's pretty old, don't youz tink? Elizabeth be only fifty von years olt. She look still like a young fraulein. Ja? But I feel purty goot und I hopes dat yoo will not tink I be too olt to come back to yer life. I don't vant to make no truble fer anyvun."

All spoke at once, even Paul

"Oh no, no!" they all responded.

Paul was more emphatic.

"Not at all, Papa, you are not too old. Why sixty-three is not at all old these days."

He knew that he was lying but he had to reassure his father that all would be well within the family. The mood became one of joy, even giddiness on the part of Elizabeth. When breakfast was finished she and Sebastian went to the sitting room, Elizabeth to her desk and Sebastian to the book shelves.

After Elizabeth and Sebastian had reached the sitting room Paul called,

"Mama. I'm going out for a while. I won't be home until dinner time."

Without waiting for a reply, he left with a slight slam of the door. Then Johan sought out Elizabeth.

"Elizabeth, oh, excuse me Sebastian. Elizabeth, I think that I should return to Hutson City and look into that property again."

Expecting her compliance, he was surprised at her reply,

"No Johan. Please stay. Stay for lunch and then you and I will discuss business while perhaps Sebastian will take a nap."

She looked at Sebastian to determine if he understood and agreed. He smiled to her so she concluded that he did indeed wish to rest after lunch.

When Elizabeth and Johan later met in the drawing room, without Sebastian being present, she surprised Johan once more with her brash decisions. She outlined her plan in detail and when she finished Johan was still showing a state of astonishment.

"My God Elizabeth. How do you think that you an manage all of this?"

Her reply was simple.

"With the capable assistance of you and Paul, that's how."

Before departing to go upstairs to take a short rest herself she cautioned Johan to say nothing in front of Sebastian and to not talk about the matter to Paul until after she herself had spoken with him. Then she said,

"Sebastian and I will be meeting with Monsignor Tierney tomorrow morning. I have telephoned him and he will be expecting us early. I only told him that I wanted to have him meet someone very dear to me."

She left the room leaving Johan by himself. Suddenly Johan realized that his life was going to be altogether different in the future, all because of circumstances in which he had played no part. For the first time in many years, he felt very lonely.

Johan also retired to his room for the remainder of the afternoon. He had taken a book from Elizabeth's extensive library collection; a book on the subject that Elizabeth had just outlined to Johan.

At about five thirty, Paul returned to the house. Now it was his turn to surprise everyone. He had a lovely lady with him. He escorted her into the drawing room and to a comfortable chair. Excusing himself, he quickly looked into all the adjacent rooms. All were empty. He pulled the cord by the door. Margaret soon arrived, looking as though she might have been napping.

"Are Mrs. Mueller and Johan, and ah, Mr. Mueller all upstairs?"
As she looked over the strange lady Margaret replied,

"Yes. They are all resting until dinner is announced. That will be in another hour, sir."

Paul did not wait. He instructed Margaret to bring the new lady a cup of tea, then he excused himself again and bounded up the stairs. He knocked lightly on his mother's bedroom door.

"Mama….Mama…are you awake?"
He really didn't care if she was or not, he was determined to wake her if

necessary. After a very short wait, he opened the door slowly. Elizabeth was just rising from the settee in the corner by the windows. His father was stretched out on the bed, but he began to stir also.

"Paul…what is it? Did you wish to speak with me? You seem a bit excited. Is there anything wrong?

Are the shops alright?"

Elizabeth was now showing anxiety.

"Oh yes Mama. Everything is indeed alright. I just wanted you to come down stairs a little earlier and not wait until dinner time."

Paul crossed the room to her, looking as though he wanted to pull her up off the settee quickly. Sebastian now was sitting on the edge of the bed, just attempting to stand.

"Mama. While you and Papa are getting yourselves ready, I'll go wake Johan."

Paul left the room. Elizabeth looked at Sebastian.

"My, how excited Paul seems to be. Perhaps we had better hurry to go down stairs. Are you alright Sebastian?"

His reply was simple,

"Oh ya. I be ready now."

When the three recently awakened people reached the top of the stairway, Paul was waiting. He said,

"When you are all ready, come down. I'm going down now."

He hurried down the long staircase and then into the drawing room. When the three entered the drawing room, they all suddenly stopped. Elizabeth spoke

Encounters Elizabeth's
first,

"Why Paul! You didn't tell us that you had a guest. Please introduce her."
She smiled and extended her hand to the lady.
Paul was beaming,

"Mama, Papa, Johan, this is Kathy, .. Kathy Frazier. She is a very good
friend of mine."

"Well, hello Kathy, we're very glad to meet you",
Then Johan spoke, trying not to look too surprised.

"Well, Kathy! I'm very happy to meet you. Paul has kept you a secret, for
whatever his reasons."

"I be happy to meet yoo too, Katty."
Sebastian extended his hand. Elizabeth, as always, was the most gracious.

"Oh my dear. Do sit. We don't need to be formal here."
Kathy had arisen from the chair the moment that the three had entered the
room. All was quiet for a few seconds, then Paul spoke.

"Well, I know that you're all anxious to know about Kathy. Actually I
was going to tell you about her a few day ago, but other things came up.
Right?"
They all knew what he meant.

"Kathy and I have been seeing each other for a few months and I thought
that it was time for you all to meet. You see, we have intentions of being
married."
Now all three rushed to Kathy.

"Well that is wonderful! Just wonderful!"

Elizabeth was the first to show happiness at the astounding announcement. Sebastian and Johan too extended their hands to Paul, then to Kathy.

"Why Paul, you old sonovabi...bachelor! Why didn't you tell us that you had found such a pretty girl".

Johan was pounding on Paul's shoulder. Paul was stuttering to find an answer.

"Well. I guess I should have mentioned it earlier, but I wanted to be sure that Kathy would accept me as her husband before I said anything. Last night ago, she did say 'yes', and now I'm the happiest guy in the world"

Margaret entered to announce that dinner was ready.

"Oh just a few minutes Margaret. Tell Stella to keep everything hot for a few more minutes".

Elizabeth was not yet ready to sit, not without knowing all the details of Paul's first meeting with Kathy, and of her entire life story.

"So, Paul, Kathy, tell us all about it, how did you meet? When? Where? And when will the wedding take place?" Elizabeth was gushing like a young woman.

Paul began. He told of how he first saw Kathy many years ago, when she was the young bride of Kevin Frazier, a fellow bargeman. He remarked that he often saw her meet Kevin when he returned from a trip, and that she was always there on payday. With that, Kathy and the others laughed. Paul continued to explain.

"I remember when I saw her with their first baby, then a few years later, she would arrive holding the hand of a toddler and with another baby in her arms. When Kevin would greet her, it was evident that they were a very happy couple. After that I left the barge job and never saw her again until I went to our shop to see Antoinette one day about five months ago. Kathy was in the shop and I reintroduced myself. I didn't know then that Kevin had died. Well, a few weeks later I met her again in the bakery. This time I asked her if she would like to join me for dinner that evening.

She said 'no' to that evening but we made a date for a couple of week later."

Elizabeth interrupted,

"So that is why you made so many visits to our shop in Riverford lately." Then teasingly she added, " I wondered why!"

Kathy explained,

"I had to be sure that my mother-in-law could stay with my children. Kevin and I had three children, all girls. The oldest, Colleen, is now in her second year of high school at St. Jerome's in Riverford, and Emily and Grace are still in elementary school."

Elizabeth looked greatly concerned. Kathy knew the question in Elizabeth's mind.

"My dear husband Kevin died about four years ago. He died during that terrible winter that we had that year, do you remember?"

Elizabeth went to Kathy, placing her arms about her.

"Oh, you poor dear. Yes, that was a terrible winter. Many people died. There was so much influenza that year! And you were left with three little girls. Aren't you a brave one! Are they all well?"

Paul smiled to show his happiness that his mother was so kind to Kathy, but he said,

"Come on! Let's go eat. I'm starved, and I'll bet you are too Kathy. We can talk more at the table".

The conversation at the beginning of dinner was inconsequential, generalities about the weather. After Margaret served the main course and left the room for a time, the matter on everyone's mind was reopened. Elizabeth inquired further about the girls, then about Kathy's background, and finally brought up the matter that was really on her mind.

"So, when do you two plan to be married? And where? Would you like Father..that is Monsignor Tierney to marry you? Oh, Kathy, I'm assuming that it will be a Catholic wedding."

Kathy's reply pleased, but disappointed Elizabeth.

"Yes, we plan to be married by a priest, but I would like it to be in my hometown, in Cheltam, at St. James, so that my parents can be there."

"In Cheltam", Elizabeth replied. "Why that's where we lived when we first came to America. Do you remember Paul? Oh no, you wouldn't you were too small."

Suddenly she remembered Sebastian's presence.

"Well you certainly remember don't you Sebastian?"

"Oh ja, I vemember da little haus, Frau Huber's. Ja, I vemember dat."

Johan finally spoke up.

"Tell us Kathy. What was your maiden name? Before you became Mrs. Frazier."

"It is Garrity. Kathleen Garrity.", Kathy replied.

"Oh, I remember a Sean Garrity. He worked with me on Mr. Aldrich's farm. He was a cripple...Oh, I'm sorry. He had a bad leg. He was a little older than me, but he tried to join the artillery regiment with me. They would not take him. He argued, saying that in the artillery he wouldn't have to walk. Is he your dad?"

"Yes. And my mom's name is Esther. I'm the middle child of seven. Yes, Dad did work for Mr. Aldrich all his life, before retiring just last year. Mr. Aldrich was very kind to him. He hired Dad right after he came from the old country."

The conversation went on about Kathy's children, and about where they would live. Then Elizabeth became more pointed.

"Kathy, you are still a young woman, still young enough to bear more children if you wished. Do you plan to?"

Now Paul reddened,

"Mother! Isn't this a bit premature. Don't you think that Kathy and I and her children need to adjust to our new life before we think about things like that?"

Elizabeth laughed lightly.

"Yes, Paul, you're right. But sometimes events are not planned, you know. But whatever the future, Kathy and her children are certainly welcomed into our family."

Kathy smiled, showing a little more relaxation, now that the questioning seemed to be at an end.

When dinner was finished, and after a few more words of pleasantry, Paul said that he was leaving to take Kathy back to Riverford, that he would be home very late, possibly not at all this evening. Everyone bid them goodnight and then Johan, Elizabeth and Sebastian went into the drawing room again. All was quiet for a time.

"Isn't it wonderful that Paul finally found a girl friend", Johan commented,

"after being a bachelor now for almost thirty-six years. Do you think Kathy is much younger than Paul?"

"Oh, perhaps a few years. But I think that she must be in her earlier thirties. If they do plan to have children, they had better not wait too long."
Though she did not express it, it was obvious that Elizabeth was hoping to become a genuine grandmother, and hoping she had not too long to wait. Sebastian and Johan both recognized her hopefulness and laughed lightly.

"Vell Elizabeth, if yoo goin' to haff gran'chil'ren, it won't be by yoo dauter, vill it?" Johan chuckled but Elizabeth showed irritation.

"Why Sebastian, that's almost a sacrilegious thing to say. And remember, she is your daughter too. We had better pray that she does not disregard her sacred vows."
Sebastian reddened,

"Oh, ein bein sorry Elizabeth, ein not mean to be naughty."
Elizabeth lightened,

"No, Sebastian. I'm sure that you did not. Well Johan, I think that Sebastian and I are ready to retire. Aren't you Sebastian? And by the way Johan, that matter that we spoke of this afternoon. We'll have to put that off for a few months."

Encounters Elizabeth's

CHAPTER TWENTY THREE

An Encounter with Responsibility

"Good morning Fath…Monsignor Tierney. I would like you to meet some one, someone very dear to me…my husband Sebastian. Sebastian this is Monsignor Tierney."

Tierney was flabbergasted. He had trouble finding his voice. Finally he blurted,

"What! Elizabeth! Did you say your husband? Wasn't he killed in the….."

From the look on Tierney's face it was obvious what he must he was thinking,

'My God, what an old man! Can he really be Elizabeth's husband? He's alive? He is such an old man!'

He decided that he had better say no more, but to let Elizabeth explain the situation. The two men shook hands, Tierney being more vigorous, Sebastian the more timid with their clasps. Naturally, Sebastian was nervous, very nervous.

"Well come right in and sit. Elizabeth it is a pleasure to see you again. In person I mean, not just in church. Oh, you know what I mean."

The Monsignor led them into his study. After they were all seated Elizabeth began the explanation of Sebastian's life while away from her. She did not bring up the matter of the 'other woman' and Sebastian's other children. She thought it best that Sebastian explain that part of his life to the Monsignor in the confessional, in which she hoped Sebastian would wish to partake.

Monsignor Tierney was again openly expressing his great surprise that

Sebastian was alive. The manner in which he expressed it almost made Sebastian feel like he was intruding into Elizabeth's life, just as Cyrus had said would happen. Now Sebastian wondered if he had done the right thing, though Elizabeth certainly had made him feel welcome, in their bed as well as at other times. When Monsignor addressed Sebastian, he almost didn't realize that he was being spoken to, he was still in a bit of a trance.

"Sebastian. Say Sebastian, how are you? Are you feeling well?"

The Monsignor recognized Sebastian's far off look. Elizabeth did also. She took Sebastian's hand.

"Oh, I think he is alright. Aren't you Sebastian? He is just naturally nervous and is still adjusting to his grown son, learning of his daughter, and wondering where all the years have flown. Isn't that right Sebastian?"

Sebastian only nodded, still saying nothing. The Monsignor decided that he had better be low key with Sebastian, not be his normal upbeat self, like he is with Elizabeth and other parishioners. After a few more words of conversation, he inquired,

"When would you two like to renew your vows. If you wanted it to be on a Sunday after Mass, it will be a couple of weeks before we have an opening. We have many baptisms scheduled. How about on a weekday?"

Elizabeth answered,

"Well, to tell you the truth Monsignor, we were hoping that we could do so as a family. We were hoping that Mary could be with us. Do you think that you have any influence with Mother Superior? We don't even know where Mary is stationed. We would love to have her here but if she is still far out

249

west, I suppose we'll have to proceed without her."

Tierney replied,

"I'll make inquiries Elizabeth, and let you know. In the meantime, is there anything that I can do for you, Sebastian?"

Elizabeth recognized the cue, as did Sebastian.

"Oh, yes, Monsignor, I'm sure that Sebastian would like to make his confession, wouldn't you Sebastian?"

Sebastian knew that this moment would arrive sooner or later. He nodded a sheepish 'yes'.

"Good! Come with me Sebastian. We won't be long Elizabeth."

The Monsignor took Sebastian's arm, almost as if he expected Sebastian to want to dash away from him. Elizabeth remained in the study.

Soon the two returned smiling broadly.

"I hope that I will see you both at Sunday Mass. Goodbye Elizabeth. It was a great pleasure meeting you Sebastian. I am so happy for the two of you, and pleased that God has bestowed the blessings of life and reunion on you both. We must never underestimate the Lord, and His wondrous way of fulfilling our earnest prayers. Elizabeth, I'll see if there is any possibility of Mary's return, but…."

Elizabeth nodded that she understood.

As Elizabeth and Sebastian walked back to the mansion, they were both walking on air. Elizabeth was elated.

"Isn't he a wonderful man Sebastian. I told you that he would be kind and understanding, didn't I? You felt comfortable with him didn't you Sebastian?"

"Oh, ja, ja. I be wery comvor'ble mit him. He be a wery nice man, Ja!"

The next morning Elizabeth had arisen a little earlier than was her custom, so Sebastian had also, though he could have slept somewhat longer if allowed. Johan also was up early. They had their usual breakfast, then Johan said that he was going to go to the bakery to see Mr. Arnsmeyer. He said that after that, he would likely to the Riverford bakery also, to visit Antoinette, the manager there. He wanted to keep busy. Besides, he felt that someone should indeed take charge of the business, since both Elizabeth and Paul certainly had other matters, important matters, on their minds. Although he did not tell Elizabeth, he decided that tomorrow he would likely go back to Hutson City to search out the deed for the property for that future bakery. He thought that he himself might wish to establish just such a business in case Paul decided to finally get serious about taking over his mother's business. Should that occur, would he and Paul both remain in Elizabeth's bakery business? Or would he choose to leave…or have to get out.

In a few weeks Elizabeth and Sebastian did renew their marriage vows after the eight o'clock Mass on Saturday morning. Paul and Johan were present, but Mary was not. Monsignor had inquired and learned that she was still in Montana working on a reservation. Elizabeth soon sat and wrote a long letter to Mary, relating all that had happened and all that was yet soon to happen. In conclusion she wrote,

"Oh Mary, will you please, please request Mother Superior to let you return home To meet your long-lost father and to attend Paul and Kathy's wedding. How can she refuse such a plea?"

In just a week or so, Elizabeth did receive a letter having the return address of:

"Mother Superior St. Bernadette Mother House, Sisters Of Charity, Philadelphia, PA"

Elizabeth was puzzled because she knew that it was too soon for Mary to have received her letter, and write a reply. With trembling hands Elizabeth opened the envelope. While doing so she was terrified that it contained possible bad news; that Mary was ill, that she was scalped, that she died! Elizabeth slit open the letter, only to find that it contained a letter from Mary that had been forwarded through the Mother House. Elizabeth quickly slit open Mary's envelope.

The news from Mary was startling;

"Dearest Mother,

I know that you are surprised to hear from me after all these years, but I had to write and tell you that I am fine, and very much enjoying my missionary and teaching work here on the reservation in Montana. I sincerely hope that you, Paul and Johan are all well. I pray for all of you daily.

An unusual circumstance has occurred. About three months ago a young Negro couple arrived here from Kentucky. They are brother and sister, not a married couple. They came west from their Kentucky home looking for opportunities that would better their lives. They arrived here, expecting to stay only a few days, but decided to remain with us. They are a great help in many areas, teaching, (they said that their father taught them to read and write at an early age) cleaning the children's dormitories, playing with the children after their school hours, and many, many other items of assistance. In the evening of the day of their arrival I felt happy, for I dreamed of father. Even though I never met him, he seemed very real and very close to me, in my dream of course.

In addition you will be happy to learn that Mother Superior is granting me a short sabbatical, then I am to be assigned to a new school that Mother Superior wishes to open in Kentucky. She has chosen me to be the founder of this new mission and school. When I learned of this wonderful opportunity, I immediately spoke to my new friends, since they were from Kentucky. What an amazing coincidence, is it not? These two wonderful people volunteered to travel to Kentucky with me and seek a good location for a school, one that will benefit the negro children there.

More good news! Mother Superior will allow me to come home to visit you for a few weeks before traveling to Kentucky. Isn't that marvelous! You must have been praying for such a development! I will be leaving here in two weeks and Annabelle and Rudy will accompany me and be with me when I visit you. I hope that you will be kind to them and offer your home to them for a few weeks.

Annabelle and Rudy said they had a wonderful father. After they were older, he told them that he was born in Germany. Can you imagine! The same country from whence father came. No wonder I feel so close to father's spirit when I am with Annabelle and Rudy.

I am looking forward with much anticipation my visit with you, Paul and Johan. I hope that they are well also. May God be with all of you!

Your loving daughter Mary"

Elizabeth was ecstatic! She could hardly contain herself. She rushed to find Sebastian and Johan. She called loudly to them from downstairs. In the few seconds that it took for them to respond, Elizabeth was thinking of how she might reach Paul soon. She called each of the bakeries and left word that Paul should call his mother immediately.

When Sebastian and Johan came into the drawing room they could see that Elizabeth was intense, but smiling. She began to almost shout at them.

"Sebastian! Johan! Mary is coming home! Mary is coming home! Can you believe it! Mother Superior has granted her a short sabbatical and permission to come home for a short time before taking up her new assignment. Oh! Thank You Lord for your loving kindness."

Johan reacted with great joy but Sebastian did not seem to absorb Elizabeth's quick statements. Elizabeth went to him and gave him a great hug.

"Sebastian my darling! Your daughter is coming home to meet you! Isn't that wonderful!"

Mary made no comment to either Johan or Sebastian about the two other guests that would be arriving with Mary.
Sebastian was now displaying a great smile.

"Ach du lieber! Mary iss comink home to wisit us! Oh, dat iss wonderbar. Oh tank de goot Lord, eh Elizabeth?"
Elizabeth took Sebastian and Johan by the hands and danced a circle. The two men laughed when they saw how joyful Elizabeth was feeling. Then a new realization came to Elizabeth. Mary could be in attendance at Paul and Kathy's

wedding! She thought,

'Oh, I hope that I reach Paul soon and tell him the good news. He must ask Kathy to arrange for the wedding while Mary is at home!'

In a short time Paul did call, having received the message to call home from Antoinette at the Riverford bakery. Elizabeth gushed as she told Paul the good news. Paul said that he was delighted. He spoke to Kathy immediately. Kathy said that they would speak to Fr. Nolan at St. James church and be sure to perform the wedding on a date on which Mary could attend. That date could not be determined until hearing from Mary again. In addition to Paul's family, Kathy's parents, Kathy's three daughters, and Kathy's mother-in-law would also be attending. Earlier Kathy had praised Kevin's mother greatly to the others, commenting on how supportive and helpful she had been after the death of her son. Mrs. Frazier was a widow of many years and was living with Kathy and Kevin when Kevin died. She remained in the house with Kathy. It appeared that Paul was inheriting a mother-in-law and a boarder at the same time.

In three weeks Mary arrived home, bringing with her Annabelle and Rudy. Elizabeth greeted them all warmly. Paul and Kathy had arrived a little earlier so Mary and her friends were introduced to them. They seemed puzzled with the two friends of Mary. Sebastian and Johan were in their bedrooms upstairs. Elizabeth asked Paul to go immediately and fetch them. Paul bounded up the stairs and soon all three came into the drawing room. Sebastian let out a loud whoop when he saw Mary's friends. He ran to them, gave each of them a great hug and shouted their names. Everyone except Elizabeth was dumbfounded. Mary stood motionless. As soon as Sebastian settled a little,

Elizabeth introduced Mary to her father. Sebastian went quickly to Mary, giving her a great hug and a strong kiss on the forehead. Mary had still not absorbed the impact of her father's presence. She hugged him and said,

"Oh my dear father! I am so very happy to meet you! But Mother said that you were killed in the war! How is it that you are here!" She could not hide her shocked reaction.

For these few minutes, Annabelle and Rudy stood anxiously by. Now they ran to Sebastian, giving him great hugs and kisses. They shouted "Papa!, Oh Papa! We are so happy to see you again! Oh Papa we love you! We love you! We missed you! How is it that you are here? How is it that you are also Mary's father?"

Paul, Kathy and Johan were standing like statues. They could not understand what they were seeing and hearing. Yes, they knew that Mary was meeting her father for the first time!

But who are these negro people calling Sebastian "Papa"?

Now Elizabeth spoke,

"Now calm down everyone! Calm yourselves! Sebastian and I can explain all. Please sit and calm yourselves."

As everyone sat nervously, Sebastian and Elizabeth explained what was the true situation. Annabelle and Rudy clung close to their father. Mary hugged her mother. Paul and Johan were shaking their heads in disbelief and Kathy was appearing to still be in shock.

Elizabeth spoke,

"I believe I was the only one to know that Annabelle and Rudy were

256

Sebastian's children. He had told us of them the night that he arrived back home. Don't you remember Paul? Remember Johan? But he did not tell us their names. When I received Mary's letter I was amazed at her statements. She said that she felt the closeness of her unknown father when Annabelle and Rudy arrived at her mission. At first I wondered about this. Then I was able to get Sebastian to tell me the names of his other children, his southern children, without raising any suspicion of my reason for the question. I awaited this reunion of all of us with great happiness, and with great thanks to the Lord for His many blessings on our family. I hope that all of you will thank the Lord each day for his loving care."

After several more minutes of joyful celebrating, Paul announced that he and Kathy had purchased a larger house in Riverford where they decided to live. It mattered not to Paul because he had to travel to the several bakeries on occasion from wherever he was residing.

After several months, Elizabeth did request both Paul and Johan to meet with her, at the office of the Altady bakery, not at her home. She did not want Sebastian to learn of this meeting. At this meeting she explained to Paul what she had already spoken to Johan before the wedding, of seeking out a vineyard in Oscala county. She explained how his father had always hoped that he would again be able to work in a vineyard, which he loved so much. She told of the reason that his father had entered the war, to secure the bounties, the money that would have allowed him to purchase a vineyard here in America, working among the vines as he had in Germany. Paul was completely overwhelmed at hearing this plan, just as Johan had been many weeks earlier upon his first learning of it. All that Paul could muster was,

"Ohmygod! Ohmygod!"

Elizabeth requested Johan to travel to Oscala alone, since Paul could not now leave his new family for any length of time. Elizabeth and Johan estimated that it might require as much as two months for the search for a vineyard to be completed, of the type and location that she desired. Then, as usual, Elizabeth had another shocking plan to reveal. She announced that she had decided to incorporate the bakery and merchandise businesses, with Paul, Johan, herself and Sebastian as directors. She announced the division of ownership that she was intending, and said that they would all meet with her attorney in two days to legalize the matter.

Her plan was simple she said. The stock was to be divided so that she retained thirty percent, the controlling stake. Paul and Johan would each be issued twenty-five percent, Sebastian ten percent, and Mary ten percent. Paul immediately asked,

"Why Mary Mom? Why give stock to her. I don't mean that I want more, but what can she do with stock. She's taken an oath of poverty."

"Yes, I know Paul. But whatever income portion is to be Mary's will be donated to her Order, to be used for their charity work."

Elizabeth looked at the two men to see if they understood and approved. They both nodded 'yes', and agreed to abide by Elizabeth's wishes. Elizabeth continued to explain the future arrangements. Without commenting on Sebastian's age, Elizabeth stated her wishes for the assignment of Sebastian's share after his death. They were to be divided between Paul's three step-daughters. Elizabeth then expressed her feelings,

"You both deserve this, you have worked very hard for it. And after Sebastian and I have moved to Oscala, if you two decide to expand the number of shops, or whatever else you decide is best, I will not be disagreeable."

After a pause she added,

"I hope that you did not object to including Sebastian."

They both heartily responded

"No!" "Oh no! Certainly not!"

The two men kissed Elizabeth, one on each cheek, then hugged each other, shook hands, and all three smiled broadly. The future was cast. Within six weeks Johan had found a vineyard owner willing to sell, but also to remain as foreman of the workers for two years. Within a few months, Elizabeth and Sebastian were ready to depart to Oscola.

As Elizabeth and Sebastian boarded their heavily loaded carriage for the long ride to their new home and vineyard along the beautiful lakeside, they called to all that were waving to them, including Monsignor Tierney and the household staff,

"Be sure to come and visit us. We welcome you! Do not forget us! And keep us in your prayers."

The carriage left, taking Elizabeth and Sebastian on their way to yet another life, the third major existence for each of them, ... their final encounter, ... this one happily together 'til death.